MW01670791

Tales of the Fallen
Book II

by

Nescher Pyscher

Argus Enterprises International, Inc.
New Jersey***North Carolina

A-Argus Better Book Publishers, LLC

For information:
A-Argus Better Book Publishers, LLC
9001 Ridge Hill Street
Kernersville, North Carolina 27285
www.a-argusbooks.com

ISBN: 978-0-6155526-3-7
ISBN: 0-6155526-3-3

Cover Art by John William Waterhouse
1849-1917

Printed in the United States of America

Dedication

The efforts of a number of people over a period of several years went into the writing of these two books. I am grateful to all of them, with many deserving of special recognition: God, because He rules and reigns. The Connors and Argus Publishing, for taking a chance on my stuff and proving I could do it. Laura Kepner, for her stellar edits, constant encouragement, and unyielding belief in my ability to write a story. You rock, home-skillet. John Gower, Mark Kelly and Christopher Modderman, for poking, prodding and generally being the kind of friends I most needed when I most needed them. Jennifer Gephart Horton for . . . well, you know. Jeremiah McDole, for swallowing his disdain long enough to read a piece of fantasy fiction, divorced from science, and enjoying it; my family and friends and the good people at Fanstory.com. Finally, I'd like to thank my beautiful wife, Christine. She is all the fan I will ever need, and I dedicate this book, as well as every effort I make hereafter, to her and our son, Geir. I love you, Mud-Duck. And I win.

Congrats, Will!

Prologue

(from Book One)

Weaver stopped. A light, bright enough to throw his shadow in crisp, sharp-edged relief across Jack's hurrying back, was shining from behind him. The light had a strange blueness to it. Weaver turned to look.

Something hit him across the face. Jack held up a freshly blooded fist in warning, shaking his shoulder with the other hand. "No, you idiot! Don't fucking look! You want to be a dragon breakfast? Run, you stupid, fucking retard! Run!"

With that, Jack began to sprint away into the gray, leaving Weaver to run as best he was able.

Something behind them roared with a dull, brassy ferocity that shook the ground, the sky, the teeth in Weaver's head.

He ran.

Chapter One

". . . one-hundred-fifty-three-one-thousand. . .one-hundred-fifty-four-one-thousand . . ."

****

Weaver suddenly stopped. He couldn't help it. He turned to look back, fighting himself for control, unable to prevent it. Something far stronger than he was—something older and more ancient than a mere mortal father's love for his son pulled at his mind and made him stop. If someone had held him down, he would likely have broken his own neck, trying to turn it to see.

The light increased. Weaver squinted his eyes against it. The light grew still more, becoming briefly unendurable, and then he saw it. Or rather, he experienced it: it was too large, too much, too real to see. His mind tried to make sense of it, tried to explain it to him, tried to break in into manageable information, and then it gave up. When he thought of it later, it was in fragments of impression; like a dream. Something rose like the sun or the wrath of an improbable god from Stones-Falling-From-Sky's hut. It was shaped like a perfect arrow: an immensely long shaft, topped by a diamond wedge for head. It rose into the sky like an erupting volcano; a star falling from earth into the sky. It radiated the blue-white light like a cosmos full of stars.

If filled the sky like an eclipse, spinning as it rose and flaring wings of incandescent flame. Weaver saw that the arrow analogy was complete; its tail become visible, and there were feathers, scales or hairs on it that mimicked an arrow's fletching.

The dragon twinkled and sparkled, like precious jewels under the light of a bright sun. It was bigger than anything Weaver had ever seen; bigger than the moon, bigger than the world, bigger than life. It was impossible. It defied the existence surrounding it, forced its way into the universe and made the universe conform to it. Reality, in the loose way that Weaver understood it, cut a dragon-shaped hole, and the dragon rose into that hole: beautiful and contemptuous. It sparkled with all the colors that are, were, weren't and will never be.

The dragon bellowed a triumphant, life-affirming hunger at the sky. The noise was like a chorus of volcanoes roaring in harmonic sequence. The sound was savagely glorious.

"It's magnificent," Weaver breathed, his eyes wide and his mind splintering. He could not look away. He was unable to take his attention, bordering on worship, off the dragon. Love was surging through him in hot waves, erasing everything.

The dragon spun higher into the sky, searching; hunting. The mighty head turned toward them.

Weaver looked into the eyes of a dragon and felt himself being regarded in turn. Even from this distance, Weaver was close enough to see, in those brief, impression-filled-flashes, the enormous interlocking plates—My Scales. Aren't They Glorious?—as thick as he was around the dragon's face. He had time to register the glowing eyes, as big as moons, with a slit pupil like a knife's blade. He saw the enormous teeth; like an endless hedge in a mouth deeper than a sea.

"Little Man. I Could Snatch You Up Without Even Realizing I Had Something In My Mouth."

Then the fear came. It was insidious. Under the weight of it, the small animal that lived in Weaver's mind—the animal that cowered in the dark around the fire; that lived in caves—took over. It turned Weaver's body and pushed him into the shambled, boneless beginning of a run, a helpless keen pushing from his mouth.

Jack looked behind him, noticing Weaver was no longer sprinting beside him. He saw the dragon rushing toward them, Weaver trying to run from it like a squirrel under the shadow of a truck tire.

"Awwwwww, fuck," he muttered. He turned to run on but the dragon was already upon them . . .

. . . and blasting overhead, missing them by inches.

Weaver didn't have time to blink. The dragon had been above Stones-Falling-From-Sky's hut, and then it was roaring toward them with that noise like the destruction of the world.

The air of its passage, so close to where they stood, knocked them over and sent them rolling several dozen man-lengths away. Weaver heard a noise like the snapping of a god's spine.

"*My Teeth And Scales, Snapping And Brushing Against Each Other,*" the lizard voice said, whispering it but crashing at the tender center of Weaver's mind.

The dragon rocketed into the sky, blaring its frustration at the near miss. A boom that shook the sky sounded after it passed over the two of them, knocking them flat once again.

Jack bounced up. Weaver took longer to recover. He smelled the stink of the dragon. It was like an ancient predator's long-lived-in den, mixed with the smell of the foul odors that came from the lands of the sky-rent: it was the poisoned smell of the place where the earthfire boils up into the sky.

The dragon was soaring and spinning above them. Weaver felt that strange fascination fall upon him again. He fought it, with more success this time. Something told him he was being ensorcelled, but he did not have the strength of will to fight it completely.

And then Jack hit him in the face, hard enough to break three of his teeth.

"You better get up and run, Weaver! It just hatched so it's still learning! We can get away, but only if we hurry! Move your shaggy ass!"

Jack's voice was panicked, and that did more than the blow did. Weaver, still gibbering, ran.

****

" . . . one-hundred-fifty-five-one-thousand. . . .one-hundred-fifty-six-one-thousand . . ."

****

The chase took them into the grey nothing lands surrounding Stones-Falling-From-Sky's house. They did not have any sort of a destination to run to; they were running away from the dragon. It would boil out of the grey mists toward them, bellowing in its trumpet-voice, and knock the two of them rolling and spinning. It would snap its enormous jaws at them as it flew overhead.

"How the fucking hell am I supposed to outrun something that makes a fucking sonic boom when it flies by?" Jack shouted at the sky. "A little help would be most appreciated!"

Weaver knew only to run. They tried to make sudden direction changes that seemed to throw the dragon off. For all its power and beauty, it was still trying to learn how to fly.

Weaver ran under the impetus of his inner survival drive, not thinking of anything but the run.

"Just keep running, Weaver. Eventually it'll get tired of chasing us and go find something to eat someplace else. Just keep on running."

Weaver grunted in wordless reply.

****

". . . one-hundred-fifty-eight-one-thousand. . .one-hundred-fifty-nine-one-thousand . . ."

****

After ten-thousand years that may've only been a few hours, Jack stopped. It had been quite a while since the dragon had flown by. He rested his hands on his knees, panting in relief. He heard Weaver's feet running on into the grey, and sighed.

"That fucking kid's gonna be the death of me, yet," he muttered to himself, running after Weaver.

They had been running for several minutes before Jack finally caught up to him and managed to grab his shoulder.

"Stop, Weaver. Stop. It's okay. I think the dragon's gone."

Weaver keened in fear. He kept straining against Jack's hand, trying to run on, running in place.

"Weaver, stop! It's okay!"

Weaver shook his head violently and tried to pull Jack after him.

"Alright. Fuck you, then."

The last thing Weaver saw was a fist the size of a mallet, descending with a booming noise all its own, right between his eyes. The darkness swallowed him for a while.

****

". . . one-hundred-sixty-five-one-thousand. . .one-hundred-sixty-six-one-thousand . . ."

****

"You have failed, Weaver-Of-Shadows. The People have come and they have consigned Moonlight to the fires and the flames. There is nothing left of him for you to save. Is that not a fine jest, Weaver-of-Shadows? After everything you have endured, after all the promises and dark bargains made, slitting off pieces of your very soul, there is nothing for you to save!"

Weaver looked around him frantically. He sat in his furs near a guttering fire on the ice. The ghost-filled winds of night howled and blew around him. The stars wheeled and spun overhead, as they had done for many, many, many turns of the skywheel. But the stars were wrong. They did not form the familiar shapes of Otter and Beaver and Great Stone Whale. They were strange, those stars; alien. And they shone down with a sick, cold light that made Weaver's bones ache and tremble.

He shivered beneath his furs. Something scrabbled on the ice nearby.

"Do you hear me, Weaver-Of-Shadows? I speak only that truth you have so long denied yourself."

As Weaver watched, something low to the ground, something with four legs, something as white and as evil as bones left unburied, skittered away into the further darkness.

"Weaver-Of-Shadows. Brave hunter who fears nothing in the lands of the People. How your boasts irked me; how your love and pride in your son ruffled my fine, soft fur. I tell you the truth, Weaver, not since the People came to the land have I so wanted to see a hunter destroyed. When you defiled your palm-scar in eager bargain to me, you disassociated yourself from all the people. Even if you somehow survive—for are you not the mightiest hunter of the People?—there is nothing for you to return to. Your people are cut off from

you. 'We are the People. We are one.' So say the Shamans, do they not? And what of the one who cuts himself off; who defiles what is holy and flaunts the laws and traditions? What is the punishment for such a one as that?"

Snow Fox laughed. The sound shook the ice all around.

"Ahhh, Weaver. I almost hope you do survive. I hope you return from this place of death and dream, lurch home to your wife and find there what awaits you. When I ate that bit of common soul with your blood in front of the World Gate, it tasted like finest wine. I could have stopped then, content, but you gave me even more! You have been my special project for long and long, Weaver-Of-Shadows. You have been marked by the one I serve, but you are mine first and foremost. I have so desired to have you in my teeth! How I have longed to crunch your strong heart, to eat your spirit, to drink your blood, to crush your bones in my jaws and rip the skin from you with my strong, sharp, cunning claws."

Weaver shivered.

"I have broken you, Weaver; brought you to this place of madness and death. And you lie here, unmourned, with all you have most loved taken from you. Is that not a fine jest, Weaver? Moonlight is dead and so are you, and neither of you will ever return, and you both belong to me for all eternity."

"No! No! That is not true! You lie, foul creature! Eater of carrion, swallower of death! You are a liar and the giver of lies! I will bring my son back! I will bring Moonlight back!"

He stood, his fists clenched, screaming into the freezing night around him. He could barely hear his voice over the ghostly whine and howling mutter of the wind.

"Do I? Perhaps. It is ever my place to be a trickster god, even in this benighted place at the end of all things. But tell me, Weaver: do you still fear nothing in the lands of the People?"

And the voice laughed. The noise rose into the night until the ice and sky echoed with it.

"And if I lie, what of our bargain, Weaver-Of-Shadows? If I lie, where is Moonlight's carefully guarded corpse? Should it not be here?"

Weaver turned frantic eyes around the ice, searching for Moonlight's body, knowing deep inside what he would find while a voice intoned solemnly from the death of Weaver's father.

He had stood there, watching, holding the torch while Otter sang the words: "We are the People. We keep to the old ways. Without the ways, the People die. When one dies, all are less. Lay the torch, Weaver-Of-Shadows, and let the spirit fly—"

The fires.

"No, no, no, no, no, no!" he said, keening in fear and desperation. He searched for Moonlight's body and could not find it.

His traitor mind boiled the memory of his desperate bargain up at him. He felt the dull, painless bite of his knife snipping his fingers away, one by one by one; the mighty sense of pain and loss as he sliced through the scar on his palm, and the light that had bled out of him.

*"**Yes. You do remember**,"* the voice called.

Weaver heard something small squeal and die. He heard something patter on the ice. He heard something digging with claws and teeth.

"How many days has it been, Weaver-Of-Shadows? How many days have you chased this mad quest into nothing? How many days have I sat here, watching them prepare the burial fires for the body of your son?"

"NooooooоOOOOOOOOO!"

The echo of his scream of denial chased him into wakefulness.

****

Weaver groaned, rolled over onto his side, and wished he could still weep.

He felt as if his spirit was trying to fly into ten-million different pieces; to leave the central 'He,' and become one with the surrounding nothingness.

He wiped his face and looked over at Jack. Jack was lying on his back, his hands beneath his head. Without looking at Weaver, he said, "You alive? Relatively speaking?"

"Did you strike me?"

"Yep. Hit ya' right between the eyes. The sweet spot. See, you draw, like, an invisible 'X' from the outside of the eyes, up across the forehead. You hit somebody there juuuuuuuust right, they're gonna go down like a sack of dead fish. You could kill an aurochs like that, you hit it just right."

He paused, as he often did, and looked thoughtful. "Matter of fact, I have killed an aurochs—"

"That would explain why my brain feels like it is stuck to the back of my head, I suppose."

“Beats bein’ dragon-chow, homie,” Jack said, and grinned at him.

Jack lit one of his burning tubes and rolled his head on his neck.

“I am grateful to you, Jack. Without your help, I would’ve succumbed to the dragon’s magic.”

“Yeah, well, be thankful it wasn’t a full grown dragon, dude. Otherwise you’d’ve succumbed, I’d’ve succumbed, and the world would be a hell of a lot less interesting.”

Weaver could still hear sharp claws digging away at frozen, bloody ice in the back of his mind. “What?” he asked, distractedly.

“I said, be glad it wasn’t a full-grown dragon.”

“That was not a full grown dragon?”

Jack barked a mirth-filled laugh at the sky. “Not a full grown dragon? Not a full grown dragon? Weaver, that was a fucking hatchling. It’s a baby! What have I been saying all this time?”

He looked at Weaver’s stunned expression. Jack laughed for a very long time.

****

Looking over at Weaver, Jack exhaled a cloud of smoke that smelled vaguely of burning bone.

“Okay, dude. Now, I’ve got to leave you here. I’ve got to—”

“Leave me? Here? But Jack, if you leave me I’ll—”

“Shut up, Weaver, and calm down. Chill. Okay? It’s just for a little while. If I don’t leave you, you won’t come back. Capisce? You’ll be stuck here, with nothing to come back to, and restoring Moonlight will be the very least of your problems.”

Weaver looked around him at the gray nothing. The ever-present wisps hung in coagulating strands that moved independent of any breeze. They looked like grey, weightless, bones, or the constructions of ice one sometimes found on the glacier further north of the lands of the People. They were frightening, those wisps; more so as they had no substance, but followed them as they moved about.

Weaver, a proud hunter of the People, trained from birth to reject fear, shivered violently.

"Hey, neh-grow. You ain't skeered? I mean, big, tough dude like you, you aren't lookin' fer yer blankie, are ya'?"

Weaver stared at him, mystified. "What?"

Jack sighed. "Slang, dude. Get some. You're a little too monochromatic. What I said was, 'You aren't afraid, are you'?"

Weaver took a deep breath, squared his shoulders, and looked Jack in the eye. "I am Weaver-of-the-Shadows, hunter of the People. I fear nothing."

"Well, that's bullshit, but if it makes you feel better. Stay put, okay? Don't go getting into trouble."

"When will you be back?"

Jack grimaced. "Weaver, you startin' to sound like a needy bitch. I'll be back as soon as I can, dude. I got to get back to where the rest of you is and take care of some bidness. In the mean time, sharpen some arrows, take a nap, or do whatever it is you monkeys do to kill time."

Weaver-Of-Shadows cocked his head.

Jack grinned; sharp and mad. "Just nod, Weaver."

Weaver nodded.

"Good!"

With that, Jack began to walk in a sky wise circle, pulling great clouds of smoke off the burning tube clamped in between his lips. He grew misty, insubstantial. By the third circuit, Jack had gone, leaving behind only the smell of his burning tube. It smelled exactly like heavily cooked meat and blood.

****

Jack re-entered himself to find Due Dareaga fully absorbed with the corpse of Weaver-Of-Shadows. Jack's mind had become a place of blaring light and pounding hunger. He entered that space and tried to shout down the awful count going on in his voice.

***

". . . one-hundred-sixty-seven-one-thousand. . .one-hundred-sixty-eight-one-thousand . . ."

***

Due Dareaga had drawn its mouth close to Weaver's mouth. Due Dareaga, blind, unseeing hunger was in the driver's seat, fully emerged, and in control of Jack's body. The part of him that was 'Jack' could do little more than watch and attempt to reason with a primal hunger.

It clamped Jack's hands harder on Weaver's corpse and threw a menacing snarl at the separate consciousness that was Jack.

"No!" Jack shouted at it, "No! Not this one!"

"MEAT," Due Dareaga said.

"No! Not meat! Not meat!" Jack shouted.

Due Dareaga stopped what it was doing and looked at Jack. But that awful count continued in their shared voice, shaking off the trees and rolling across the sky.

***

". . . one-hundred-sixty-nine-one-thousand. . .one-hundred-seventy-one-thousand. . . ."

***

What's that? Three minutes? Something like that? How long can an ape brain live without oxygen? Four minutes? Five?' How long was he dead before I pulled his plug? How fucking long do I have here?

Due Dareaga sat over Weaver's corpse like a predator defending its prey. Jack knew he couldn't fight it. It would be pointless to try. He had something like a minute or so to do what was necessary to save Weaver's life, and Due Dareaga had full control of his body.

Jack heard something that he'd been listening for and it gave him an idea. It was scrabbling on the turf near them to gloat over what it thought was a victory. He swelled with anger.

Due Dareaga couldn't be fought, not by Jack. Due Dareaga couldn't be controlled, not by Jack. But Due Dareaga could easily be distracted and redirected; a new target given to it; one that deserved to be eaten.

Jack looked out of his eyes into the moving gorse and saw a flash of low-slung white. Due Dareaga looked with him.

"MEAT?" it asked.

Jack grinned. "Meat."

****

Weaver sat down in the grey nothing, trying not to look around him at the wisps. It would not be right to say that he was afraid. He was Weaver-Of-Shadows. He feared nothing that lived.

But that was the problem, wasn't it? Nothing here was alive.

"Including you," a voice of oiled smoke whispered in his mind. Weaver clamped down on that with a hunter's discipline. He would not fear. Fear was for the weak. Was he not Weaver? Did he not face the great white bear armed only with javelin, knife and spear? Did he not climb the face of the glacier? Did he not spring from a line of … a line forever broken hunters that stretched back to the time of the sky-rent?

No. He would not fear grey wisps of nothing. He would sit and he would wait. And he would not fear.

Weaver tried to find a comfortable position on the ground beneath him. It was cold and slightly damp, like freshly turned grave dirt as though it had rained recently.

Weaver looked up into the sky. He could see nothing but endless grey wisps. This was a nothing, nowhere place. Rain had never fallen here. He ran his hand over the ground and smelled his palms. It smelled of metal.

"It is blood, oh Weaver-of-Shadows. The blood, sweat, semen, urine and tears of ten-million generations of souls," said Snow Fox.

Weaver jumped up and spun around, looking for it. He saw a white flash, slung low and close to the ground, moving into the grey. "Aiee, Snow Fox! I see you there, lurking in the grey!"

The white flash had disappeared into the hanging murk. Weaver could see nothing beyond a few feet. The murk gave off confusing shadows and moved in a wind that Weaver could not feel.

"Lurking, am I, Weaver?"

The voice came from behind him once again. Weaver turned around, trying to keep Snow Fox in front of him.

"Skulking and hiding, am I?"

This time the voice came from far off to his left.

"And what else would you be doing, oh, trickster? I know you for who you are! False one and eater of small bones!"

There was a high pitched series of yelps. Snow Fox laughed at him.

"Weaver! Weaver-Of-Shadows! How you amuse me! How you provide infinite jest! Trickster, am I? False and eater of small bones? Very well. Let it be as you say."

Weaver spun around, still trying to track Snow Fox. The voice had come from behind him again, but above him as well.

"I come for your benefit! I come to save you much toil! Further striving on your part is useless. The People have come. The women have taken your son's body and dressed it for the Fires of Lamentation and Memory. Even now the charred and smoking bones of Moonlight lie upon the last ashes of the pyre built for him. The wood was collected for months, Weaver. Small pieces, here and there. The fires burned for three days, and the aurora danced the entire time. It was moving and beautiful. The People waited for you to return, to throw the torch, but you dallied over-long. And now, your striving is pointless."

It paused for just a second; a brief eye blink. When it resumed speaking, the voice was from behind Weaver yet **again.**

"And where is his father? Where is Weaver-Of-Shadows? Where is the one who should sing Moonlight's soul into the lands beyond? Why, Weaver is nowhere. He is no place. His body lies, gently decomposing, beneath a tree that does not exist. Or perhaps he sleeps just this side of death on a glacier, waiting for one final cold to push him into the beyond. Whichever is true, glacier or tree that does not exist in the lands of the People—dead as they are in the river of time—his spirit wanders in the nothing. Weaver-Of-Shadows, proud hunter of the People, is being chased by the phantoms in his own heart and mind. Moonlight will wander the lands of the People, an unmoored ghost. He will feel the keen knife of his father's betrayal forever and ever and ever."

"You lie," Weaver whispered, his fists clenching.

Snow Fox scrabbled in the grey, laughing its high-pitched laugh again.

"Do I? Perhaps. It is my role to lie to the hearts of the brave and show them the fear they deny. But answer me this, Weaver-Of-Shadows: if I lie, then why does the fear of my truth snail its way even now across the walls of your heart?"

Weaver closed his eyes, and clenched his body into a tight, human bow.

"YOU LIE!" he roared into the grey.

"Perhaps," Snow Fox's voice slyly wheedled.

"There is no 'perhaps,' Snow Fox! You lie! You come here to taunt me. What do you here otherwise, Snow Fox? What place has an eater of the weak in a place like this?"

Weaver saw nothing but the grey wisps all around him. When Snow Fox's voice resumed speaking, it came from very high above him. The voice sounded a bit like the poisoned thunder rolling in from the lands of the sky-rent.

"Ahhhh, Weaver. Even now you do not recognize your doom. You are betrayed, Weaver. Betrayed by everyone and everything. But as for what it is I am doing, oh Weaver-Of-Shadows, here in this place where I am the one to be feared; when the glory-songs are sung, they are sung about me; here, where I am the predator, and you are the prey, what I do Weaver-Of-Shadows . . ."

And now Weaver could see something moving around in the murk. He could smell its breath, its hide, long before he could fully see it. It smelled of small things that had died in fear and in pain. It smelled of blood and bones splintering under sharp teeth. It smelled of ripping meat. It smelled of the madness of the blood-drinker and the fear of the prey. The white shape of some obscenely large form was coming toward him. Its footsteps thundered under him, shaking the ground with each footfall. It towered above Weaver, moving with the slow, swaying gait of an enormous predator.

Now the silence was absolute. Even the ever-present wind was still. He could still feel the impact of gigantic paws striking the earth beneath his feet, but he could hear nothing.

It came into focus and definition all at once, starting with its amber eyes, burning down at Weaver from out of the grey. They were glowing with every hate since the beginning of time down at the suddenly trembling, mewling Weaver-Of-Shadows.

"What I do, Weaver," Snow Fox's voice said, rolling out of a cavernous mouth full of poison teeth, ***"is hunt!"***

Weaver-Of-Shadows, first hunter of the People, turned and ran into the grey, screaming.

****

". . . one-hundred-seventy-one-one-thousand. . .one-hundred-seventy-two-one-thousand . . ," the voice in Jack's shared head boomed.

****

Jack watched the small form of Snow Fox find a good place to lie down, blending itself carefully into the surrounding vegetation. He admired the way it made itself invisible against all the green and gold of Middangeard. It wouldn't be easy for anything to do that, but a god of ice and snow? That'd be even harder.

So, yeah. Mad props for crazy skill, but the little bitch is still disrespecting me.

Jack had told Snow Fox to leave. Snow Fox hadn't left. Snow Fox had come back. Snow Fox, little, itty, bitty trickster god Snow Fox, had defied him.

Snow Fox is gonna make a mighty nice fur hat.

Due Dareaga smiled its lipless, hungry smile at Jack from its place inside his shared consciousness.

"MEAT! MEAT! MEAT!" it said, bouncing up and down in its eagerness.

Jack smiled. He'd never eaten a god before. He had to wonder what it would be like.

"Go get 'im, dude."

Due Dareaga flowed like silver ink across the ground to where Snow Fox lay hidden in the gorse.

****

Jack ignored the high-pitched squeals of fright and the happy moaning sounds coming from behind him. He ran to Weaver's corpse. It wasn't easy, splitting yourself into different pieces, but sometimes it was necessary.

"The things we do when somebody's got us by the olives," Jack muttered, while he checked Weaver's pulse.

Nothing.

He knew that, but these things had to be done correctly. It was magic, with its own rituals to be followed, one after the other, and all magic is defined by the person casting the spell. He watched Weaver's chest for a moment, looking for any kind of a rise and fall. He put his ear close to Weaver's mouth.

Nothing.

He squatted and interlaced his fingers. Putting his locked-together-hands directly over the bottom of Weaver's breast bone, he began chest compressions.

"One, and a-two, and a-three, and a-four, and a-five, and a-six, and a-seven, and an-eight, and a-nine, and a-ten, and ah-'leven, and ah-twelve, and ah-thirteen, and ah-fourteen, and ah-fifteen," he said, counting down with each compression.

****

Due Dareaga made a slobbery feeding noise, much like an oversized-toddler eating spaghetti mixed with cereal.

****

Jack tilted Weaver's head back and pinched shut his nose. He blew two perfect breaths into Weaver's mouth. "C'mon, Weaver. Your mouth tastes like fish, and I don't feel like doing this all day."

****

Snow Fox mewled piteously.

Even doing CPR, Jack couldn't help but smile.

****

Weaver was beyond fear, beyond panic. At least, when the dragon was chasing him, he had Jack's form and Jack's voice to focus his attention on. Jack kept him running, kept him moving, kept him alive. Now, it was just Weaver running through the grey while Snow Fox chased him.

High above him, the sky-shaking voice of Snow Fox roared in high mirth.

"Ha, ha! Yes! Run, little Weaver! Run, little Weaver-Of-Dreams, Weaver-Of-Nothing! Run, you maggot, and feel the fear that is Snow Fox!"

Weaver ran.

****

Jack checked for a pulse.

Nothing.

"Shit."

Time was running out. These things were very specific. If he didn't bring Weaver back, he'd've failed. And if he failed....

Well, there was no real point in thinking about that. He just couldn't fail. Due Dareaga was having a wonderful time chasing Snow Fox around the place, but Weaver wished he'd hurry up and get it over with. The yelps were distracting.

"Settle down and digest, you albino fuck!" he yelled, while focusing his will. There were dark and forbidden magics that Jack knew would have Weaver up and dancing the Macarena in seconds . . . if he were inclined to use them. But this was his choice, and being Jack, there was a certain question of style.

"And I ain't trying to get all necrophiliac on this throwback fuck, anyhow," he muttered.

He reached into nowhere. His hand disappeared halfway to his forearm. He pulled out a very large syringe, full of a clear fluid. Reaching in to the nowhere again, he pulled out a complete defibrillator kit. He hooked the EKG up to Weaver, and turned the monitor. The EKG read flatline, as he knew it would.

Jack counted Weaver's ribs, and with a practiced flourish, he shoved the syringe's needle in between two of them and injected nearly 100ccs of pure adrenaline right to Weaver's heart muscle.

****

Weaver shuddered and stopped, grabbing at his heart. It felt as though something had just bitten him deep inside his chest. It hurt more than anything ever had, and it momentarily drove all other concerns from his mind, even the hunting Snow Fox.

"Here, my Father! Come this way!"

Weaver looked up. From out of the grey mists, a dim, blurry outline was waving an arm toward Weaver. The head was sitting on the torso in ungainly way, as if it had been nearly ripped off.

"Moonlight? Is that you, my son?" Weaver gasped.

****

Jack put an oxygen mask over Weaver's face. Firing up the defibrillator's electrical pulse mechanism, he watched the EKG monitor. Flatline. Jack started working on the gaping hole in Weaver's neck, sewing the torn edges shut with fingers that tapered down until they disappeared at the molecular level. He was literally gluing Weaver's torn neck molecules back together. He did this quickly and efficiently, pumping O2 into Weaver's face. The EKG remained flat-line.

"Alright, you sumbitch. Get ready ta' ride the lightning!"

Jack applied the paddles and shot Weaver full of juice.

****

Weaver screamed. It felt like his bones were on fire.

His muscles clenched. They were afire, and freezing, all at once.

"Here, my Father! Come here!"

Through eyes now streaming with bloody tears, Weaver looked up. Through the grey mists, he could see the ill-proportioned, broke-back, hulking shadow of Moonlight waving him forward.

****

". . . one-hundred-eighty-one-thousand. . .one-hundred-eighty-one-one-thousand . . ."

****

Jack checked Weaver's pulse again. *Nothing.*

"Alright. I played by the rules. Time to cheat." A flat, clear, opaque plane, like an explosion in space, radiated out from Jack.

". . . ooooonnnnneeeeeeeeeeeeeeeeeeeeeeeeeeeeee-huuuuuuuuuuuuunnnnnnnnn . . ."

The voice sounded like it was trying to make its call heard through a foot of amber.

Jack grinned down at Weaver's corpse. "I can't stop time. That's beyond me. But I can slow it down to a pace that'll do us some good."

Next, he very delicately took matters in his own hands.

"I can't believe I'm gonna pull this Neo-Loves-Trinity shit. I should totally kick your ass for making me use a pop-culture cliché, Weaver. In fact, I think I will once I get done fondling your heart."

Reaching in-between the molecular layers, Jack drove his hand into Weaver's chest, his hand and fingers wiggling slowly with the effort, and grasped Weaver's heart.

****

Weaver screamed. He could feel Jack's hand closing around his heart. The hand squeezed with a force that buckled Weaver's knees.

"I am sorry, my Father, but you do not belong here."

Weaver couldn't see. He couldn't speak. He couldn't do anything but lie there, cradling his arms across his chest, whimpering in fear and pain.

Something grabbed him by the hair and began to drag him across the ground.

****

The hunt was going badly. Snow Fox couldn't smell Weaver. There was no trace of him. It criss-crossed its own tracks, snuffling and sniffling, trying to find some evidence that Weaver was even still in Nifleheim.

Curiously, it could also feel itself losing power. It was shrinking, reducing. It had no explanation for this, but it could not feel all of itself, either.

This was not unusual. Being a multi-dimensional entity meant sometimes losing track of bits of yourself. And when one was as deceptive and tricky as Snow Fox, it was possible to lie to oneself so convincingly as to believe everything one believed.

It could find nothing. It looked up, its amber eyes easily piercing the grey gloom around it, trying to see Weaver. Off in the distance, just disappearing into the mists, Snow Fox saw Moonlight's mangled spirit dragging Weaver's body.

It grinned and ran toward them. *'Two for the price of one!'* it thought, already anticipating the crunch of bone and the spilling of dead blood.

****

".nnnnnnnnnnnnnnnnnnnnnndddddddddddddddddd dddddddddddd . . ."

Jack squeezed Weaver's heart in a rhythmic pattern while simultaneously flexing his diaphragm muscle to force air in and out of his lungs. He delved further and began pushing the red blood cells through Weaver's arteries and veins, going so far as to load the blood cells with oxygen and to pull the waste gases off of them. There was a lot of necrotizing going on already, and Jack did what he could with the cells that had expired. He suspected that a lot of this was posing. Weaver had killed himself. It could be argued that Weaver had sacrificed himself to the not-wind. If he managed to bring Weaver back, he wasn't entirely sure what would arrive. It would be wearing Weaver's skin, but . . .

Potassium and glucose were produced, and he fed them to Weaver's cells like a mother spoon-feeding an infant. Sodium; vitamins; minerals; carbohydrates; he fed Weaver's cells everything he could think of. He even fed them minute levels of caffeine, nicotine and some cocaine, figuring it could only help at this point.

If it ends up I was wrong, Weaver'll just be dead, he thought, spooning another load of electro-chemical necessity into Weaver's red blood cells.

It was as advanced as advanced life-saving could get.

****

Moonlight released Weaver's hair.

"My Father does not belong in the land of the dead," Moonlight said, his voice was toneless and monotone.

Weaver heard Moonlight's voice, but it made no sense to him. The returning sensations of life overwhelmed him. He felt the burn of air in his lungs, the flow of blood in his veins, the prickle of pain. His eyes were tight shut, but suddenly, he saw Jack's face. It was bent over his, and Jack's eyes were also, as if he were concentrating.

"He labors to save your life, my Father," whispered Moonlight's dead voice.

Weaver could only stare. Moonlight reached a hand down and covered Weaver's mouth. "Be silent, my father. Snow Fox comes."

Snow Fox reached them an eye-blink later. He saw Weaver's slowly fading form with Moonlight standing over him.

***

"rrrrrrrrrrrrrrrrrrrrrreeeeeeeeeeeeeeeeeeeeeeeeeeeeee eeddddddd . . ."

Jack continued his CPR. He periodically checked Weaver's pulse and his brain's electrical-chemical system. It was taking a while, but Weaver's brain was beginning to respond. The electrical-chemical reactions were increasing, and Jack felt autonomous twitches and flutters under his feverishly working fingers. He had a long way to go, but Weaver was coming back.

"It's like givin' a car a jump. You just gotta keep feedin' the fucking thing juice. Eventually you'll either get it started or it'll burn down to the axles. Either way, the car's battery being dead isn't an issue anymore." he said, to no one in particular.

****

Weaver opened his eyes one last time. Moonlight

stood over him. He looked down at him with sad, dead eyes.

"My Father does not belong in the land of the dead," he said. And Snow Fox appeared, his eyes blazing.

"No! Moonli-" he screamed, through the soul-burning pain, before the full return of life silenced him to Moonlight utterly.

****

Jack sighed in relief when he heard the EKG give a feeble beep. Weaver's heart was starting to beat on its own. He kept up his CPR, but began pulling back, putting more of the load on the heart itself.

Time passed.

"C'mon, Weaver, ya' smelly sumbitch. I don't like you enough to be inside you like this!"

"eeeeeeeeeeeeeeeeeeeeeeeeeeeeeeeeeeeeeiiiiiiiiiiiiii iiiiiiiiiiiggggggggggggg . . ."

****

Weaver heard a rushing noise. It was a strangely rhythmic sound, and one he'd felt he'd heard before. It took him a long moment to realize that what he was hearing was the beating of his own heart. He closed his eyes to Moonlight's face, and opened them to see Jack.

"Jack . . .?" Weaver's voice was weak and thready, muffled under the oxygen mask.

Jack opened his eyes and looked down at Weaver. Weaver was looking back up at him. His eyes were half-closed and lethargic, but awareness was there. From behind him he heard the sound of Due Dareaga feeding ecstatically on Snow Fox.

****

Snow Fox saw the mangled and twisted body of Weaver's son Moonlight. It was well. If he couldn't have Weaver, he'd at least have the satisfaction of consuming the son's dead spirit. It wasn't as good a jest as breaking Weaver and killing him, but taking anything away from Weaver, no matter how pointless was still a wonderful prank.

"Turn and face me, Moonlight-on-Water. Face me and see your final oblivion!"

Moonlight shuffled listlessly around. His dead eyes met Snow Fox's. With a leap and a closing snap of jaws, Snow Fox finally began to feed.

****

They didn't emerge from smoke and shadow, nor did they suddenly pop into existence. This far out on the reality curve, they were everywhere, and in a very real sense, already here watching. The Three, in one of their many aspects, stood over the scene, brought here by the moon's death in this forbidden place of power. The killer was male. He knew the rituals, and all was done properly, but they had been offended, and by a man. Men should not dabble in the affairs of women.

Weaver didn't see them. His eyes were closed and he lay on the grass in a sort of half-doze, recovering from his recent exertions.

Nothing goes unnoticed, nothing goes unpunished. And if they refuse to act, that is their decision as well. They are the Three Who Decide, and they stood over Jack, watching.

The Three watched silently, observing things and keeping their own counsel, as was their usual way.

Jack felt the presence of the Three, but he made no

move to recognize them. His heart hammered in his chest, sweat ran down his face, and he suspected that his hands were covered in bits and pieces of Weaver that he didn't want to examine too closely. It wasn't an auspicious way to meet anybody for the first time, much less an aspect of a power you've just pimp-slapped.

For its part, Due Dareaga was aware of the Three, but Due Dareaga's awareness of things was suspect at best. For instance, it could not determine the differences in sex between members of the same species, nor could it accurately judge chronological age. Subtlety was lost on it, and it tended to view things in the black and white of 'MEAT' and 'NOT MEAT.'

Most everything that existed was 'MEAT.'

Due Dareaga noted the three of them: a young, man-thing, holding a bundle of yarn; an older man-thing, holding knitting needles, and an ancient man-thing, holding a sharp but rusty knife.

Due Dareaga picked what was left of Snow Fox up, looked at them, and measured their strength with a practiced predator's eye. It knew, somehow, that here, if ever there had been in the long centuries of its existence was 'NOT MEAT.' Its other, the Jack-thing, tried to keep it from 'MEAT' by telling it 'MEAT' was 'NOT MEAT,' but Due Dareaga knew better. The other, the Jack-thing, just wanted the 'MEAT' for himself! That was why he kept it from Due Dareaga.

Due Dareaga held Snow Fox tightly in one fist and waited to see if the three man-things would try to take its meal from him.

When the three women ignored him, Due Dareaga mentally shrugged.

'MEAT,' it said, in its silent voice of pumping blood and growing bone. It shook Snow Fox by the scruff of its neck at the three women, waited briefly for a response, and then lifted Snow Fox's face to the hole of its own and went back to its noisy feed.

***

"The hunter wakens, my sisters," said the Young to the other two. "He has died. Twice. He lives in the forbidden beyond: the third life. And he has pulled our sister-moon from the sky. Should he go unpunished for this?" Her voice was like sweet music under a wakening sky of purest blue.

"Not he, my sisters. The fairy. But it was at the hunter's cozening that the Stranger acted. Yes, my sisters. He awakes. He died the first death, and the second. Now he wakes to a new form; one I think he'll not be grateful for. He swims through the healing sleep, but he awakes," replied the Brooding. "And what shall we three do with him?" Her voice was like the buzz of somnolent insects, late in summer, during the hottest part of the day, but there was that of it which reflected the Young's voice. It was as if she spoke from the same place the Young spoke from, but with a different mouth.

"What's to be done, my sisters?" replied the Ancient in her cracked voice of splintered bone. "He's made his choices. He's paid his debts, and now he reaps his reward. He's stuck with it, as are all of his People. He is human. They pretend to control their own lives. Let this one try." Her voice was like the crack of final thunders; the melting of fatal ice; the doom in the night that comes with a groan and the fall of ages. She too sounded as though she were echoing her sisters, and indeed, when the Ancient spoke, the lips of the other two moved in soundless concert with her words.

"And what of the Peer; the Green One?" asked the Brooding.

"Ah, yes. The fairy," replied the Young. "He lives in the Story. He pays part of his debt, and by paying, seeks to undo the things that bind him. That has naught to do with us, though he helps the hunter who insults us so. We choose instead to remember his dread insult to our other sister."

"Yes. He killed her, did he not?" said the Brooding.

"He did indeed," replied the Ancient. "The fairy insults us much, my sisters. Should this be borne?"

"The fairy is of no matter, my sisters," replied the Brooding. "Fairies lie under the Earth. They are the Strangers and Of the Green. Our own dear sister will deal with him as she sees fit."

"The fairy has chosen this?" asked the Ancient.

"He has, my sisters. Chosen it of his own free will," replied the Brooding.

"And what of the godling? Do we let this aspect of it die the death of Due Dareaga?" asked the Young.

"What is a godling to us, my sisters?" replied the Ancient. "One trickster godling of ice and snow is as bad as any other, wouldn't you say? There are other aspects of it. Let it find them and rejoin it later. We have come, we have seen. Perhaps we will punish the fairy later. Perhaps not. But we are no longer needed here."

The Three stood for a moment longer, watching. Their eyes were now as white and dead as ice under water. They turned toward Yggdrasil, nodded to it as equals and friends, and disappeared.

Jack sighed in relief.

Weaver slowly opened his eyes. "I am alive, Jack?" His voice was feeble, but gaining steady strength.

Jack wiped his hands on his trousers. He grimaced at the slimy, greasy feel of them.

"Relatively. For somebody who's never heard a Fender turned up to eleven, I guess. You're about ready to finish things up, aren't ya'?" he said, lighting another one of his burning tubes.

"I am," Weaver replied. He felt within himself. His injuries—the scrapes and bruises, cuts and knocks; the tenderness of his healing fingers—it was all there, but it felt . . . right. He removed the strange mask blowing air into his face and with a tremendous effort, stood up. He swayed, took a few steps forward, and locked himself into position, standing on his own feet with an effort, but standing.

He looked at Jack. He looked beyond Jack to see the rapidly desiccating corpse of Snow Fox disappearing—like blood down an ice hole—into nothing.

"It won't bother you no more."

Weaver nodded, grateful. He was still very weak, but he felt his strength returning, moment by moment.

"I must go, Jack! I have a kiss to deliver!"

"Yep. Go that way," Jack pointed toward the west. "You'll soon find your way home, Dorothy."

Weaver began to shamble into the direction of the setting sun. He was back! He was free of Snow Fox! Soon Moonlight would live again!

****

Jack sighed. He drew heavily on his cigarette. It smelled of burning bone and long-forgotten, dusty hallways. He watched as Yggdrasil opened a hole into reality, into which Weaver ran with more high-pitched whoops of delight.

The hole closed with an anti-climactic 'pop' and Jack sighed again. Due Dareaga crawled back, with a torpid-lizard's lack of grace, into their shared skull, and settled down to digest its meal and have a bit of a nap.

"Welp, that's that, I guess," he said, to no-one in particular. "I 'magine I'd better go see what other trouble I can get into."

****

Jack began looking for a thin place into reality. There were any number of holes here and he was a master at finding them. He needed only to feel the static tingle of world membranes rubbing up against each other to make his way to his next destination.

Yggdrasil blew a leafy goodbye at him and Jack smiled.

"Yeah. You too, brah," he said.

Jack smoked his cigarette, inhaling each puff until the entire thing was gone. There was nothing left to do here, except . . .

A wind picked up, blowing leaves and dust into Jack's eyes. He coughed and spit, sneezed, and wiped at his suddenly running eyes. When he opened them, Snow Fox stood in front of him, fresh blood dripping from its muzzle. A single, small finger, well-chewed, was caught in the twisted mat of its coat. It was much smaller and thinner than the last time Jack had seen him, but that was only to be expected. You don't get an aspect of yourself consumed without losing part of the whole.

"You know he will fail," Snow Fox said, licking a pink tongue slowly over the still-warm blood. It noticed the finger and nipped it free of its coat.

"Thought I told you to beat it, dick-hole."

"And who are you to tell me anything, fairy?"

Jack grinned. It was a hard, cold, mirthless smile that promised death. But first there would be pain; pain like slowly broken glass. He lit another cigarette, savoring the taste of fresh-mown grass. He looked down at Snow Fox, cracking his knuckles, one by one, still smiling his daft, cold smile. He released his hold on the form he wore, letting Snow Fox see him as he truly was.

The bargain he made was forcing him to help Weaver, and he couldn't do that if Weaver was gibbering in insane fear at his true form. So he wore something a little less threatening. There was no need to do that with Snow Fox.

Snow Fox backed hurriedly away.

"I'm the guy that's gonna pimp-slap you into the next time zone, Snow Fox," Jack said, his voice like trees falling or oceans evaporating. He stood nine feet tall, and almost as broad. His hands were enormous paws, tipped with claws of glass. His eyes dripped sparks and the horns on his head gave off multi-colored flashes of light. "Then I'm gonna come find you, reach down your throat, and pull your tail out through your asshole. Then I'm gonna get really creative with your inside out, upside down carcass. I might pop your eyes out and skull-fuck you for the sheer pleasure of hearing your brain mush against the inside of your head-"

"He will fail, fairy! He will fail, and then he will die, and then he will belong to me!" Snow Fox yipped, backing still further from Jack.

"So?"

Snow Fox stopped and looked up at Jack quizzically. ***"You do not care?"***

Jack shrugged.

"I don't give a flying fuck, Snow Fox. Ain't my problem. Weaver's life is his to do with exactly as he pleases. If he wants to jump off a bridge wearing a bra with his dick tucked between his legs and an umbrella shoved up his ass, that's his thing."

Snow Fox grinned. It was lascivious and servile. ***"Then we should work together, Jack! If you do not care."***

"No. See, the problem is I do care. Not about Weaver. I mean, if we boiled him so the muscles fall off the bone, he's just another mortal. You turn your back for a few hundred years, and he falls over dead anyway. The boss seems to think otherwise, but I think one fuck-up's pretty much the same as any other fuck-up. Weaver just happened to be standing under the pipe when the universe pulled the chain. No, I could care less about Weaver. What I do care about is you disrespecting me in my hood."

Jack made a sudden grab for Snow Fox. Snow Fox

yipped in alarm and jumped nimbly out of the way into one of Yggdrasil's branches.

Yggdrasil, one of the foundation stones on which the universe stood, blew a quiet warning of moss and sun-warmed branch into Jack's face. Yggdrasil never spoke in words; couldn't if someone asked it to. No, it was a sensation of warning, mixed with a smell, combined with the texture of warm broth being slowly poured over your head.

Jack got the idea. Shedding blood here, in Yggdrasil's branches, innocent or otherwise, would be punished. Sacrifice was one thing; it was allowed most anywhere. But the violent shedding of blood was quite another. Three feet away would be fine, but here Yggdrasil would get pissy. And while Jack and Snow Fox were mighty powers in their own right, neither one of them was about to disrespect Yggdrasil, the World Tree.

Jack glared up at Snow Fox, clenching and unclenching his fists.

"I could reach up there, walk five feet away and rip your skin off to use as toilet paper, Snow Fox. You know it and so do I. But I'm gonna respect Yggy's space. Know this: you can only run so far, asshole. Eventually I'll find you. And when I do, I'm gonna make a sandwich out of you."

Snow Fox grinned and turned around three times on his branch, sun wise.

"Yes," it said, as it disappeared. ***"I will be looking forward to our next meeting as well, Jack O'Green. I think perhaps it will hold surprises for you."***

Chapter Two

Weaver floated, unconcerned, he drifted in and out for a time. At one point he was sure Moonlight stood over him; his hands strong, his arms hale, his body whole. He smiled down at Weaver, his eyes shining with love.

Jumping-Ice-Spider came and railed at him in languages he could not understand. Her anger mystified him, and left him hurt and befuddled.

Otter came, as did Bear Claw. Each one saying things to him; touching him, reaching out to him with imploring hands. Faces, voices, all intertwined and mixed, cascading on him like fallen ice or drifting snow, one chasing another and another.

After long enough for the universe to end and begin again, Weaver opened his eyes to the roof of his own skin hut. Recognizing the pattern of well-tanned skin immediately, he drew a sharp, involuntary breath of excitement and regretted it. It was only with the greatest effort that he stifled a groan. The pain in his body was exquisite. Every inch of him ached, and intense twinges inside him spoke of damage done on a deeper level; internal hurt that may or may not ever heal. Still, he was looking at the roof of his skin hut. He made it! He'd done it! Everything would be fine now!

Smiling in relief, he tried to stand. The pain that coursed through him was like lightning. Bones shifted inside him that grated and clicked against each other in their torment. The scream he gave did little to relieve his agony. His vision grayed, and he felt himself slipping back into the comfortable nowhere he'd lost himself in for a time. Gritting his teeth, he forced himself to stay conscious. When he returned to himself fully, opening his eyes, his mate, Jumping-Ice-Spider was wiping his brow. Her eyes swam with concern and Weaver felt himself floating away into the love he saw reflected there.

"You must lie still, Weaver-Of-Shadows," she said, her voice as soft as snow on the eyelash. Her face was as beautiful as it had always been. Weaver felt hot tears of love threatening. He swallowed as she wiped a gentle hand down his cheek. "The injuries you have suffered will take you from us if you try to-"

Weaver shook his head, smiling gently. He lifted his hand to her lips, and it was like moving the earth backwards. Arms weighing as much as mountains, a single finger managed to make the journey to her silken lips and touch, for an instant. His mouth worked as he tried to speak. So dry! He was so dry! It felt like he'd never had a drink of water or anything like it. His tongue felt like a torn rag, useless and filthy. Jumping-Ice-Spider saw his discomfiture, and lifted a skin of water to his lips. The first few drops were like heaven, and he could feel them working through him. He sucked greedily at the skin, but Jumping-Ice-Spider pulled it away.

"You must rest, Weaver. You have been through much, and you body cannot accept more than the smallest portions. Please, try to sleep-"

"M . . . Muuh . . . Moonlight . . ."

Jumping-Ice-Spider turned away, her lips thinning and her eyes closing.

"We will speak of Moonlight later, Weaver. Please rest."

And she laid a hand on his brow, and sang a song only the women know. Despite himself, and despite his best efforts, Weaver felt himself falling away into the slow, drifting darkness.

****

More time passed, and he drifted in and out, sometimes for only an instant, sometimes for what felt like days. He was as weak as an infant, and he never woke for more than water, food, and the basic utilities of his toilet. Jumping-Ice-Spider was never far from his side, and her love was a constant beacon. Weaver marshaled his strength, speaking little when he could return from his comfortable healing darkness, and smiled the wise smile of the victor.

He would live. He would heal, he would grow strong, and then he would return his son to a full and rich life that could shine like all the stars in the sky!

****

"I do not think he realizes it yet, Bear Claw. His body is so changed. His heart, I can hear it beating in his chest during the night. He breathes so slowly now, and his body is like ice, his muscles like stone! But the worst of it is Moonlight. I think he believes Moonlight is yet-"

"There are many secrets beneath the sky, Spider. Who can say what Weaver has seen? What he has been through? What he has done? He lay on the ice for a time longer than any man of the People. We live our lives in the very shadows of the gods. Who can say what Weaver heard or saw or did? Perhaps Weaver sought their favor and they changed him. I think you can only let him sleep. The time for hard truths will come. Be patient."

Weaver heard the words and followed them fully into consciousness. A lamp burned nearby, casting shadows that danced. He wondered if the voices he had heard were real or more of his healing dreams. For the first time he felt as if he knew himself fully, and could finally participate in the activities of life.

"Spider?" he called, shocked at the weak condition of his voice.

Jumping-Ice-Spider's face swam into view. Love and concern shone in her eyes, and nothing more. "Weaver? Are you awake?"

Weaver closed his eyes. "I think . . . I think perhaps I am, Spider. Will you help me sit up?"

"Ho, Weaver-Of-Shadows! How good it is to see your eyes shine in the light!"

The voice rang. There was only one man who could sound like that.

"Bear Claw," Weaver said, his voice thick with remembered failure. Bear Claw had been the hunt leader. Bear Claw had been the one who had led them onto the ice. Bear Claw had not protected Moonlight from the mother bear's falling claws.

"We have kept long vigil over your corpse, Weaver-Of-Shadows!" Bear Claw said, his face smiling and his eyes watching and weighing. Weaver remembered the feel of the spear in his hands after Moonlight . . . after Moonlight fell. Why hadn't he run the man through then?

Ah, well. Time to fix that after.....

"I am not dead yet, Bear Claw," he said, forcing a smile into the rigid, hate-locked muscles of his face.

Bear Claw laughed, throwing his head back and roaring. "No! No, you are not! And I expect you won't be for a long time yet, Weaver! You are harder than stone and sharper than a spear!"

He beamed at Weaver. "I must tell the rest of the tribe you have returned to us. Be well, Weaver-Of-Shadows."

"And you, Bear Claw," Weaver said, finishing the ritual greeting out of habit.

Jumping-Ice-Spider busied herself in a corner of the hut, doing things that seemed to require all of her attention.

"Spider?"

His voice was so weak! How broken he felt, and how like a powerless child!

Clearing his throat, he tried again. "Spider."

She stopped her work and knelt beside him, smoothing a gentle hand down his chest. She smelled of the cold, clean wind and the snow.

"Yes, Weaver? Are you hungry? I have some broth set aside that Otter says may help."

"No, Spider. I am not hungry. Where is Moonlight?"

Jumping-Ice-Spider looked away, her eyes darting. "We can speak of that later, Weaver. Perhaps I should fix you some of that broth. I imagine you are very hungry."

"Spider," Weaver said, reaching out to her.

Spider's chest hitched, and she made a small sound. She covered her face in her hands and her entire body clenched, just once.

"Spider? What is it?"

For a moment longer, she sat there, her face in her hands. And then she looked at Weaver, her eyes running tears.

"Weaver," she said, her lips trembling and her voice cracking with every syllable. "Weaver, Moonlight is dead. His body was consigned to the flames many turns of the sky ago. The Lamentations for the Dead have been sung, and the time of mourning is long past."

Weaver shook his head. "No, no. No. I have only slept for a short time-"

"Weaver, you lay on the ice for an entire turning of the moon. The men said that your mind slept, but your body kept them away from you. Night after night they tried to bring you home and night after night you chased them from you with drawn spear and knife. The men said that winds blew around you and your head was veiled in darkness. Your eyes were closed and you made no sound, but no one could approach you. It was only after the moon had turned that your body weakened enough for them to subdue you and you bring you here. From that time to this, you have slept! You have slept for seven turnings of the sky! The time of the hunt has passed seven times! Look at me! Am I as you remember me?"

Weaver looked at her, confused and scared. He'd not noticed the changes, seeing only his beloved Spider. But now that she'd drawn his attention, he saw the hints of white in her long, dark hair. He'd thought it a trick of the light. Spider saw him peering myopically at her, and she thrust her face into his.

"Look at me! I am older, Weaver-Of-Shadows! The scars of time have touched my face! Your son is dead seven times over!"

Chapter Three

Shadow's voice tailed off into silence. He dropped his hands and the skeins of Story melted into the nothing from which they came. Shadow's eyes were still closed. He opened them to see Solly Mont's boring into his.

The only noises were the cracking of the fire and the howling of the not-wind outside their haven.

He sighed. "The rest we have through mighty magics, indeed. Much of what we know we had to speak to the long dead to learn. Many Shamans lost their own connection to life, dwelling too long in the land of death and dream.

"This all happened long ago. The story was told, Shaman to Shaman. All of the People know the story of Weaver, but the last tales of his life are tellings that only the Shamans know."

Shadow swallowed and took a deep breath.

"Weaver . . ." Shadow sighed again. "Weaver has become one with the winds of madness, Solly Mont. By defiling his common soul—scaring his palm and offering the blood to Snow Fox as he did in front of the World Gate—Weaver defiled the commonality of the People.

"It is a hard thing, but we survive as we do because we are one people. The laws and traditions ties us one to another, so that all may live. Our gods gave us the sign of the aurora, flowing in our blood to remind us of our oaths and common life. When Weaver rejected all of that, he rejected his place among the people. He rejected the rights of all of us to live in favor of his own needs, wants and desires. He was to be cut off in our traditions, and left to make his way as a man alone. The tribe of the Glinting Badger took him back, however, as you have heard, and overlooked or ignored what is right and holy to do according to our laws.

"I think perhaps that mercy for Weaver's loss clouded their judgment. But they paid for their lack of discipline.

"The not-wind used the hole Weaver had cut into the commonality to force its way into Weaver. His mind left him. He killed his mate, Jumping-ice-Spider. He choked her and then crawled, naked, from his bed to the place of the Dead Fires. When Bear Claw confronted him, holding a spear, Weaver tore it from his hands and killed him with it. Arrows broke on his body. Spears refused to pierce him. Knives shattered on his skin. Otter fired one of his precious beads at him, and it bounced off, caroming into the night and killing another tribesmen.

"He crawled on his hands and knees, weeping the entire way, killing or maiming those who tried to come between him and the fires. A powerful gust followed him, with screaming voices of the damned riding it.

"Though he was weak, starved and barely alive after his ordeal, no-one could stand against him. He was borne on the arms of madness; indestructible and unstoppable. Weaver crawled to the ashes, broken and weak as he was, and began eating them. He did not stop until he had reached the bottom of the pile."

Solly made an involuntary noise of horror and disgust.

"When he had finished eating the ashes, he stood to his feet, naked, and loped off onto the ice. The ones left behind did not try to catch him. He killed the strongest hunters in the tribe. Everyone who stood against him was killed, crippled or mauled. In one act, Weaver effectively killed them all. No-one was strong enough to hunt, and the Tribe of the Glinting Badger was no more. Some survived, but they were a tribe no longer.

"Time passed. Those left of the Tribe of the Glinting Badger made way for stronger tribes. They were absorbed and intermarried, becoming other people. The People tried to live their lives. After one full turning of the sky, the killings started.

"The People started to die, Solly Mont. First, all the remaining members of the Tribe of the Glinting Badger. They moved to many different hunting grounds, spread among many different tribes. Some were very far away from the evil of Weaver, but he soon found them. One by one they died, one a year.

"When all of the Badger were dead, Weaver turned his hand to the other tribes. One by one. Always in the darkest, coldest part of the night, and always in secret. We heard their screams in the night, and though the hunters searched with torches and what magic we command, we have never been able to find them. And always that screaming. The bodies are found on the ice much later, torn and twisted; some of them appear to have been feasted on, and tortured in ways that I will not speak of here.

"Every turning, on the anniversary of Moonlight's consumption, someone dies in horrible screaming agony. We have sent hunter after hunter, and no one has ever found anything other than broken bodies. The killer leaves no trace of himself behind and nothing we can do stops him. We believe it is Weaver-of-Shadows, and we believe him to have become a creature only the Shamans speak of, and only in secret: a Reaver. We have no magic to fight the Reaver. It is harder than our spears and arrows, and it is a creature of un-ending hunger, fear, sorrow and evil. It serves the wind that briefly kissed your brow in coming here. None of the people can stand before it and live.

"The People are spread thin, Solly Mont, and we are few. The children born to us are small and weak. The hunters die and no food is brought to the suckling mouths.

We die in pain and screaming agony, but we also die in hunger and want. If this continues, the People will die. If the People die, then man will die. The lands of the sky-rent are still poisoned, and nothing can live outside of the lands of the People. I have waited here for longer than you could possibly imagine, for one promised to come. I hoped to find answers, and I find you. So I charge you, Solly Mont, as the hospitality price owed me and the People: save us. Save us all."

Solly stared at Shadow for a long moment. "You don't ask for much, do you, Shadow?"

Shadow smiled grimly. "I seek the payment owed me. I have sung the song I was taught. I would rest now. Perhaps you have a story? Shared waters of wisdom lead to deeper pools of insight, so say the People."

There was a long silence as the two men weighed the responsibilities amassed between them. It was Solly who broke it.

"Yes. I think I do have a story. Mine's not quite so grim as yours, Shadow. Not by half. But Jack's got a starring role, and if the universe runs the way I've been taught it does, you need to hear this story. This happened a long time ago as I reckon things: years and years before I had the slightest idea of what magic really was; long before I'd ever met you or Taliesin. It starts in a little town I've come to believe may be home. It seems this place, a town by the name of Oakenfeld, celebrates an important holiday once a year, remembering a battle that took place a long way from there . . ."

And Solly Mont took up the skeins of Story. He was not yet the Storyweaver he would become, but he was better than most. And he was a sungmeister born. He could weave a story that would hold back the night for a time, and perhaps find the solution to the problems the two of them faced. He took the loom from Shadow and began to weave his own skeins upon it.

Chapter Four

The place was nameless and that gave it a certain power. It was a tattered scrub of earth. Even the local, fanatically xenophobic tribesmen avoided it.

Namelessness forms a protective bubble; a kind of invisibility. So long as a place, a person, a thing, hasn't got a name, it can be unnoticed for millennia. Once you name it, it has weight, gravity, presence. It begins to pull people and things toward it.

The place in question was a bare-faced escarpment rising from the desert sand like a hang-nail; a basalt cliff, several hundred feet high. It was the only landmass for a hundred miles that hadn't been weathered into sand.

There were some tough plants atop the cliff that provided meager sustenance for a small flock of goats. A pool of tepid water sat at the cliff's base, fed by a weak, underground spring.

If one cared to, you could work your way up the sheer sides of the cliff, climbing and struggling in the pottery-kiln-like temperatures of the sun-blasted desert, and have an unparalleled view of several thousand miles of naked wasteland flowing from dune to dune like an endless sea, just in time to die of heat stroke. It was important to no-one.

Men on thrones, however, have very different ideas about what is important and what is not. When men on thrones begin drawing lines on maps and looking at the lines on their neighbor's maps, even forgotten basalt cliffs growing out of remote deserts in the sun-baked Outrealms can suddenly be of tremendous strategic importance.

The king looked at his map, saw the area in question and proclaimed it of dramatic strategic importance to his empire. In ringing royal tones, he declaimed that it would be the spot of a fort known to all the realms as Fort Legueone.

The spit of land, which now had a name, would be guarded year round by a full rifle company: one thousand men, of His Royal Majesty's Own.

There were no volunteers.

The king, being no prouder or stupider than any other king anywhere, was forced to populate his spanking new fort with a less-than-desirable force of mercenaries, discipline-problem-soldiers, draftees and other dregs from around the empire.

If a man was able to see lightning and hear thunder, the king was willing to pay him the princely sum of one crown a year, for a commitment of ten years; burial expenses and all the sand he could eat. In no time at all, the roster was full and one thousand men found themselves en-route to the extreme edge of the king's empire, in hell. The local tribesmen, previously indifferent to the desert strip, became determined to take it back from the "barbarian invaders," especially after said barbarians had the bare-faced audacity to build a fort in the only place for a thousand miles with any sort of shade. Such are the evils perpetuated by ill-informed men given unfettered access to badly drawn maps.

Men came and went. Every ten years, a new company went out, and the survivors of the previous incarceration came back.

So it was one bright spring morning that a fleet of ships sailed from the capital of the empire, bearing one thousand men and their commander, Solly Mont.

The coast itself had only one safe harbor where ships could land. A tattered town of sorts had sprung up and this was the only place for thousands of miles that had a bazaar or a tavernasi. The rest of the 'human outposts' within the fort's jurisdiction were the tents of nomads huddling around thin puddles of water and the occasional encampment of tribesmen.

The ships, cheaply built for the sole purpose of transporting the King's majestic army to their new home, were tossed and battered by the waves. They sprung leaks, grew mold, and threatened at every swell to fly into a thousand pieces. The soldiers within, land-lubbers to a man, suffered accordingly. They were wracked with fevers, agues, seasickness and diarrheas. The food went bad. The water grew stale.

There were fights. Blood was drawn, bones were broken. Small mutinies, conspiracies of two or three, were put down once every few days with a liberal flogging by the fort's new Sergeant major: Fergus Ingersoll, as ill-tempered and evil a man as ever lived. He was also the fort's chaplain.

Sergeant Major Fergus Ingersoll feared only one thing and that secretly: his new commander, Solly Mont. There was something about the wise, knowing look in those fierce, black eyes that made goose-pimples rise. Like many bred-in-the-bone bullies, this infuriated Fergus beyond words. It was shameful to fear any man, but even worse when that man wasn't white.

To his way of thinking, any man who wasn't born white and serving the same God the same way Fergus did had one foot in hell anyway, and he lived by his convictions. The black and yellow men under him suffered indignities that brought on far more disciplinary problems than would normally be the case.

As for Solly Mont, he moved shipboard as ferociously as a tiger. His every step was sure. The captain of Solly Mont's vessel, on watching his stalking passenger moving from stem to stern on his daily inspection, remarked to his first mate, "Ah'd hate ta' have a piece a'that lookin' down at me from th' far end o' a'cutlass. Tha' one's made a'teak."

Solly's back was straight, his stomach firm. His hands, as strong as steel cables, were flexing constantly. One could almost hear the knuckles creaking. His black eyes blazed at the clouds above them and he seemed to take the rough crossing as being a personal affront. His stern, warrior's face never evinced the least sign of discomfort, and he ate at every meal, defying the seasickness that so plagued everyone else. With the waves crashing ten and twenty feet high, Solly Mont was always in a neatly pressed, spotlessly clean uniform; his saber ever present at his side, his tri-corner hat sitting firmly on his head, his boots polished to mirror shine.

Brave, handsome and dashing, Solly cut a very different figure from his less-than-savory command, and his command responded to his military bearing with a surprising affection and loyalty before the ships had even landed.

"There's summat about tha' one; do y' ken it?"

"Aye. E's got th' eye o' a king, th' hands of a chief, an' th' bloody muscles of a bull. There's summat about 'im. Too right!"

He was a hard, fierce man, but a wise and just leader as well. He often stopped to speak with his men, learning their names and holding conversations of little importance with them. He never spoke of much, but to the demoralized, ignored criminals that made up the vast bulk of his command, the little was often more than enough.

No one knew much about him. In the rumor-plagued confines the men found themselves in, this was odd enough to be remarked on in its own right. No one could say much about where he came from or who his people were. Some said he had come from somewhere in the outlands outside the empire. His curly locks, cut to regulation length, and his dark skin and black eyes suggested the Orient, but his voice had the clipped accent of the northlands where the wind was cold and the sun never rose far above the horizon. Stories swirled around him like lazy smoke. It was said he'd lived for many years on a palatial estate some distance east of the empire on a barbarous island. It was said he was married to the Princess of the Night, and he ran from her vast anger.

Some people even went so far as to say he wasn't human at all, but a dark and powerful spirit wearing human skin. Some said that his eyes spoke of a wanderer whose whims took him out of sadness.

Solly let people think what they would. While secrets and rumors covered him like grease, he was also the only person of command who'd asked to be sent. He'd walked into the king's very castle, asked to see the commander of the king's forces, and told him he'd like to be sent to Fort Legueone as commander. The general, only too glad to have someone willing to be in command, left his past unexplored.

The fort itself was built directly into the cliff. It was generally round, like a boil, with thirty-foot-high, crenellated walls. Five-hundred men had died slow, heat-blasting deaths building it.

The common people of the empire didn't know or care that Fort Legueone existed. Even the king had forgotten about it.

Only the recruiters remembered Fort Legueone and they sent men there every ten years. It was a place where a man came to forget, or to be forgotten.

Were it not for the barren inhospitality of the surrounding desert, the posting would be relatively easy. The tactical ridiculousness of Fort Legueone left the men with little in the way of soldiering. The only people who cared about it were the local tribesmen, who sent occasional parties to harass and annoy the troops stationed there. There was no command from his Royal Majesty to extend the empire's jurisdiction, no need to improve what couldn't be improved in the lands around the fort, and no towns or settlements to protect. Aside from keeping the fort from falling apart and keeping themselves alive, the soldiers were left with very little to do. Solly Mont's job was mostly keeping them from going insane with boredom.

The men spent their time fighting the occasional skirmish with the aforementioned tribesmen, their Sergeants, and each other. A ship sailed from the empire once a year, laden with such supplies as the quartermasters felt the fort needed, mail and pay, and the men made trips once every three months back to the ratty little landing-town on the coast. If the ship was due in, they'd meet it. If not, they fought, drank and whored as much as they could for a fortnight. They marched back to the fort with their meager supplies, poorer, sore and ready to start it all over again.

Day followed day, week followed week, and year followed year, with a drudging sameness that challenged the very fabric of the human soul.

The soldiers of Fort Legueone, sheltered by the wise hand of their commander, Solly Mont, managed to stay a desperate, dancing half-step ahead of a crippling boredom that approached homicidal insanity.

They called the place Fort Nowhere, going so far as to erect a sign over the gate in every language of the Empire.

In naming it, with a True Name, they drew an awesome power to them that would change and save all of their lives. For out beyond the dreary, hot walls, the tribes were gathering with one goal in mind: the eradication of this place and all the men within it.

****

It was the beginning of their third year in this place that the magic that had been unconsciously woven by a thousand desperate men was let loose upon the weave of the world.

Fort Legueone was on full alert, the men pulling double shifts under a nervous command. They had been instructed, after numerous sightings, to keep a keen eye out for a large band of tribesmen that had been seen in the area.

The tribesmen usually had no more than five or ten in any one encampment at any time. It was believed these were families of one or two groups, at the most.

A group had been sighted that numbered more than a hundred. At first it was believed to have been a migration of some kind; tribesmen leaving the area because of the fort. Then other large groupings were sighted, and the sightings were increasing in frequency. Then the smaller, usual encampments of men, women, children and even livestock started throwing themselves at the fort. They died under a freezing hail of bullets every time, but their attacks were increasing in frequency and ferocity. The command of Fort Nowhere believed a large-scale attack was imminent.

It worried Solly. He doubled the watches and patrols. He'd sent dispatches back to the king, asking for additional materiel, but he had a strong suspicion that Fort Nowhere would be on its own in the event of any kind of a real attack. He had been hoping to see the larger band of tribesmen for himself and get some kind of an idea of their strengths and their intentions. Thus far they'd remained little more than flitting shadows in the far distance and harassing groups.

On the day when everything changed, the men reported to Solly Mont that something strange was happening on the eastern horizon. The Sergeant of the watch sent his junior to report to Captain Mont. The junior, having more enthusiasm than sense, burst into Solly's bedroom without knocking.

Solly had been eating, but not enjoying, his usual breakfast of water, barley griddlecakes, and a nettled cactus apple. The cactus was a rare and wonderful find. It grew in the cracks and crevices above them, sipping delicately on a thin rivulet of water that dripped with glacial slowness. It tasted a bit like boiled shoe, but it fruited every three days—against all probability—and it grew everywhere. It was proof against the all-too-real possibility of scurvy. He'd just taken a mouthful of cactus apple when the young soldier broke in upon him.

The young soldier leaned on his musket, gasping and panting for a long moment. He threw Captain Mont a very casual salute, and through the breathless wheezes, hiccups and snorts of a fast run, he reported what he had seen.

"It looks like there's green . . . growin' like, in th' sky, sir!"

Solly chewed his cactus apple, taking care to spit the spines.

"What?"

"Th' sky, sir. It's gone all green in th' east!"

Swallowing and staring at the young man, Solly wondered if he was seeing evidence of insanity.

"My Sergeant's seen it too, sir. You'll have ta' come take a look."

Solly donned his tri-corner hat of command, grabbed his pistols and his saber, and followed the soldier to the keep.

When he got to the highest tower, he stared out at the eastern horizon, being careful not to place his bare hands on the scorching stone. Sunrise in the desert surrounding Fort Nowhere was preceded by a blistering wave of heat. Two to three hours before the sun rose, the sand would begin to warm, pulling in heat from the air. The men of Fort Nowhere called it the 'oven effect.'

The men assigned to night duty often spoke of the disconcerting way the temperature would change, within a few minutes, from the chilly cold of night to the blistering, clay-baked heat of day, all before the sun had pinked the sky in the east.

Captain Mont stared at the roiling clouds. They were lying on the horizon and extending no more than a few hundred feet above it. In the brightening light of day, Solly could see that the sky was the exact green of a summer meadow. The clouds were as thick as ink.

He watched the east until the sun stood overhead. The green clouds moved with a slow but steady purpose, directly toward Fort Nowhere.

Solly could feel something. It was like a prickling of his thumbs. He watched the boil to the east with a curious mix of apprehension and anticipation. Curiously, the clouds grew thinner as they neared the fort.

It wasn't until well after the third hour of the second watch that Solly spied a small figure walking down the road towards the fort. Solly's eyes were keen, so he'd spotted the figure long before the watch would. The green clouds had been thinning until they were no more than the merest suggestion. When the man-shaped figure materialized from out of the edge of Solly's vision, the clouds disappeared altogether.

This was magic of the very highest order. The thing, whatever it was, was still several dozen miles away, and Solly could smell the ozone reek of magic boiling off of it from here. Something, however, held him back from issuing a general call-to-arms. The figure walked the day with a casual, unconcerned lope that brought it steadily toward Fort Nowhere on an unvaryingly straight line. Solly couldn't see any gear on the man, or for that matter, any clothes.

Shortly after being assigned to Fort Nowhere, Solly had acquired a camel, a hardy beast much more suited to a harsh desert environment than the horse he'd been given for this command. He ordered his camel saddled with an extra ration of water and set out on his own to investigate.

He rode for an hour before he came even with the small figure. It looked up at his sally and waved in an unconcerned fashion.

"Hey! That's a soldier! Awesome!" The figure spoke the common tongue of the empire, but with a thick, strange accent. It sounded like the up and down lilting of a dulcimer.

"It" turned out to be a "he." The figure's unashamed nakedness left this in no doubt. He seemed not to even notice the heat coming from the well-traveled, beaten-sand of the road. There was a suggestion, much like a smell, of enormous strength from him that belied his size. He was like a gnarled old weed, or a vine root that pushes its way through granite.

His skin was palely white, like someone who spent a great deal of time underground. His hair was a bright, brassy, shining blonde, and his eyes were as green as jade. They were smiling on the outside, but Solly Mont, attuned to the difference between appearance and intent, saw that they were as deadly serious as cancer. The thing's eyes looked as if they were lit from somewhere inside its skull. A bright, gleaming, too sharp and too toothy smile completed the strange creature's look. Despite his ever-so-slightly menacing appearance, he had demonstrated no ill intent as of yet and Solly decided to give him the benefit of the doubt.

A scar, the mark of three talon-tipped claws to Solly's eyes, rode his left cheek, and was the only blemish on the skin displayed to Solly Mont's gaze.

The man had no protection of any kind from the sun and appeared to be unaffected by it. It looked like he was enjoying a casual stroll in temperatures that could glaze pottery.

Solly saw the heat rising from the road, could feel it up here atop his camel, and yet the little man stood there, barefoot and unaffected.

Solly slithered from his mount and tossed his canteen to the curious figure. The man caught it easily, and with a polite "To your health!" unscrewed the top and took a healthy swig.

He spit it out almost immediately.

"Fuck! Water? C'mon, dude! Ain't you got somethin' a bit stronger than that?"

Solly decided to try and bluff his way into more information. Playing dumb worked sometimes.

"Not here, I don't. Who are you, and why are you walking out this way? Where are you coming from? Why are you naked? And for pity's sake, where is your water?"

The man tilted his head to one side, the precious water he'd just spit out running down his naked chest. He looked like he was considering the questions. He smiled to Solly and handed him back his canteen.

The man bowed floridly at the waist, one hand reaching to the sky, the other curled about his naked abdomen. One foot was presented forward and the other was crouched behind. When he spoke, his accent changed to mimic that of the realm.

"Why, 'tis Jack O'Green, I am, an' at yer service, I'm sure."

He stood from his bow and looked Solly in the eye.

"As to why an' where I'm comin' from, why, I'm comin' from tha' way."

He turned and pointed toward the east. An empty hell lay in that direction. It was several hundred miles of bleak, baking wasteland that held only lizards, cacti, and the occasional snake, half-cooked and insane.

The man turned and pointed toward the fort. "An' I'm goin' tha' way,"

He smiled that dangerous smile and bowed again, clicking his bare heels together.

"As fer water, well, me boyo, there's water everywhere, if a one knows where ta' look!"

"You're not going to tell me you stepped out into the bloody desert and expected to just fall into a puddle, now, did you? It's hot enough to melt glass out here!"

Captain Mont wiped his own dripping face, as if in demonstration that it was, indeed, quite hot.

The camel made a noise that was half-way between a belch and a snort.

Jack looked at him, his strange smile unchanging.

Solly was stalling for time, and they both knew it. Solly sighed. This was going to be a problem. He took a swallow off his canteen. The mouth of the canteen was still wet from Jack's lips. Solly tasted mint. There was a suggestion of thyme, cloves and cinnamon as well. It was somehow like getting a kiss from springtime and it was odd, wonderful and uncomfortable, all at once.

The water had grown tepid and dusty in the airtight confines of Solly's well-made canteen. Were it not for the taste of Jack's lips, the water would taste like hot, dry air.

Jack watched Solly, waiting for a response.

Solly wiped his mouth and closed his canteen. If there was any kind of discomfort from what he'd just experienced in drinking after Jack, he made no sign of it.

Jack's smile spread and he looked away. "Well? Are you gonna answer me then?" Solly asked.

Jack turned in a half-circle, his eyes touching Solly's on his way around.

At that briefest of touches; that miniscule eye contact, a psychic arc of understanding jumped from Jack to Solly and back. It said, 'I understand you. I know you understand me. What are you going to do about it?'

It was statement, threat and promise, all rolled into one neat, hot, little ball of thought. It was meant to be a focused, lightning-like attack that overcame Solly's defenses in an instant and revealed who and what he was. Solly was quicker than that, however, and made no acknowledgement of the instantaneous sizzling on the surface of his brain. It was a game the Faery played; one Solly had seen before, and had been anticipating.

Jack's circle faced him back into the sun. He stood, saying nothing, staring into the ball of flame above them. He turned back toward Solly Mont after a very long time.

"Is it hot out here? I hadna noticed."

Solly blinked. He understood what Jack was doing. The creature in front of him was daring him to acknowledge that he wasn't human; that further, he knew it, and could recognize it. Jack looked like he'd just stepped from his boudoir and he was making sure Solly knew he knew. He was daring Solly Mont to ask; to acknowledge; to open the door to the impossible and see what lay on the other side. He was daring Solly Mont, a fearsome adept in every definition of the word, to name him; to attempt to control and confine him; to dominate him. He was making himself available as slave, servant and familiar.

It was the circle of magic—as man understood it—given its ultimate form. 'Call me. Control me. Put me in your power . . . if you can. I'll give you everything your heart desires if you can keep me in your control.'

One the circle was drawn, there was no turning back. And Jack was psychically handing Solly a thick chunk of chalk.

The other half of that offer was too evil to give much contemplation. If Solly attempted that fearsome control; if he tried to draw the circle around Jack and Jack's will was beyond his, then Jack would have Solly under his horny thumb, to do with as he pleased, for all eternity. He would take from Solly everything there was to take and then he would take some more.

It was the conversational equivalent of going all in when you've got nothing to win, never mind having nothing to lose.

He hadn't needed to play these kinds of games in a very long time. Fort Nowhere was good for that. In the epic struggles of gods and powers Solly'd found his life becoming since Wisdom had sent him out into the world to learn, Fort Nowhere had seemed to him to be a resting spot. Relaxing, almost. He'd thought Wisdom's purpose in sending him here was to learn to endure; or to take a vacation. His guard against the creatures of Faery had fallen a bit.

These games, they weren't something you forgot, but it wasn't something you dealt with in the day-to-day among mortals, either.

The gnn had their rules and courtesies, and they were very careful to follow them to the letter, as did the gods and powers who wandered around at the edges of human existence. The Faery, however, had their own set of rules, and they tended to change.

In his very best voice of command, he said, "You'd better come with me, Jack; if that is your name. The locals are none too friendly, and we've been having problems with them of late. We'll see you on a camel and back out to the border."

Jack obviously wasn't having any of that. His smile widened. He was enjoying the chase, the cut and thrust, the pirouettes and the somersaulting.

"Well, suren tha's why I've come, me boyo! Ta' answer tha' fair call o' danger, an' defend th' glorious empire against all enemies, furrin' an' domestical, under th' shinin' command o' Solly Mont."

Solly swallowed a sudden urge to vomit. It wasn't his True Name, of course. Not even he knew that anymore, but it was a name he was known by, and that this powerful creature knew it, meant that Jack could wield some power with it. Oh, the game was getting tricky.

And then inspiration, like lightning from a sunny morning, hit Solly Mont with the force of a bomb.

He looked into Jack's strange green eyes, took a deep breath and gambled.

"You've come to enlist. That's what you want me to believe. You walked, naked, across the blistering face of hell, in order to enlist."

Jack's smile spread across his face, revealing the double and triple rows of his teeth.

"Aye, Solly Mont. That I have."

He shrugged. Needs must, when the devil holds the reins. He took a deep breath and plunged headfirst into the deep, pulling heavily upon his fearsome will to start the spell he wanted, one of the few he'd managed to learn from his few human teachers.

Solly knew there was more magic out in the world, but he'd not learned it, not yet. Taliesin had not yet taught him what he would later learn and while he was numbered among the strongest of spellcasters among humans, he was not yet a hundredth of what he would later become.

"Very well, Jack O'Green. We'll make a soldier of you, then, if that's what you're pining for. There's an oath to be taken, first. Will you take it?"

That was one of the rules: you couldn't just spring the oath. You had to tell him about it and let him decide. An oath was not binding if it was forced or tricked onto them, and then the spell wouldn't work. They had to decide to take it, and then play with the boundaries of the oath as they saw fit.

Jack stopped smiling, all at once, like a blown candle flame. He looked at Solly for a moment that stretched across time and back.

"An oath," he said, making statement and question of it, all at once.

"Yes," Solly replied, "an oath of service, loyalty and blood. There's not a man in that heap of stone behind us, didn't take the same. And I hold all and one accountable to it." Solly sped up his spell-weaving as much as he dared. He'd only have a brief moment to spring his trap on Jack, and it was hard enough to do while multi-tasking like this. It had to be perfect and doing it by will alone as truly testing his abilities.

Jack's smile spread across his face again. It even bled into his eyes. He threw his head back and laughed long and loud.

Solly was grateful for the heat. Fear sweat suddenly seemed to pop out all over him. Solly was sure Jack could take him on the arcane level. His only hope was to catch him by surprise.

Jack continued to laugh. He chortled and snorted, giggled and guffawed. When he had laughed himself out, he wiped the tears of mirth of his eyes and looked at Solly with something like admiration.

"An oath. That's a good one, Solly Mont. Verra well. I'll take whatever oath ye'd have of me . . . on one condition."

"And what might that be?"

"You are Solly Mont, right? Wisdom's Servant, Wisdom's Slave? I ask as . . . well, yer a tricky one ta' find, so ya' are, an' I'm thinkin' I might've gone too far back. Answer me, an' answer me true, an' I'll take yer oath. Answer me not, an' . . . wellllll . . ."

Jack's grin widened further, and he flexed the muscles of his hands, arms and chest.

And there it was, right out in the open. No more pretense, no more games. Jack knew exactly who he was. This was all just game-playing and preamble.

Solly sighed. What choice did he have? Stopping Jack without some kind of a leash was beyond him at this point.

"I am, Jack O'Green."

"Good! Then I do take your oath, and swear to keep it as best my kind's able."

Solly's sigh of relief was only just audible.

"Raise your right hand, then, Jack, and lay your left upon your heart."

Jack raised his right hand and gripped his dangling testicles with the left.

Solly said nothing.

Jack laughed again.

"Well, it's closer to my heart, anyway, Solly! Only funnin', boss. Only funnin'." Jack raised his right hand, his face turning serious.

"Do you, Jack O'Green, swear to serve his Royal Majesty's interests here, knowing that such service may result in the loss of limb and or life?"

"I do, Solly Mont."

"Do you, Jack O'Green, swear that you will obey the commands of those placed in authority over you?"

"I do, Solly Mont."

"And do you, Jack O'Green, swear by all that you hold high or holy to lift no hand against those who serve beside you, above you, or below you, here, in this place, on pain of oath-breaking and all that implies?"

And he dropped the spell he'd been weaving across Jack's naked shoulders.

Jack's hand fell and his face went as grey as stone.

Solly watched Jack's eyes as he felt the Oath-Cage falling around his shoulders. They could both see the invisible strands of silvery light cross-hatching over Jack. Jack winced as he waited for the net to close, to contract around him in a cell and force his will. It was a fearsome spell, and he would be Solly's puppet for as long as Solly lived.

The two of them stared at each other.

Jack lifted a tentative hand and touched the strands. The material was unbreakable, but it was flexible, yielding; like strong cloth instead of titanium.

Solly stared at him, letting Jack figure it out. This Oath-Cage was everything Solly had, magic-wise. He'd woven the Oath-Cage around Jack in such a way so that it was as binding as anything could be, but not confining enough to chafe. It gave Solly the power to contract Jack's will into nothing, should he so desire, giving him absolute, puppet-like control over Jack, but it took precious seconds to enact. He'd woven it loose to demonstrate his power in a way that he hoped wouldn't be insulting.

The Fae respected might, but they respected style even more.

"I won't have you wandering as you please, Jack."

Jack ground his teeth together and punched the material of the oath-cage. It stretched with the force and rippled, like a stone dropped in a lake.

"And if I refuse the oath?" he whispered, through clenched teeth.

Solly lifted his right hand and closed it slowly into a loose fist. The Oath-Cage closed around Jack until he could feel the cloth-like material on his skin. It lay there, like silver fish-scales.

"You know the answer to that, Jack."

"I'll do it!" he said, his faux accent returning. "An' ta' hell with th' consequences! Been an age since I've had so much bloody fun wi' one o' yer kind, so it has!"

He laughed with unbridled enthusiasm.

"Aye! I do swear, Solly Mont, by dark o' Moon, an Shadow Fall; by dew's drop under leaf and by twilight's Silent Whisper, I'll nae lift hand against those who serve beside me, above me, or below me, here, in this place, on pain o' oath breaking and all that implies, an' ta' hell wi' ye, Solly Mont!"

Solly slowly lowered his fist and opened his hand.

"An' may th' irons o' hell be my bed mate if I'm lyin'!" Jack said, grinning from ear to ear and laughing.

"May God, who hears every word uttered by men, beast and element, hold you to your oath, Jack O'Green, and punish you as your crime would merit," intoned Solly, closing the oath as was appropriate.

And may I have the wit to keep him occupied long enough to get him moving on, Solly silently prayed.

Chapter Five

The sun had crossed the mid-point of the sky in the time Solly had been out there with Jack. He shook his head irritably. Most of a day lost to this foolishness! He'd had plans for the day, duties he'd wanted to assign and see carried out. There were three disciplinary matters awaiting his attention, and he'd long been meaning to see about trying to find another well in the area. There were scouts to be sent out and reports to sift through for valuable intelligence. He'd tried explaining to his scouts how important it was to watch for things that stood out, but all too often he got a very detailed, badly-written report about rocks, sand and lizards.

Solly hoped that by combining multiple reports from different scouting teams, he'd get some idea of the tribesmen's movements. Instead of getting any of that done, he'd been out here, dealing with a fickle creature that had far more power than sense.

He sighed. He was frustrated. There was only so much time! Working during the blast-furnace heat of the day was a sure way to injure and kill his men. He didn't have the manpower he needed, his men didn't have the skills they needed, and there just wasn't any way he could get everything he wanted done, done.

The command required too much of him. That was the problem. A thousand men relied on him for everything: their food, their drinking water, their health and welfare in this baking hell, it was all Solly Mont's direct responsibility. His Sergeant major, who should have been a wise and seasoned right hand, was a bloody abusive bastard who got into fist-fights with metronome-like regularity. If he thought anyone would listen, he'd complain about the unfairness of it all.

"And to top it all, now I'm stuck with a Faery to amuse," he mumbled.

"Won't be tha' bad, Solly! I'm a rum one when ya' get ta' knowin' me proper," Jack replied, grinning.

Solly looked at his newest charge with a beady, commanding eye.

"You'll be needing to get dressed, Jack. I can't have you wandering into the place mother-naked."

Jack looked sly and wrapped a hand around his member.

"Don't want me offendin' th' sensibilities of yer precious men, do ya'? My dangling tallywhacker's intimidatin'?"

Solly continued to stare.

Jack's smile faltered.

"Well, I just thought I'd ask. Ya' ne'er can tell with soldier-types. And anyway, where am I gonna find a set of clothes out here?"

"Jack O'Green, you'll not come into my fort if you're not dressed."

Jack stared at Solly, testing, probing and poking for a crack. Solly stared back.

"Verra well then," Jack said. He grinned and cast a spell.

Solly was an adept. He'd sat at the feet of masters all over the world, learning their techniques and secrets, and teaching the things he knew in return. He'd long surpassed his teachers in workings and ritual. He knew smokes and fumes, charms and runes. He knew songs and stories, dances and chants. He knew objects of power and the secrets of paths. But Jack's casual mastery made him look like a fool. Jack's eyes closed in concentration, and he held his hands, palm up, to shoulder-height. After a moment, Solly felt the weight of Jack's concentration. It felt like being squeezed between two gentle but indifferent hands. Jack's hands were rock steady, and his eyes remained closed.

The air around them coalesced and thickened to a bright, silvery-green stream that flowed over Jack's naked body. It boiled and ran like soup spilled on a hot hearth stone. It solidified on Jack's chest, his arms, and his legs. It took the color and form of a pair of non-descript breeches, a tunic and a pair of fine, soft boots. A filigreed sword took shape at Jack's left hip in a tooled leather baldric with a gold-etched scabbard. A tree, cunningly worked in gold, sat on the cap of the pommel. From where Solly was standing, it looked like an enormous oak, done in miniature.

Jack lowered his hands and opened his eyes. Green light poured from them in an uninterrupted stream. The light ran down Jack's face like tears. It was too bright to look at. Solly blinked in pain and the light disappeared as if it had never been.

Jack looked at himself, twisting this way and that, examining what he had wrought.

"Better?" he asked, drawing the sword and cutting the air with it a time or two. It made a high-pitched whistling whine as it passed through the air.

"Yes."

Solly mounted his camel and turned back to the keep.

Jack followed, whistling a tune.

The ride back to the fort was thoughtful. Solly was wrapped in his own megrims and Jack sang salacious tune after salacious tune.

"And t'was her usual cuuuuuuuuuuustoooooooom to let them craaaaaaaaawl up her ass-"

"Jack!" Solly thundered, trying very hard to hold on to the pommel of his saddle.

"Sah!" Jack said, glee bleeding out of his voice.

"You will not—and this is a direct order, Jack O'Green—will not finish that chorus."

"Sah!" Jack said.

Solly rode ahead of Jack toward the fort. He waited until he could see the sentries' eyes atop the wall and waved at them in what he suspected was a pointless gesture. Being a masterful student of human nature as he was, Solly knew the sentries had watched nothing at all of the surrounding desert while he'd been talking with Jack. No, they'd kept their eyes glued to the fascinating spectacle taking place between their commander and the newcomer. But there'd be a pile of detailed reports for him to peruse, he was sure.

'Sited: one lizurd, yelloh-gren markings; thurd hower of furst watch, on northeast crenuhlashun. Lizurd sat for sevurul turnings of the glas, making no efurt to moove out of lite of sun,' and so on and so forth. Solly suspected there was a pile of master copies somewhere, and the men followed it, letter for letter.

The gate was opened, and Solly rode in, Jack at his heels. The men on duty were not openly gawking at Jack, but there was an unusual amount of milling about: waiting for orders, changing of the guard, a look at the duty rota, and the overenthusiastic performance of pointless duties. Solly watched from the corner of his eye as a corporal instructed a private, in loud, ringing tones, no less, on the proper way to check the mortar between bricks. The men were hard-pressed, bored to the point of insanity, and possessed of morale lower than a snail's bellybutton. They needed a distraction. Jack would do.

Jack, for his part, was obviously enjoying the spotlight very much. He swaggered and strutted, cat-called and whistled. Solly led Jack into the keep proper, heading straight for Sergeant major Fergus' office. He wanted to get Jack processed as quickly as possible to keep his mischief-making to a minimum.

Solly barged into the Sergeant major's office. The door was little more than a plank with hinges and provided only the illusion of privacy. The office, a hole painstakingly cut into the side of the cliff, very like a small cave, was just big enough for Fergus to have a quiet place to drink and nap. Fergus slept on a mat, naked, and sweating. The sour reek of wine filled the air.

Solly stared down at him in pity. The man was a wreck. Too many wars, too many years spent shedding his blood for the empire. But he was a survivor. He'd been all that, done all that, and come through the other side. He was the kind of hard-edged, surviving soldier Solly needed in this oven; someone the men could look to and say 'Fergus not only did it, he did it more than once. We're gonna be just fine, lads.'

If only the man wasn't so unremittingly evil! And that was the problem, wasn't it? The man was evil. It would've been easy for Solly to dislike the man, but Solly understood Fergus. Underneath the drinking, the whoring, the malevolence, Fergus was a good soldier. He wanted, desperately, to serve his king and his country, and he wanted to see his service acknowledged by the country he so loved.

He was a hard, brutal man, yes. He'd committed crimes in the name of soldiery that would shrivel the souls of anyone. But he was also, first and foremost, a soldier of his king. And despite the disappointments of his thirty some-odd years of service; despite the lonely, impossible demands placed on him and the absolute lack of recognition, there was still a part of him that was a shining-eyed young boy, marching off for the first time.

Fergus was as tall as an average man, but he was astoundingly wide. He looked like an ambulatory brick. His shoulders were five feet wide. His chest was as deep as an ale barrel. Fergus' gravelly, ravaged voice came broiling out of it like smoke from a flue. Fergus moved like a bear; with quick, short bursts of speed that were surprising on a man so large. He was a hard-muscled ox of a man. Thick ropes of twisted, hawser-like tissue crossed his shoulders, his arms and his back; dramatic evidence of his many vicious battles with all comers. His muscles moved under his scarred skin like puppies playing under a blanket. He could exert unbelievable power with his hands, arms and back: destroying stone attack dummies during sword drill; tossing the troopers about, three and four at a time, during close-combat drill. Tattoos of every posting he'd held covered him in scrawling pictures of violence and lewd behavior. A disciplinary branding marred his left breast. He'd once knocked a duke's bastard through a tavern wall. The boy landed on his back and lost several teeth and the use of his left eye. The boy still flinched at loud noises and spoke with a mushy, mangled lisp. The duke had branded Fergus himself.

Hair like the hide of a boar, cut close on the scalp, covered the rest of his body in a furry, tangled coat. His hands were like two pigs, hanging off the ends of his arms. Awake and sober, they were fearful, those hands. Strong and implacable, utterly undefeatable. When Fergus made a fist and threatened one of his troopers with it, that fist filled the sky.

His eyes were close-set and mean; narrowed into thin slits under the well-defined muscles of his face. Most of his left ear was gone. The right had the torn appearance of something that had been chewed on and forgotten; a warning about wearing earrings in a fight. His teeth were rotted, blackened stumps in his mouth. Even the man's lips were scarred, thick and mangled to some degree.

Sergeant major Fergus' alcoholism was no secret.

Solly could've reduced Fergus to the ranks, but he needed someone in a position of leadership at Fergus' level. And in this time of increased stress, only Fergus fit the bill.

Th' man has me over a barrel, Solly thought as he watched Fergus snore, snort and gurgle. He waited until he was sure Fergus had a lungful of air, fetid as it was, and then took a deep breath, pulling the damp, musty smell of the man deep into his nose.

"Sergeant major!" he bellowed, in the drill-ground voice every soldier since the beginning of time has learned to dread.

With no intervening time between passed-out drunk and standing at perfect attention, waiting for orders, Sergeant major Fergus seemed to levitate from his filthy mat and stood on his feet.

His eyes were burning holes into his self-constructed hell; bleary and unfocussed, he still snapped off a perfect salute.

"Sah!"

The unmistakable sound of Jack snickering filled the air. It was pitched to carry, and Fergus' bloodshot eyes narrowed in threat.

This should be interesting, Solly thought.

"This," he said, indicating the still snickering Jack, "is Jack O'Green. Whether you believe it or you don't, our bonny lad here has walked across the bloody desert to join us in our hell. He's gonna be a new recruit, and I want you to see personally to his kit. He's already taken the king's oath, and as you can see, he has no need of a sword. Get him a uniform and a bunk, Sergeant major. I'll be in my office."

Solly turned on one heel and left Jack in Fergus' dubious care. He had no doubt he'd be hearing about Jack soon.

****

In fact, it was no more than two turnings of the glass. He'd been in his office, going through the latest badly written surveillance reports, listening with half an ear to the activity in the yard.

Fergus, nursing what had to be an evil hang-over, had apparently decided to spread the pain around a bit, and set up a close-combat drill class in the cool of night. He was running the troopers through their paces. Solly could hear the man's enraged shouts through several thicknesses of wall.

"Suren I've never seen such a group of lily-waisted poofters! Yer all poms an' sons of poms! Put some balls into it, dam' ya'! No! Yer not doin' it as I showed ye! Ye've got ta' grab him here, like so, an' here, like so, an' then ya' toss him, like so!"

There was a thunderous noise as a body hit the wooden fence surrounding the drill ground.

"There! Now ya' gone an' done it! Ye've broken our beloved commander's wee fence! An' what he's gonna have ta' say ta' tha', I'm sure I don't know. Get up, ya' pale-assed faggot! Get up an' try again!"

Solly went back to reading a report about a buzzard eating something unidentifiable. It was almost a pleasure to read, as the trooper who'd written it had a more than passing acquaintance with proper spelling and punctuation: 'The buzzurd, having pulled for a long time, then was hit in the face by suddenly snapping tishew.'

"An' what have we here? Is our newest trooper too much of lady ta' join us in a bit o' exercise?"

Solly's ears pricked. His attention zeroed in on Fergus' voice.

"Is tha' right? Well. Why don't ya' just step up here, an' let me be th' judge o' that, princess."

Solly didn't realize he was running until he'd made it to the courtyard.

The keep was built around the central square that was the exercise yard. All of the daily business of the keep was done in the large central square in the keep's center. It was a hundred paces to a side, with a central square that formed a sort of boxing ring. This ring was an 'instructional area.' Fergus would choose a trooper—supposedly at random, but Solly suspected the trooper had gotten on Fergus' bad side somehow—to help demonstrate a tricky bit of close-combat technique.

The trooper was more often than not carried from the ring on a stretcher. If Fergus was in a good mood, he might be allowed to crawl out.

Solly rushed to this central ring just in time to see Jack and Fergus enter it. The men of Ft. Nowhere surrounded the square, ostensibly to have some instruction. They were silent but watchful. Fergus was a bully, but he was a known entity. Jack was an unknown and subject to speculation. Fergus stood inside the ring, gleaming with sweat, bare to the waist, his massive arms crossed over his heavy chest, leering at Jack. Jack stood on the other side of the ring, an unconcerned smile on his face, still wearing the uniform he'd conjured.

"Well, boy? Here we are. Are ya' gonna come give yer uncle Fergie a kiss?"

Solly began the process of closing the oath-cage. Jack had given his oath; his solemn promise that he would not harm any of these men. Fergus was a loud-mouthed bully, but he didn't deserve Jack's teeth. Solly closed his fist and Jack whipped around to face him. Their eyes met: Jack's strange green to Solly's black.

Something bled out from Jack's eyes, something Solly could not articulate. It was a wordless plea; a silent request. It was so uncanny, most especially coming from Jack, that it stopped Solly. Before he could make a decision one way or the other, Fergus chose then to charge, bellowing as he came.

Fergus crashed into Jack with the force of a wall falling over. He did something complicated with his hands, and Jack was knocked down by the impact, landing several feet away in the dust. His eyes were unfocused and his mouth was open.

Fergus stood where he was, grinning evilly.

It took him several tries, but eventually Jack got to his feet.

"Well, boy? How do ya' like my kisses?" Fergus called.

Jack stared at him for a long moment. He dusted himself off, stretched and then he walked back toward Fergus. "I'm sorry, Sergeant major. Could ya' show me tha' again?"

The silence in the yard was complete. Fergus stared at Jack.

"Verra well," he whispered, shaking his head. He turned away from Jack, took a few steps away, and then charged, bellowing words full of hate. Jack stood there, unconcerened as Fergus came on, filling the sky with his voice.

And then it was over.

****

When Solly thought about it later, it was hard to reconstruct. It looked like Jack took gentle hold of Fergus' right wrist, and then Fergus performed a somersault, in mid-charge, and landed on his back, arms and legs spread-eagled.

Solly thought he recognized the throw to some degree. It looked like a Ju-jitsu toss, but it was done with a lazy grace and elegance that nothing mortal would ever be able to replicate.

Jack turned back toward Solly.

"Do ya' ken?" He ignored the gasping, spitting Fergus at his feet.

Solly thought he did. Fergus' own force was being used against him. So long as he didn't get within reach of Jack's hands, Jack couldn't and, for that matter, wouldn't hurt him. If Fergus chose to attack Jack, Jack was going to toss him—and here was the beautiful part of it, the part that allowed him to stay within the boundaries of his oath—using the power of his own momentum against him. In effect, Jack wasn't doing anything. Fergus was attacking himself.

Solly nodded. Jack grinned a fierce, dangerous grin at Solly and nodded back.

****

Fergus stood up, still gasping for breath. His face was terrible to see. A wide gamut of emotions crossed it, but all of them promised pain and a horrible, slow, lingering death for one Jack O'Green.

"Ohhh. You'll pay for tha', boyo. You'll pay in blood," Fergus whispered while Jack just stood there, grinning.

The men watching were still silent. Yes, Fergus had been knocked down, but they'd seen him get knocked down before, rare as it was.

Fergus circled Jack, making feinting motions with his fearsome steel-cable arms and his horrible hands. Jack stood on his side of the ring, keeping his face toward Fergus. His hands were out toward his side, palm outward, and his feet were shoulder-width apart. A beatific look was on his face that must've been unnerving for Fergus to look at.

Fergus' second rush was almost too fast to see. He came at Jack in a blur; arms spread wide open, cursing in a black rage. He threw a fist out and the noise it made as it connected with the side of Jack's face was like a thunderclap.

But Jack was moving too. He took a single step forward, moving even faster than Fergus was, absorbed the punch to his face somehow, and lifted his right hand. He gripped Fergus' right arm at the elbow, and with his left, gripped Fergus' right wrist. Still holding Fergus, he spun around on his own axis, lifting Fergus above his head. Fergus, still bellowing, flipped over and landed on his back, skidding across the grit-covered ground, some twelve feet away. When he stood up, long moments later, there was blood running down his back. His eyes were dazed and a confused look was on his face. It took him a few moments, but sure enough, he staggered back into the ring, muttering threatening imprecations.

Jack's right eye was swelling shut, and Solly could see he was in real pain.

Fergus wiped at his face, spreading the gooey mixture of spit, sweat, dust and blood away from his eyes. He looked at Jack with murderous hate blacking his eyes.

"Luck. S'all tha' was. Luck th' first time, an' luck tha' time, too. I'm gonna pull tha' pretty dress of yours off an' do such things ta' ya', boy. You'll be beggin' me for mercy. I swear it!"

Jack yawned.

Fergus went mad. He howled a curse at the sky and rushed Jack again, this time going for Jack's knees.

Jack jumped above Fergus, his legs coming up to his chest, his arms spreading wide. Fergus charged beneath him and spun back around for another pass almost before Jack landed.

Jack put his right hand on Fergus' throat. With his left hand he gripped Fergus' right wrist. With an elegant tug and a simple twist, he threw Fergus over his own hip, onto his back yet again while Fergus tried once again to tag Jack in the face.

If he'd connected, the fight might've been over. But Jack's head moved like a snake's.

Solly felt the impact through his boots from where he stood, some twelve feet away.

Solly watched Fergus looking up into Jack's eyes. From where he stood, Jack's eyes were flat, polished orbs of perfect green, and they held not the promise, or the threat of Fergus' death, but the imminence thereof. Solly looked into Jack's eyes and he saw the future as it would be if Fergus pursued this course of action. Solly suspected that for the very first time in his entire life, Fergus saw his actual death at the hands of something harder, stronger and far, far meaner than he could ever hope to be.

Jack stood up. He was weaving just a little. It was subtle, but Solly noticed it. Apparently Fergus' punch had taken more out of him than Jack wanted to admit.

The cheers, when they came, started like a summer thundershower. There were a few small, timid voices at first. These were joined by others, who were joined by still others, until the walls of the fort shook with the resounding cheers of badly put-upon, beleaguered men who'd just seen the primary source of their torment get his ass kicked.

They lifted Jack on their shoulders and carried him off to the barracks.

Fergus, ignored and forgotten about, got to his hands and knees and crawled out of the ring.

Solly watched the men carry Jack into the barracks and found himself waxing poetic. He had no doubt there would be a sorry collection of sore heads and sour stomachs at dawn's inspection.

To this tired, hot, desperate place of walking death, Jack brought with him a perfumed whiff of strangeness, of newness. To the men of Fort Nowhere, Jack wasn't a dangerous predator, a creature of ambiguous morality. The men didn't care if Jack was 'good' or 'bad.' Out here those distinctions weren't white or black. Solly knew that the men only cared that Jack O'Green was alive, that he carried life with him in his pocket like a handful of precious coins.

Their shouts were still shaking and echoing off the walls when Fergus finally managed to stumble to his feet. He stood weaving and panting, holding his ribs.

Fergus straightened, giving a barely audible groan. Solly heard the crackle of joints and abused tissue. He suspected Fergus had a cracked ribs, maybe even a sprung vertebra or two. Given the man's almost preternatural constitution, this wouldn't put Fergus down for long.

Fergus was an old soldier. You learned how to take a beating when you had to, or you died.

Solly waited, giving the man time to regain a measure of his dignity. When he did speak, his voice was gentle.

"He'll be a good trooper."

Fergus turned toward Solly. He stared at his commander with an unreadable look in his eyes. Sweat covered his body in a thick lather. It was mixing with the gritty sand of the circle to form a grimy plaster that Solly knew added an abominable itch to what must be his many aches and pains.

He said nothing. Solly sensed the weight of unspoken words and unasked requests; the torture of unfulfilled needs.

"Aye," he softly replied.

Solly's heart swelled with pity. He didn't like to see anyone in pain. His mouth made the offer before his brain decided to make it.

"Come to the officer's mess with me, Fergus. We'll pop open a bottle or two and tell each other stories and lies."

Fergus stiffened as if he'd been stabbed. Coming to rigid attention, he saluted with a snap. "Beggin' th' commander's pardon, sah! Fraternizin' as th' commander suggests is strictly forbidden by regulations, sah!"

Solly stared. He returned Fergus' salute.

"Permission to retire, sah!"

"Permission granted, Sergeant major."

Fergus executed another salute, turned smartly on his right foot, and marched, with parade-ground-perfect steps to his office, leaving behind a spotted trail of blood and sweat that the thirsty ground of Fort Nowhere eagerly drank.

Solly watched him go. There was a sadness in the way Fergus clutched his strength, his masculinity around him, even after he'd been so out-classed. Still, he had his bed and his soothing bottles of wine. Solly had no doubt the man would be good as new and twice as bad in a few days.

Solly saluted the singing, cheering knot of noise to his left, turned, and made his way to his own office, careful not to step in the small puddles Fergus had left behind him.

Chapter Six

Life, that great, laughing mocker of all things mortal, went on.

The tension caused by waiting for the impending attack was electric, arcing between men; discharging and grounding in petty fights and stupid brawls. It was too hot, they were too crowded, there was too much hanging over them, and there was just too much of a mess on their hands.

Jack submitted to the necessary lifestyle changes required of a king's trooper, assimilating into Fort Nowhere's overall command structure. He was not a perfect trooper. He refused to do some things required of him, but there wasn't a soldier there who didn't behave in exactly the same way.

Fergus' humiliation at Jack's hands had obviously created a rabid, frothing hatred within Fergus' heart. He made it his personal mission to make Jack's life as miserable as was possible. Jack responded by grinning his most engaging grin and asking "An' how's yer ribs today, Sergeant major?"

The men loved Jack. Like all Fae, Jack knew an endless number of ribald, hilarious stories—more precious than diamonds and rubies in this place of stifling boredom. He could dance; he could sing—raunchy, rollicking songs that had the men laughing too hard to join in. He could juggle and do sleight-of-hand and impressive magic tricks that never grew stale.

His every utterance was suited to his audience of young men, and there wasn't a single moment in Jack's waking hours when he wasn't surrounded by a grinning, laughing knot of them, enlisted and officer alike. Every chore was accompanied by a song. Every forced march was made less onerous by a long, rambling story that often had an achingly bad punch line. He was always ready with a quick jest or a delightful, inventive prank. He never hurt anyone, and he laughed as hard as anyone when the men pulled a prank on him. Theirs were never as good, but they were enthusiastic.

Solly couldn't understand it. The Fae were quick to take offense at the slightest gesture, yet there Jack was, laughing like a loon after a four foot fall from a sawed-through ladder into the cesspool.

When thinking back on it later, several of the 'Jack Reports' stood out with a crystalline clarity. Solly's mind, an organ that operated as much on non-conscious levels as it did on conscious ones, imparted them with an importance it was aware of that Solly's larger consciousness was not.

The Fort's Head Cook, Liam Curtchett, brought him his favorite of these reports, and he often reflected on it later.

Sunday was Liam's day to make his weekly report on the fort's food situation. It was usually a very dry, depressing recital, made only the tiniest bit interesting by the fact that Liam was the one giving it.

Liam had the technical rank of a Leftananet. But as he was the cook, he was ignored as a part of the overall command structure. A wizened old bit of horsehide, Liam was crusty and usually unwashed; dirt covered him in a literal and figurative sense. Filth was caked under his fingernails and animal and vegetable matter was sprinkled on his clothes. There was a sour, pickled odor about the man of sweat and rotted onions. It was said among the men that the greatest threat facing Fort Nowhere was "Liam's fingers in th' bread."

Liam's hair was reduced to a wispy fringe around his ears, and his face was a mass of dirty, gullied wrinkles. Unlike cooks in happier environments, Liam was a skinny as a rail. Despite his unpleasant personal appearance, his appalling lack of any kind of hygiene, and his abominable cooking skills, he managed, somehow, to be good at his job. He and his rotating staff of thirty men used what was available to put a hearty, if awful, meal in front of the men, three times a day.

Liam was likable enough, possessing a certain rough amiability. As the men of Fort Nowhere put it: "Stand upwind, an' Liam's a right agreeable bloke."

He had the irritating habit of apologizing, mid-sentence, for his language, to any of his superiors in rank and then using the very same phrase in the next breath. None of his juniors could even so much as hope to match him in a cursing contest, and there were quite a few of his superiors who took furtive notes when Liam was under full sail and berating some quivering private who'd dropped a pot.

Solly found himself hard-pressed to persevere through the apologies. He'd once asked Liam not to worry about his language. "We're all bloody soldiers, after all," he'd said, with his winningest smile.

Liam had been mortified, scandalized to the point of shocked silence. After a long, painful moment of gaping like a fish, Liam had managed to stutter out, "S-si-sir, ye shouldn't say such fookin' things, or use such fookin' language! You're our bloody commander, dammit!"

Solly surrendered to the helpless look in the man's eyes.

Three months after Jack arrived, Liam reported to Solly's office with a smile eating up most of his face. He saluted his superior officer, and before Solly could say a single word, launched into his weekly report.

"Sir, I dinna ken it t'all. Th' soil here's damn-all for growin' anythin' more than them toxic, scraggly weeds, pardonin' yer presence, sir. We've tried everythin'. There's nae use in fertilizin' it, nor irrigatin' it. It's just dam' stubborn dirt, sir, pardonin' your presence. We'd nae have enough ta' feed even th' dam' goats if t'weren't for th' supply wagons, pardonin' yer presence, sir.

"But tha' Jack . . . I dinna ken how he did it, but he's fookin' gone an' started a garden, sir, pardonin' your presence, sir. Th' fookin' corn's three feet high, th' tomaters are growin' like they're racin' each other, an' th' man's got strawberries, blueberries, an' fourteen other fookin' kinds o' bloody fruit an' vegatabalers I ain't never seen nor heard tell of, sir! 'E's a bloody fookin' miracle-worker is what 'e is, pardonin' your presence! An' do ye take a fookin' look at this!"

Liam reached a hand into the pocket of the filthy apron he habitually wore, and brought out a tiny cluster of tied stems, a bright reddish orange in color. He handled the stems as if they were made of delicate stardust. He held them out to Solly, grinning like a mad man.

"Take a fookin' whiff o'that, sir!"

Solly cautiously lifted the bundle of dried flowers to his nose and took a delicate sniff.

The scent which rose into his nose was tantalizing. It made Solly think of thick slabs of tender meat sizzling over a slow, careful fire. The slabs were delicately spiced, glazed with some sort of gelatinous sauce. On the same brazier were chunky slices of dill-covered onions, peppers, lemons, pineapple-

"Nah, nah, sir! Let me get it in th' fookin' food, first!"

Solly looked up at Liam in surprise, the fantasy of meat dissolving. Liam was holding his hand out and trying very hard not to laugh at his superior officer.

"Thorry, Liam," Solly said, and took the tiny bundle out of his mouth. He wiped his spit off and handed it back to Liam.

He could taste those thick, generous slabs of meat in his mouth, still.

"S'alright, sir. Shoulda fookin' seen me when Jack fust brought it to me! I only dam' near bit th' boy's bloody arm off, savin' yer presence sir."

"What is it, Liam?'

"Be fookin' damned if I know, sir. I've never heard nor seen anythin' like it afore. All I can tell ya' is that the wee-est amount of this here fookin' miracle weed'll make dam' near anything taste like a feast fit for angels, pardonin' yer presence, sir. I had to bloody fookin' threaten Sergeant major Fergus with a fookin' spoon ta' make 'im stop lickin' on one of me pots, pardonin' yer presence, sir."

When Solly reported it in his daily log, he called it 'Jack's Fookin' Weed Sunday.'

****

Mondays were always the same, and they were never pleasant. Monday was the day Solly sat down with Fergus. As Chaplain, one of Sergeant major Fergus Ingersoll's duties was to ensure the men were as morally pure as military duty would allow. As he was Sergeant major Fergus Ingersoll, none of the men had a penny's chance in a whore house on Saturday night of every going to any kind of heaven.

The discussions since Jack had joined the men had one topic. After only the most perfunctory review of various soldier-related issues, Fergus would start in.

"Sir! He's a bloodthirsty, whore-spawned, gutter-ditch-waif o'th' devil! Ye saw the powers 'e had an' used on me! He's a warlock an' worse, sir. Will ye stand by an' allow th' men ta be infected by such? He's a pagin, an' worse than a pagin, sir. A right devil, an' ya' should chuck 'im out. He won't wear boots, sir! By all that's holy, how'm I expected ta' maintain any kind of order wiv such as that runnin' 'round loose?"

This went on for a while. Solly understood that this was Fergus' way of soothing his tortured ego, and as he was a very wise man indeed, he made no issue of the fact that his senior enlisted man was questioning Solly's ability to command. These conversations were in private, and it would do Solly no good to alienate Fergus further by pointing out that he was the NCO and Solly was the officer.

Jack, in his corner, smiled a slow, secret smile.

****

The following day wasn't as pleasant. It brought the 'Jack Problem' to an immediate and frightening head. When he was awakened by the thundering knocks on his bedroom door late that night after a long and tiring day, Solly was as afraid as he'd ever been in his life.

That night he'd been dreaming a sad, hurting dream and watching himself as he dreamt. He was who and what he was, and he'd learned long ago to enter a wakeful, dreaming state; taking note of everything around him while his mind told him stories. He could decide what to dream about and he'd taught himself to control the course of the dream. This taught him more about himself and the world around him then he'd learned after a thousand years of sitting at the feet of learned masters.

He'd learned, in his dreams, of weaknesses, ignorances, bigotries and prejudices he was unaware of in his waking life. He'd faced them in his dreams, acknowledged them for what they were, and learned to defeat and overcome them. His dreams were a teacher; a gift from her to lead him down hidden paths of wisdom. The painless, effortless realm of dream had allowed him to learn complicated, complex things he'd struggled to teach himself. Stripped of the ten-thousand distractions every moment of wakefulness brought him, he'd taught himself a thousand different things undisturbed in the silence of his own head.

On one memorable occasion, he'd journeyed to a jungle in Africa to learn the martial art, Mutamba. The word meant 'Throwing the Spear' in the language of the slight people who lived there. Solly's teacher was an old man of seventy summers, no taller than Solly's waist. His name was Lugada. He'd been a master of Mutamba for the past sixty years and taught it to all comers for the last fifty. There was no one, anywhere, who could so much as touch him, and Solly was eager to learn this art from him.

Lugada had learned Mutamba at his father's knee. His father had learned it from his father. His grand-father had learned it from his father, and so on, and so forth, on back into the hazy realms of human history. Solly suspected that Shem, Ham and Japheth would probably recognize Mutamba. It seemed changeless and ancient.

For three months, this wizened, grinning gnome, with his skin of blackest night and his hair of pure snow, had tossed the much larger, much stronger and wildly overconfident Solly Mont around like a helpless kitten.

Solly, finally fed up with bruises and the high-pitched laughter of the village children—all his betters in Mutamba—decided to swallow his pride and spend a week watching the practices and then dreaming about them. Lugada had demonstrated the intricate, confusing, and sometimes contradictory steps of this martial art so many times that he no longer thought about it. It was as natural to him as the sun rising and setting. For a week, Solly didn't participate in the practices, he sat back and watched Lugada's every movement. And then he dreamed.

He learned what he was doing wrong. It was obvious to him now, away from the good-natured jeers of children who'd never seen a giant before, much less one that spent so much time on his back in the dust. Mutamba wasn't like the tree-breaking punches and swings of other lands.

Mutamba was closer to being like the ocean: a wave rolled in, followed by another, but before the second wave rolled in, the first rolled out. It was like breathing: a continual, flowing dance of movement. And Solly was chopping around, stomping and flailing when he should've been waiting for the pauses between breaths; the fractured moment between crashing waves. Take a breath, and then let it out, but punch, twist, throw or kick in the minute pause between breathing in and breathing out. There was more to it, of course. He wasn't compensating for his greater size and weight, for one thing, but he learned everything he was doing wrong in his dreams. He was trying to do the same thing Lugada was doing the same way Lugada was doing it. What worked for a man who was three and a half feet tall and weighed less than sixty pounds would not work at all for Solly Mont. He was a fool to think it would.

When, in the hot light of morning, he threw a move on Lugada with a small correction he'd devised himself to compensate for his much larger, heavier frame, Solly had the pleasure of seeing Lugada's helpless, ear-to-ear grin beaming up at him from the ground.

"When it does work, even a teacher can learn a few things, eh?" Lugada said, after picking himself up and dusting himself off.

"A teacher can't help it if he has a hopeless fool for a student," Solly replied, grinning back at the man.

The lessons from that point on were much less painful.

Solly Mont was the world's wisest man partly because he knew to listen to his dreams.

On that night, he stood in the darkest corner of their bedroom and watched, like a sad voyeur, as he made love to her for the ten-thousandth time. They hadn't yet been reunited, and this was an important dream because he couldn't remember her as she really was. That had been taken from him by Wisdom. He could only remember this pale, dream-shadow version of her. He remembered things that could never be taken away; things that had been stitched into the surface of his heart and mind: her taste, her smell, the feel of her skin. But he couldn't remember her name. When she spoke to him in dreams, she spoke to him in his voice. And it felt like the cut of a dull blade against his soul.

The dreams of her were bittersweet agony. They were a painful, graphic reminder of all he had lost, all he had forsaken when he had stopped up his ears. But they were important, because the time was coming when he would have to remember, would have to rediscover who he was.

His forever love; his perfect queen. The passionate, overwhelming soul-mate.

She made the blood roar in his ears; made the surging tides within him beat against the walls of his spirit with a frantic urgency that would not be denied. The sweet touch of her tongue against his; the gentle swell of her breasts; the taste of her salt on his lips. She was moving in that slow, timeless way of hers; he was drinking in the beauty of her every breath.

The window was open, and he could hear the gentle rustling of the diaphanous curtains in the cool breeze, scented with the blossoms that grew so thick and full below. The only light was the moon reflecting from their skin, their eyes, their laughing, eager lips, tongues and teeth.

He loved her. She loved him. They loved each other in the quiet still of the night; breaking and crashing into each other with the gentle movements of their love, the ferocious sounds of their mutual sexual hunger. With naked love, with urgent need, he cried her name out as he gave himself up to her; wholly, totally, completely hers.

It was the same dream of her he always had and he never failed to wake in misery. When Wisdom had reduced him, separating them—or so he thought then—forever, the relief of forgetting the woman he would later learn from, marry and call 'Ana' had been almost worth it.

Almost.

When the thundering knocks began, he'd torn himself, with relief, from the dream. The tears on his cheeks were hot and plentiful, as they always were.

He didn't really think about his responses over the next few moments. Long years of living at the edge of human existence had ingrained a set of responses for every eventuality. While he was still shaking away the dregs of his dream, he reached with one hand for his pistol-belt. With the other he reached for his saber. He didn't bother with clothing. Still operating on those autonomous reactions, he yanked the door open and stuck the barrel of his pistol into the face of the person standing on the other side of the door, whose fist was raised to knock yet again.

In the pale glow of the oil lantern outside his door, Solly saw an obviously very frightened and very drunk Fergus standing there, blubbering to himself. He paid not the least attention to the barrel less than an inch from his face, or the fact that his commanding officer was mother-naked. Fergus' face was streaked with sweat, dirt and several hours worth of beard. His uniform was torn and stained with large, purple roses—spilled wine, Solly assumed—in more than a dozen places. He gave off the distinct reek of drunken fear in billowing, choking waves. Solly smelled a sharp, ammoniac odor he identified as fear-piss. It mixed with Fergus' sweat to create a truly noisome miasma.

Solly felt his eyes begin to water. He ever-so-gently eased his finger away from the trigger, thankful for the brief moment of lucidity that had allowed him to make out Fergus' features. Fergus looked at his commander, his eyes wide as dinner plates. A thin string of drool dribbled from the corner of his mouth.

"Pagins, Cap'n," he mumbled, mush-mouthed. "I warned ye, did I not? Pagins an' th' devil's spawn!"

He turned a half-step to his right, leaned a hand against Solly's wall and vomited a generous stream of purple fluid. The smell was apocryphal. Solly felt his insides begin to quail. The man had been drinking something other than wine. From the smell, and the truly degenerative state Fergus was in, Solly wondered if Fergus had broken into the paint locker and sampled some of its contents.

Fergus groaned and began mumbling inanities non-stop from his place against the wall.

"Tol' ya', so I did. An' now he's runnin' loose among us, feastin' an' rapin' at will, an' it's all yer fault, so 'tis. They won't find me accountable for this evil what lurks in th' hearts of men. Black an' twisted-"

"Sergeant major Ingersoll!" Solly bellowed, his patience snapping, U-teeennn-sHUN!"

Fergus, his mind scarred to a depth of three inches with drill and ceremony, snapped to a loose-boned, sickly approximation of attention.

"Sergeant major! Report!" Solly ordered, the tone of command in his voice over-riding Fergus' disabled nervous system, tapping into the core of the man; speaking to the wide-shouldered, straight-backed Soldier that lived in his most secret soul.

Fergus saluted. "Sah. Th' new recruit, sah."

"Yes? What about the new recruit?"

"Sah. I dinna ken how ta' tell ye, sah. It's a bloody mess is what t'is, sah. I warned ye, did I not? Warned ye about pagins an' such . . ." His voice degenerated into a loose series of rambling mumbles. He tottered for a moment, his gaze losing what little focus it had. Fergus' eyes rolled into the back of his head and he collapsed. It was like watching a slow-motion landfall, or an earthquake. He fell against the wall and slid, face-first, into the filth he'd just produced outside his commander's door. His head hit the mud-daubed wall with a hollow, echoing noise.

Sighing, Solly looked down at the man in exasperation. He did not envy Fergus the way he would feel for the next few days, assuming he didn't have him hung. With a grunt of effort, he rolled Fergus onto his side, out of the puddle of vomit. Fergus mumbled something incoherent, gave a thick, guttural snore, farted twice, and moved no more.

Solly went back into his apartment and dressed, taking his time. Whatever it was that had driven Fergus to drink himself into a stupor, Solly Mont wanted to be sure he faced it with his uniform on, with all the bells and whistles of his command regalia.

"This'll be about Jack," he muttered, walking to the barracks his newest trooper occupied. He could just see some kind of an oily, greenish cloud hovering over it against the flickering light of the fort's many torches and oil lanterns.

With a sinking feeling of dread, he hurried his steps.

****

The scene was one Solly Mont would never forget. All the men of the barracks were lined up against the wall furthest from Jack's bunk. They were wide-eyed and staring. Some were muttering and one brave man had pulled forth a large, silver, holy symbol. He appeared to be trying to perform an exorcism.

"Dear Lord, chase this here beastie back ta' hell, as we're as scared as we can be, so we are," the man said.

The scene was something that harkened back to the very primal beginnings of man's existence on earth. It was terrifying to see a true predator sleeping, its mind utterly relaxed.

The fault was his, of course. He'd had the men of Jack's platoon out on patrol all day, and Jack's lot had been drawn for the kitchen rota this week as well. Even with his supernatural vitality, there came a point where you were just tired. Jack was snoring peacefully, sleeping and apparently dreaming.

Like every trooper stationed at Fort Nowhere, Jack had been assigned a wooden bunk and a wooden foot locker, along with a set of His Royal Majesty's Own Linen: grey as ash and as itchy as a plague wagon. After only a very short time in the oppressive, oven-like heat of this place, wood tended to petrify, becoming something very close to stone. It was as dead as it was possible to be.

Jack's bunk, however, was sprouting healthy, green leaf-covered vines that twined around Jack's arms and legs, the head of his bed, and across the wall his bed sat against. A few of the vines were burrowing into the dust-covered, stone floor of the barracks. The squeaking, grinding, rubbing sound they made as they drilled their way over, under and through the thick, ancient flags was enough to make a strong man wince. Several delicious-smelling globes of a bright red fruit depended from some of the more adventurous vines. As Solly watched, a piece of this fruit fell from a vine crossing the ceiling. It broke open when it hit the floor, and the intoxicating smell of honey, roses and ripe red apples filled the room.

Jack's foot locker was moving across the floor. It scraped a foot forward, paused, and then moved another foot. Watching it, Solly was reminded of a large sloth. It took Solly a moment to realize that the foot locker was moving under the forceful impetus of something growing inside it.

Solly strode to Jack's bunk, moving the growing moving things in his path aside, and shook Jack by one shoulder.

Jack instantly awoke at Solly's touch. He looked up into his commanding officer's eyes, and Solly recoiled in shock and horror. Jack's featureless, shining, flat eyes of perfect green shone. Solly found himself the spiritual focus of a rage so deep and full that he felt he was drowning in a burning ocean of it. He sensed that these were the very merest shallows of the anger Jack was capable of. The thought made him shiver involuntarily.

"Trooper O'Green. I need to speak with you. At once," Solly said, proud of the way his voice did not shake.

Jack shook himself, waking fully. He looked around the barracks, seeing his fellow troopers lined up as far from Jack as they could get. They were in a shivering, silent knot.

"Feel asleep, did I, sir?"

"Yes, trooper. That you did."

For the very briefest moment their eyes locked and held.

Then Jack grinned. His eyes assumed a normal human appearance. His face went very still. He looked down at his footlocker, and after a moment it stopped moving. He touched the post of his bed. The vines seemed to grow back into the dead wood of his bunk and disappear. He threw himself out of his bunk and stood before his commanding officer as if nothing at all had happened. He snapped to a parade-ground-perfect position of attention and saluted Solly Mont, naked as a babe, and just as unashamed.

Solly took a deep breath, dug deep within his reserves of strength and dignity, and took full command of the situation. He returned the salute.

"Trooper O'Green. You will dress and accompany me back to my office. You will do this with haste. Is that understood?"

"Sah!" Jack said, his eyes fluttering with a laughing mockery.

Solly Mont turned on his heel and regarded the still-cringing men on the far wall.

"You men will return to bed. You will do this immediately. You will sleep soundly, without dreaming and wake refreshed. You will remember nothing of this or my instructions to you now."

The order had the force of what little true magic Solly commanded behind it. The men walked to their bunks, climbed in and fell immediately to the very deepest of sleeps.

Solly turned on his heel and marched to his office, his back ramrod straight, his head held high. Jack O'Green walked a half step to his right and his rear.

The two men did not speak. They passed Fergus, still dribblingly unconscious, without a glance. Solly opened the door of his office and held it for Jack.

Solly's office was large enough for Solly to have a desk, a chair, several cabinets, a bed and room to pace; something he tended to do with regularity in the stress of this environment.

The office was clean, relatively dust free and smelling of stone, efficiency and the brusque, no-nonsense behavior that epitomized Solly Mont. The office had no windows but it was quite cool owing to the heavy, insulating properties of the stone.

Solly did not light the oil lamps. Though it was as dark as the inside of a bad woman's heart, neither one of the two men currently occupying the office needed any light. With practiced, unthinking gestures, Solly reached for, stuffed and lit his pipe. The match flared like a tiny star in the virgin black of the office.

When Solly had his pipe going to his satisfaction, he sat down behind his desk with a weary sigh. The dull glow was a warm spot of illumination in the cool of the office. He took three deep breaths and held them for a count of ten seconds. When he was sure he could count on himself not to over-react, he looked up at Jack.

Two blank, glowing, emerald, Jack-high-eyes, regarded him in turn.

"Cards on the table, Jack. No more guessy-games. I'm not entirely sure what or who you are, but I know better than most the least of what you are capable of. What I don't know is why you are here, and that I'd dearly love to know, Jack O'Green."

Jack took his time in replying. When he spoke, it was with the same even, quiet tone Solly had used.

"Is tha' so? Well, Solly Mont. 'Tis said if ya' name th' devil's dance, then th' devil has no power over you."

"A riddle, Jack?"

"If ya' like."

"Played the usual way?"

Jack winced visibly, and Solly knew the reason. The riddle game bound the participants to truth. It was unbreakable to man, god, beast or Fae. Once entered, if you knew the answer to the riddle, you had to answer truthfully, and your competitor had to acknowledge your truth. There were no deceptions in the riddle game as played by the higher orders of man, god and Fae. There were laws older than mankind for the riddling game. It was a sacred, honorable contest and to violate it in any way was unthinkable. Name the devil, 'eh?

Jack took a long time to answer. "I could just force the answer out of you," Solly said. He lifted his hand and squeezed it, closing the oath-cage down around Jack.

Jack slowly smiled. "I think if ya' were gonna do tha', you'd've done it by now, Solly Mont. Very well. We'll play it the usual way."

Solly took a long puff from his pipe. He blew the smoke in his lungs out in a thick gust.

"And the stakes, Jack O'Green?"

"Th' only stakes worth playin' for, Solly Mont: life an' death." Jack sighed, rolling his head on his neck.

"Look, can we drop the accent? It's bugging the fuck out of me. Holding true to the face of the thing when you're around the little throwbacks is all well and good when they're clamoring around you, but between you and me it's like eating a face full of gooey insects with every word. Can we talk the way they do at the far end? None of this "Aye" and "Nay" bullshit. Just straight-up, simple-speak. No formality, no courtesy, just direct, blunt, unpoetic language. They call it "keeping it real," but it's just a cover for being too fucking lazy to use language properly. And they've got the best slang. All kinds of stupid, offensive shit that goes right up the nose and punches the brain. I gotta tell ya', dude. I fucking love it."

Solly said nothing. He'd done very little Traveling at this point. He'd only recently discovered the way to move from the earthrealms to the Outrealms, and that was by accident. Coming here had been something of a mistake. He'd entered a World Gate with a badly-healed scab on his left knee. He'd been trying to see what the writing on it was, and he'd lost his footing and fallen in. The blood had been just enough to open the gate and fling him across space to the king's realm. At this point in his personal history, he hadn't yet met anyone who could teach him how to travel, aside from the rare and hard-to-find World Gates. He'd only heard the briefest explanations as to what Travelling was. But it never did to let the other guy know how limited you were.

"Very well, Jack. We'll speak in a manner you're comfortable with."

"Awesome. Okay. Stakes. It's like this, Solly Mont, there's a great army of tribesmen out there," he waved an arm toward the surrounding desert, "just waiting to fall on us with the wrath of ten-thousand thousands. You could force me into the fight, marching me around like a puppet and using me as you see fit. It might work. Or you could play my little game, with some stakes worth playing for and have me in your little fight as a willing, able combatant."

"What are you saying?"

"A riddle game for stakes, Solly Mont. I win, you pop off this oath cage and I take you home with me in a jar. You win, I stay here, fuck your enemies up and save all your asses on my own dime."

Solly dropped his eyes from that disturbing, polished stone gaze. He wiped a tired hand across his face. He could certainly use Jack fighting to the best of his abilities in the upcoming battle, but Jack wanted more and he wasn't offering much. And really, did it matter?

He came to the decision with resolve. Other lives than his were in the game as well. Live or die, succeed or fail, he would face this challenge as he faced every challenge since Wisdom had cursed him: head on and chin first.

"Okay, Jack. Let it be as you'd have it, then."

"Awesome. Okay. Here's the riddle."

Jack stood up and spread his hands. He turned around three times, slowly, smiling all the while and sat back down.

"Who am I, Solly Mont? And for me, who are you?"

Solly stuck his pipe in between his teeth and spoke from around the stem. One of the things he took great pride in was the forgotten, esoteric rituals surrounding obscure traditions. He was a student of the forgotten, the hidden and the unknown, or rather, the no longer known. He began to answer Jack's riddle with a very old tradition he'd learned during his time with Vaiinoreian. It was practiced by the sungmeisters of that cold, inhospitable place, and it had been handed down as tradition for countless generations. It was the riddle-song and the question-story, all rolled into one formal practice of story and response. Solly started out with his blandest suspicions.

"Everyone knows the best riddle is one that hides its answer in plain sight." He paused to puff from his pipe, his eyes growing distant with memory. "It was my grandfather, I believe, who told me that in certain tongues, the name 'Jack' used to mean 'Man.' Someone who wanted to be clever, and hide his name in the words, well, that person might just call himself 'Jack O' Green,' or 'Man of the Green.'"

He looked at Jack. Jack stared back, giving nothing away. "Further," Solly continued, "my grandfather said that there lived a Green Man. Neither man nor god, nor devil nor demon, the Green Man was an awful figure who must always be respected and feared. It was said that the Green Man would demand the life-blood of any, and many there were who fell before it. His place was the Green, the Swamp, the Tree and the Harvest. Neither good nor evil, the Green Man dwelt apart from all life, living and feeding on the edges, and it was a brave soul indeed that incurred his wrath."

To his very great surprise, Jack responded correctly. "Yes," he breathed. "So it is said."

Ahhh. A hit. I might get out of this alive, yet. "Oh, but there's more, Jack O'Green! It is said they are born of the Fae. It is said they are stronger than any ten men and are only seen by the brave, the pure and the good."

"Yes," Jack replied through gritted teeth. "So it is said."

"And yet there is still more, Jack O'Green! It is said they have covens beneath the Harvest Moon, talking of such things as concern those of the Harvest and dancing the night away. It is said they have powers over the living, the dead, the elements and the earth besides. It is said that silver runs from their fingertips and they bleed it instead of true blood. It is said their eyes are jewels, their bones are metal and their skin is stone. My own grandfather said his dear daughter was carried off by one such, and made into a Fae bride. So it is said and now I ask you, what say you to such, Jack O'Green?"

A formal ending, an answer and a challenge. Solly hadn't played in a thousand years, and despite himself, he was enjoying it.

Jack sighed. "Yes. That's as may be." Then he grinned up at Solly. "As far as kidnapping bitches . . . well, a lot of that shit is stuff I made up. It never ceases to amaze me what you tree-apes will believe."

Solly clasped his hands over his stomach, put his feet on his desk, leaned his chair back against the wall and waited. His turn was over. He'd won. If Jack could answer the riddle of who Solly Mont was, the game would keep going until one of them lost.

In a quiet voice like the wind blowing between the trees, Jack began.

"Yes. So it is said, and so it may be, as many believe. But I doubt that it was your grandfather who told you that. If memory serves, your grandfather held no truck with such as the Green Man. Your father? Perhaps. History does not say, and I don't remember for time sits on me as heavy as any. But your father was a singer; a warrior and a poet besides. He lived with a foot near the edges, and perhaps we met once or twice. But your grandfather? Tell me, Solly Mont, and tell me true. Did you ever even meet the man?"

Solly's feet left the desk. His chair hit the floor with a 'thunk.' The magic of the riddle game bound even the Fae to truth. The things he was saying, even if Solly couldn't remember them, had to be true. His pipe fell from nerveless lips. And there it was, finally, out in the open and clear air. Jack knew. He knew! Solly didn't, and neither did anyone else, but Jack knew! Solly realized that Jack probably even knew his secret name, his identity in the world of men; Jack knew it all, and the power of that knowledge was formidable.

There was a tense silence for ten heartbeats.

Jack smiled a glinty-toothed smile and went on, his voice steady and quiet.

"But what say you, Solly Mont? For it is also said by them as know that there walks the earth one who none would know, not even himself, for he was given that most wondrous of gifts and turned himself from the face of his master, Wisdom. Ahasherus, they call him; The Wandering Jew; Mordecai and still other names."

Solly couldn't breathe. Jack continued, as unstoppable as a glacier.

"It is said he bottled the gnn and trafficked with all manner of beings. It is said he walks the earth still, re-learning the lessons of Wisdom. It is said that she took from him that which was most precious to him; his True Name. He may eventually remember what he once was, but he cannot be that. Not yet."

"How do you know that?" Solly whispered.

"Are you fucking kidding me? I'm Jack O'Green, biz-natch! What don't I know? Recognize!"

Jack eyes, hard eggs of polished emerald, glinted merrily at Solly for a moment. Then he looked at the wall and his voice softened.

"I came here myself under no true flag of enmity between you and I, Solly Mont. If I tried to take you, I tried to take you in the manner of my kind. I am myself; singular and unique, and I must behave as I must behave. To do otherwise is to deny my nature and deny myself. To be as I am, as I was created, despite what the learned say, is surely no crime, is it? Is it a crime for the bear to snatch the salmon from the stream? Is it a crime for the lion to bite the neck of the wildebeest? I must eat, Solly Mont. And in you I saw the potential to feast. Am I to be judged 'enemy' for my nature? What say you to that, Solly Mont?"

The rules of the game were being bent here, but Solly felt the autonomic responses of a fight or flight reflex beginning to work inside him, and he spent a long, helpless moment getting his emotions, his hormones, his very self back under control. He did not speak for a long time. Under the sacred rules of the riddling game, there was a response required, but he was having trouble making his voice work. His mind worked furiously while he stared into Jack's green eyes. He ticked over everything he knew about the Fae: their customs, their manners, their strange games and their complicated rituals of favor and disfavor with their tempestuous queen.

Jack was being disarming, charming even. Appealing to Solly's better nature. But the rules were harder than that. Solly had to answer, to take his turn, and if he didn't, Jack would have whatever he wanted from Solly Mont. And there was the last riddle of Jack O'Green to be answered yet. What he was Solly now knew. But not who.

A voice, barely heard, whispered in the back of Solly's mind. It was hard to hear, still and almost silent. It was a voice he heard only rarely these days, and when he did, he silenced everything else. Focusing his formidable will and attention on that voice, despite the panic that still lingered within him, was hard. He'd learned, through painful, heavy experience, to listen when she chose to spoke. For he was sure it was her voice breathing what he knew but couldn't quite grasp.

Green

It wasn't actually audible, but it all fell together in Solly's mind with a click. He drew a deep breath in surprise and looked up at the featureless, shining green eyes of Jack.

Green

He nodded, sending a wordless thanks back at that voice. Once again she'd saved him as she had so many times before. It was a gift. A small one, and one he'd earned. It had been taken from him, of course; the memory. He took a deep, stilling breath. It was a gamble, but he certainly didn't want to spend the rest of eternity as some sort of a cipher in a Fae gambit for favor and control.

"Yes. So it is said, and that's as may be."

Jack's grinned widely.

"Almost had you there, didn't I?"

Solly didn't reply. Instead, he picked up his pipe, re-lit it and took several steadying drags. Wisdom's curse took his True Name from him. It stripped him of his formidable powers, his memories and his sense of self. Everything he was had been taken from him, but just now she'd given him back a small piece of his past: the feel of his love's hand in his and tricky green eyes, dancing in malicious glee.

Jack O'Green. And all of the Fae were ruled by a queen he couldn't really remember. He couldn't remember Ana's True Name at this point, nor could he truly remember her, but he remembered Jack's face in her periphery. He could see it there, hanging on the pale, shadowy, dream version of the Ana he could remember. A constant, lurking presence, with those blank, polished-sphere, emerald, glowing eyes. Yes, he was certain.

Green

"Yes. So it is said, and so many believe. But it is also said," Solly went on, and he had the distinct pleasure of watching Jack's smile collapse, "that the Fae fear their queen-"

Jack held up a hand, interrupting Solly, mid-word. It was a gross violation of the rules, and allowable under only one circumstance: "Okay. I concede. You can stop there, dude."

Solly sat back in his chair again.

"I wonder, Jack O'Green," he said, while trying to convince his pipe to stay lit with enthusiastic puffs, "what the sentence is in the lands of the Fae for losing the riddle game. You are a prince of the realm, are you not? A Green Lord. If your queen knew you were here, losing to a human, enslaved to one, no less, I imagine your life would be forfeit across all of time and space. The only place you could go that would be even remotely safe . . . would . . . be . . ."

And Solly sighed as realization crashed over him. Jack hadn't been caught, he'd surrendered.

"Oh, Jack. Please tell me you didn't think I would protect you."

He looked up at Jack in time to see him his entire body slump in defeat.

"Yes. So it is said," Jack said, completing the ritual in a hollow, dull voice.

****

Solly watched Jack as he smoked his pipe. Jack sat with his head on his arms, pillowed on Solly's desk. His every line spoke to a misery that was bone deep.

When Jack spoke his voice was leaden, dull. "I took your oaths, Solly, and I meant them." He sat back, and his face broke into a rueful grin. "Well, I meant them as much as my kind's capable of. But I swear to you by Sister Moon, by Those That Dance on Summer Stone, and The Silver That Never Forgets, I did not come here intending harm to you or yours. I was wandering through and I happened to hear you were here. I came to find sanctuary."

Solly snorted.

Jack spread his hands.

"Okay! Sure! It would have gone a long way for my own good standing to make you a bauble on milady's bedside. And I freely admit that I tried to do that. Look, Solly, Titiana is a mean bitch, dude. When she's pissed at you, you find other places to be, or you find a way to make her un-pissed. I heard you were here, figured you could protect me from Titiana. When I saw how reduced you were, I figured I'd try taking you out and presenting you to her as a 'Please don't kick my ass!' present. It would not have actually harmed you to be returned to Titiana's embrace, would it? I mean, she might eventually fuck you to death, but damn! What a way to go, right?

And you guys loved each other once, didn't you? Can you blame a brutha for trying to get back into his queen's good graces?"

When Jack said the name, it was only a word. It had no connection to the woman in his head. 'Titiana' was a person he did not remember in any way. But he didn't let this show. Instead, Solly quirked an eyebrow at Jack, trying to maintain his bluff. If Jack realized he couldn't remember the queen of the Fae .

"Fuck. Whatever, dude," Jack said, throwing his hands up in the air in defeat. "I took my shot, you beat me fair. I won't try again, as long as I'm here, and not just because you've got me by the short and curlies. I swear it by Sister Moon, by Those That Dance, and Ne'er Forgets Silver. You've beaten me twice now. I'll fight your battles for you . . . but . . . damn, man! Please don't let her take me!"

Solly looked at Jack, reading the interplay of emotions crossing his face. Jack was a scoundrel, a liar, and as far as could be measured among the chaotic, anarchic lifestyles of the fickle Fae-kind, a criminal. He couldn't take the chance of another encounter like this with the looming threats already present. There were too many distractions, all of them hungering for his blood. But he needed Jack, too. He represented an ally, a link to his past and someone with power he could rely on.

Jack stared back at him, naked hope standing in his eyes.

"Okay, Jack. You can stay. But I've got a further requirement." Solly said, coming to his feet and interrupting Jack's sigh of relief.

Jack's eyes went suddenly hard. "Yeah? And what might that be?"

"A period of service."

Jack stared at Solly, saying nothing.

"As you said, Jack O'Green, I beat you fair. I could force you to do whatever I want. I could close this oath-cage and force your brain out of your ears. But I'm not the type to do that when the stakes are life and death. The choice is, must be, yours. I need you, but I need you to enter my service willingly, with all of your powers, faculty and formidable will. You're no good to me as a puppet."

Jack cleared his throat with a loud, rumbling noise. It sounded disturbingly like the furious growl of a thwarted predator. "This service, Solly Mont. What have you got in mind?"

"Nothing too onerous, Jack. Basically what you've already agreed to. I'm holding you to it with the oaths you've already sworn, the oaths you've sworn me just now, and the sure knowledge I'll name you as Oath-Breaker if you fail to uphold. You can take that to Titiana if you like. Would she forgive a fallen, disgraced Green Lord who'd also been named Oath-Breaker? Ever?"

Jack hissed between his teeth. He clenched his fists and tensed as if to spring.

Solly waited.

Jack sighed and relaxed. "You know I could break you open and eat your heart before you even knew I was chewing on you, right?"

Solly looked at Jack. "I know you're brave enough, and yes, just dumb enough, to try, Jack. But I tell you again as polite warning: harder, dumber and quicker than you have tried before now, and I'm still standing."

Jack grinned. "You're a real hard-ass. You know that? Whip it out. We'll fucking measure."

Solly laughed.

"Do I have a choice?"

"There's always a choice, Jack O'Green. Stay here, agree to my terms and live under my protection, or take your chances elsewhere. The choice is yours. I can promise you this: you won't suffer in my service any more than I myself will." And he held his right hand out.

After a moment, Jack took it. "And when will I be freed?" Jack asked.

"When I can no longer use you, Jack O'Green," Solly said, "but first, you're going to tell me a story."

"Ahhh," Jack replied. "The First Magic. Are you testing me?"

"You can call it whatever you want, Jack, but as of right now, you're my bondsmen, and I want to hear a story."

Jack sighed. "You want to hear the real story of why I'm here, don't you?"

"That'd be good, yes."

"It's not a very good one. It doesn't have a happy ending."

Solly nodded. "Many stories don't. But I'd hear it all the same. Does it have a woman in it?"

Jack nodded. "Women. Immortal women are hard and cold. They've forgotten what that steadily burning candle of mortality feels like. You burn the passion right out doing it that way. How about you, Solly?"

Her not being there was a void in his heart. But she filled him, and the promise of somehow being able to someday return to her kept him going. If he could taste her name on his lips once more . . .

Jack leaned forward and whispered a name: "Ana."

After Jack whispered those few syllables, walls long built in Solly's mind crumbled just a little. He could see her. He could see her plainly, as he had last seen her: perfect, clear and like he was staring at her. Her skin was as dark as polished ebony, her neck like an ivory tower, and her breasts like two doves. She sat on a couch of green grass, and her fingers were dripping with the sweetest of myrrhs. His heart surged with old, remembered love, and he stood up, carelessly knocking his chair over. He gasped at the perfect power of her lovely face, arms up to embrace him . . .

. . . and then she faded into the ghost his mind knew and ached his heart with.

Solly leapt over the desk, grabbed Jack one-handed by the throat, and threw him against the wall. Jack hit the wall with a meaty thump, and tried to claw through it with his fingernails.

Solly spat incoherently at Jack, who was powerless to fight Solly back under the weight of his oaths. Solly's fingers, like steel cables squeezed Jack's throat."

"Icangiveitallbacktoyou!" Jack squeaked out, hammering at Solly's unyielding hand. "I know who you are! I know your real name!"

"No-one knows my real name, Jack O'Green. No-one!" Solly let go, and Jack crashed to the floor. Solly turned back to his desk, rubbing his face with both hands.

"I was there, Solly Mont," Jack said, rising to his knees and rubbing his throat. "I heard you tell her your name. Your real name. Wisdom may have erased your memories, your powers, your abilities. She may have stripped your name from all of existence's memory, but she didn't erase the past! She didn't erase me. Wisdom's curse doesn't erase the abilities of a multi-existential being with a unique time-signature. I tell you, I was fucking there! I heard you say it to Titiana when the two of you met! I even went back to double-check! I don't know it now, but I can go back there, relive the experience and hear it again!"

"Wisdom stripped my name from all of existence! It's gone! I've tried talking to every single person I can find who might've been there then-"

"Yes, but you didn't talk to anyone who can go back there and hear it again!"

Solly stared at him, dumbfounded. Could it really be that easy?

"I'm outside of time's flow, Solly! You humans, even those of you lucky enough to shed your mortality, you view time as a river. Your places on it are fixed in a location known as 'the present.' The past is behind you, and the future lies ahead. Events are followed by events and spring from the dubious bosom of cause and effect. While this metaphor works, it's also flawed. I see time as an ocean, and I can choose my place on it. I can exist at any point along my personal time stream. Ever since I was Fae-born, I've been 'Jack,' I'll always be 'Jack.' I have no 'present,' ever bleeding into the 'past.' Nor do I have a 'future.' There's only 'now.' And 'now' can be at any point in my existence. It only requires my presence to, like, define itself."

He shook his head, frustrated with his inability to explain it. "Look, dude. As near as I can tell, I'm unique. Because of my time signature, I'm spread across the entirety of existence like a thin covering of paint. From my point of creation, to my death, I am a continuous being, separate unto myself, across all of my personal time and space. What this means is, whatever any 'Jack' knows, all 'Jacks' know, or can know. I am in perfect communication with every manifestation of myself. Wherever I dip my toes into my personal time stream, I'm connected to that plug-in. I see what it saw. I know what it knew. I experience what it experienced. It's me in a different 'now.'"

Solly's breath came in quick, hard gasps. "And what? You want what from me, Jack O'Green? You see my kingdom! You can have half of it!" Solly swept a hand, indicating the dust-covered walls, and the sulfurous heat just outside them.

"Okay, okay. Calm down there, O.J. Let's talk for a minute. I told you why I'm here. We'll talk some more. How's that?"

Solly righted his chair and sat down heavily in it. "This is why you are here, isn't it? To torment me."

Jack righted his own chair and sat. He rubbed his neck. "Again, I told you why I'm here. I'm hiding from

Titiana. You got hands on you like a bull strangler. You know that?"

Solly counted to ten, breathing heavily. he fought himself for control. "I'm . . . I'm sorry, Jack. I'm not prone to attacks of temper, but you got me in a very vulnerable place." He rubbed his hand over his hair and looked Jack in the eyes. "I reacted badly. I apologize."

Jack waved a non-committal hand at Solly. "Yeah. Whatever."The room filled with a tense silence as the two men thought separate thoughts.

"Alright, Jack. Start at the beginning."

Jack sighed. "Well, it's funny, really, that you should start talking about women." Solly groaned dramatically, and Jack grinned.

"What, you're gonna tell me there isn't a dozen troopers outside that door who aren't running from women?"

"Tell me this: was she the queen's sister? Her best friend? Did you compromise her good name?"

"Uhhh . . . no, no, and no. She's a . . . unique? Yeah. Unique. That works. A unique case. A favorite daughter of one of milady's best-friends. She's just. . . well, it's complicated."

"Never mind. I've been alive long enough to know that stories are rarely simple. Tell me, Jack O'Green."

"Okay. Well. It started with a girl. All the best stories do, you know . . ."

And Jack lifted his hands, calling the Weaves of Story into existence. Jack's eyes were far away as he began to weave.

"This happened to me when I was hanging out in the earthrealms. I'd been just, like, bouncing around for a while when I spotted this tasty piece. She had this quality about her that I couldn't define. To this day, I still don't know exactly what drew me to her, initially."

He sighed, a rueful grin on his face. "The excuses we make for booty, 'eh, Solly?"

The magic rose, the weaves blazed, and the two men leaned into the currents of the first wave.

Chapter Seven

The sun had set three hours ago. I'd been in the parking lot, next to her jeep, watching the door and smoking cigarette after cigarette. Her peers came and went. None of them saw me.

When she stepped from the building, keys in hand, and a bevy of bags slung around her shoulders, she looked like a refugee trying to catch that last helicopter.

She was beautiful, but only in that 'tired, thin, underappreciated' way that you sometimes see in the young, professional ladies. I like to see those whispery qualities. It makes getting a slice that much easier.

She was dark; olive or umber, if you like; 'swarthy': tan skin, black hair, burnt eyes. Her color reminded me of smoked honey, or a bronze mirror like they used in Babylon. They did something there; some trick of refining that made the mirrors a darker color than bronze could ever be. It didn't patina, either.

Her conservative outfit looked like something you could buy in bulk: a blazer, a mini-dress thing that wasn't sure what it was and sensible shoes. She certainly had the gams for three-inch heels, but our Molly didn't like her feet to hurt. Her outfit was camouflage: armor. The muted colors and heavy fabrics covered her dusky, curvaceous limbs and kept dull eyes back.

Molly, sweet, lovely Molly. If a man couldn't see the goddess hiding behind the 'business casual' then he'd failed the first test. I probably should've been paying more attention at this point.

The smell of her—soap, fatigue, ambition and bad coffee—wafted over to me. Her hair was long and loose, and had that beautifully undone quality to it that really great hair does: wake up, wash your hair, and don't do a thing to it. I growled in aesthetic approval.

I put her age at twenty-five, but she carried herself like a woman much older. She was tired, and she was sad, and she was ready for something new and strange and different in her life.

She hadn't seen me yet, and I listened to her shoes making dead clicking noises on the pavement. I waited until she had gotten her keys in the door before letting her know I was there.

"So I was saying to myself, 'Here's a chick that's got it allllll figured out'."

There was a gasp, the dropping of bags and the clattering of keys. I waited until she had spun around; kicky little can of mace in hand, before allowing her to see me.

I waved. "Hi." I was proud of that. It took some doing, making sure I was posed just right. She let me know what she thought by macing me.

I let her empty the can. I sat there while she sprayed it all over my head, face and neck. It itched like getting water in your ears. When she had finished, I removed my ballcap and wiped my face with one hand.

She stood there, breathing heavily, her eyes wide in fear, and her hands thrust toward me, holding the emptied can of mace. She was even lovelier, if that were possible, and for just a moment, I could see claws and spears dancing in her eyes.

The mace had extinguished my smoke, so I shook another free, lit it and smoked it while I looked back at her. Little sparks of the stuff still dripping from my face ignited and danced across my skin. I ignored it, thinking it could only add to the effect. I ran a hand through my hair and replaced my ballcap.

After a long, tense moment of listening to her gasp and hiccup, I said, "Look. Your arms are gonna get tired, and if you don't start taking normal breaths, you're gonna pass out. Just . . . chillax, okay?"

"W-who are you?"

I grinned in what I hoped was a disarming fashion. "Ah. Normal conversation. Tell me. Do you usually mace people who say 'Hi'?"

"I don't know who you are or what you want, but I'm warning you-"

"Well, shit. It's a good thing you warned me. I'd hate to think you would just up and mace me without a warning."

Time to move things along. I didn't want to watch her freak out all night. I wove a little charm around her; something to help her relax a little.

She grinned. The magic was lowering her defenses. I've been chasing tail for a long time, and there aren't many who can resist me.

"No. Not normally."

"'No, not normally' what?"

"I don't normally mace people when they say 'Hi'."

"Good to know. I can't imagine you'd have many friends. Cigarette?" I offered her the pack, and she took one with only a slight tremble in her fingers, making it a point to avoid touching me. I handed her my lighter, itself woven with little charms.

"Normally, I'd light that for you. That's good manners, that is. But I can see you're a little nervous."

She nodded, lit the cigarette and took a drag. Then she looked closer at my lighter, seeing the spirals and swirls engraved on its surface. My lighter's pretty special. You could stun a bear with it from thirty feet away.

She hefted it. "Is this gold?"

"Nope. It's an alloy. Specially crafted for me by a friend."

"Really? What's the friend's name? Is he a local jewelsmith?"

"Well, 'local' is such a tricky word, isn't it? And his

name's . . . well, it's not one you hear very often. I call him 'Heph.'

"'Hef'?"

"Something like that."

She nodded, and took another drag off her cigarette.

I patted the grass next to me in invitation. She looked at me, obviously fighting the shivery strands of invisible magic prying away at her reason. I couldn't blame her, but I wouldn't be who I am if I couldn't overcome a bit of hysterical, female reason.

"Yeah? And I'm just supposed to trust you? What're you, crazy?" She leaned against her jeep, still twisting against the magic and the voices in her head telling her to relax, to join me, to open herself up to possibility. I could see her wanting to give in, but our Molly's a bit too practical for that. I wove faster and harder.

I sighed. "Look. I don't care if you trust me, Molly. I'd just like you to sit for a spell and have a conversation with me."

"Was . . . was that a pun?"

Now that caught me off-guard. I didn't think Molly could see I was using magic on her, and I've always thought I was too subtle for any hairless biped to catch me unless I wanted them to.

"You know," I said, stalling for time, "it might just have been?"

She grinned, but held her place on the side of the jeep.

This was getting old. I wove even faster while the silence between us thickened like cold gravy. Eventually I saw her eyes beginning to glaze.

"Am I a prisoner?"

"Do you want to be? Not really my thing, but if you need me to tie you up or something-"

"Okay. I probably deserved that."

Taking a deep breath, her eyes almost closing under the weight of my charms, she stepped forward and sat down on the grassy berm next to me. I let the magic around her do its work and lay back, looking up at the stars. We smoked in congenial silence for a long time.

She turned towards me, seemed about to speak, obviously thought better of it and smoked some more. I lay on my back, looking up at the stars, enjoying myself immensely.

Eventually she turned to me, sighed and said, "Look. Don't take this the wrong way, but are you a crazy? And who are you? I mean, you don't look like you're all that threatening, but you're giving me a totally creepy vibe. I think you might be casting a spell on me." She pointed to the school at our backs at this, "And I teach science, so I know there's no such thing as magic. Plus, I know I should be screaming my head off, trying like hell to get away from you, but instead I feel . . . really . . . serene."

She said all this in a clear, precise way, her nerves steadied and calm under the weight of my magic. I shut my eyes and took a deep breath.

"Why don't you just call me 'Jack'?" I said.

"Okay, 'Jack'," she said, the quote marks slamming into place with what I assumed was probably the weight of disbelieving irony. "Do you make it a point to lie in wait for young women late at night outside their place of work and offer them strange cigarettes?"

"No, but that's not the question you should be asking me, Molly," I said, still lying on my back with my eyes shut. I heard her stiffen and felt her pulse race a little.

"Oh? What's the question I should be asking? Besides 'How do you know my name?' that is?"

I opened my eyes and looked over at her.

She was looking back at me, her eyes wide again. I looked at myself through her eyes for a moment. I was wearing my far-realms skin. There's nothing pretty about it, but it lets me blend in: short, stocky, blond; a day's worth of beard stubble decorating the cheeks; an oversized hoody-sweater in purple; blue-jean shorts despite the cold, and a ballcap with 'Army' written on it that neatly shadowed my facial features.

She had a point. I wasn't menacing, but I probably didn't inspire confidence, either. I sighed and pointed at her with my cigarette.

"The serenity you feel is caused by the smoke," I lied.

She looked at it, perhaps noticing it was hand-rolled for the first time. "What? Is it doobie?"

I laughed. "Doobie? Seriously? Who the fuck says 'doobie' anymore?"

"What? Is that not contemporary?"

"I don't know. I guess I could ask the guys at the malt shop. Maybe the Beaver would know."

"You're making fun of me, aren't you?"

"Yeah. Yeah, I am, Donna Reed."

"What should I call it, then? I'm not up on stoner lingo."

"Well, if we're still talking about weed, you could call it "a cigarette for four twenty," but whatever. The question you should be asking is 'How'd I know you were a chick'?"

"Alright, Jack. 'How'd you know I was a 'chick'?"

I was a little disappointed in her; letting me side-step the question like that, but I soldiered on.

I pointed at her car, tricked out with a complete off-road package. "No self-respecting, heterosexual guy would be caught dead in that thing. I imagine the salesperson said something like, 'Cherry-Red' or 'Scarlet-Flame.' It looks like cough syrup! And that off-road package you've got just screams 'poser.' Besides, you need to use a different brand of wax if you're trying to convince people that you ever use this thing for mudding. Missing a wash or two wouldn't hurt, either. I took one look at this beast and said to myself, 'This thing's either owned by a chick or a faggot.' After that, it was simple deduction. If you work at a school, you pretty much had to be a chick since I don't see the school board hiring faggots."

"It was 'Tornado Red.' Tell me something, Jack. Have you heard of the PC movement? 'Faggot' is offensive and 'chick' is sexist and demeaning."

"Yeah, yeah, yeah. Next you'll be telling me about the hole in the ozone, and why I'm horrible because I still like bacon-double hamburgers with extra carcinogens. Fucking tree-huggin' hippies are ruining the world. Don't tell me how to fucking talk."

"Nice."

"Isn't it? Bet you wish you could get away with thinking like I do, don't ya'?"

"Have you always been an asshole?"

"Probably. Look, you wanna go get a cup of coffee or something?"

She snorted laughter. "With you?"

"Yes, princess. With me. I'm asking you, Molly, to have a cup of coffee with me, Jack."

"No, Jack. No, I don't. What I want is to go home and take a shower. I mean, this has been interesting, but it's been a long day. I've got to be up early tomorrow, and I've got papers . . . to . . . grade . . ."

I wish I could take credit for her sudden realization, but that was all Molly. I could see it working behind her eyes. She wanted an adventure, and here I was. I decided to help things along a little.

"Yeah. Papers to grade. I'm really busy too, Molly. Right about now you're realizing that you've got nothing to go home to but a cranky cat that doesn't appreciate you, a stack of bills, and a whole mess of papers to grade that'll be looked at once and then thrown away. You haven't had a date in three years with anyone but guys who can't be bothered to remember your name long enough to commit it to memory as anything other than 'that slutty chick with the tits.' You've been hoping for something strange and romantic and wonderful to happen to you for a long time, and that's why you're still sitting here on this wet grass, talking to me, a weird stranger, late at night, in a cold parking lot."

She looked at me with tears standing in those wide, wondering, amazing eyes.

"How do you . . . how . . .?"

"I'm a great judge of character, Molly. Besides, don't cha wanna have coffee with a god?"

Chapter Eight

Humanity has a lot of stupid ideas about things. You've convinced yourselves that you're at the top of the food chain, intellect wise, and the entire universe lies like a glittering jewel at your feet, waiting to be harvested for your personal use and benefit.

"Look!" you say. "We set foot on the moon!" Great!

You spent twenty quizillion dollars and threw a plastic spaceship at the moon. And for what? To prove that some of you are microscopically cooler than another flavor of human. Yes. We're all very impressed that you managed to fling a big hunk of metal at the biggest target in the sky. What'd ya' find up there, by the way? A buncha rocks? Some holes? Dust?

Wanna hear a really cool secret? The Chinese got there fifteen hundred years before Christ was born. Don't believe me? That's fine. I'm a prodigious liar. But spend some time looking—I mean, really looking—at Chinese Moon festivals. And the Chinese learned everything they knew about rocket science from the Egyptians.

Guess who taught them?

And if that monstrous self-centeredness isn't enough, you people go and assign us immortals qualities and characteristics. You've decided what everything else in the universe is. Here's what I mean: "Oh! The poor thing! He's been alive for forty-thousand years! He's experienced everything there is to experience, felt every emotion there is to feel! How bored he must be!" What a load of shit.

I'm guessing it was one of us that started that whole song and dance. It'd just about have to be. I'm four-hundred-thousand years old, and I'm bored?

Let me break this down for you. Do you remember being, say, nineteen years old? Remember all that boundless energy and resilience? Remember feeling like you could wrestle a bull before breakfast and then eat it? Now imagine feeling that way your entire life and only getting smarter as you get older.

Yes, age would suck, but I'm not old. I'll never get old. I'll be me, just as I am, until the end of time. Imagine being able to drink yourself blind, fuck yourself stupid and fight yourself bloody every damn day. I can eat whatever I want, whenever I want and I never have to worry about getting fat, high cholesterol or high blood pressure. I heal faster than you breathe, I'm stronger than any ten of you, and I can metabolize pretty much anything. Think walking on the moon is pretty special, huh? How would you like to do it in a Speedo?

Between 'em, the Greeks and Romans provided me with nearly ten-thousand years of entertainment. I feature prominently in something like eighty-five percent of Norse mythology, and I've got a forty-five foot statue somewhere in Egypt: gratitude for all the knowledge I dropped about rocket science.

And you humans just keep going, making more of you. It's fascinating. I'll be entertaining myself with your descendants for a million years. Still think I'm 'bored?'

I'll tell you the truth. I don't know how to be bored. Boredom implies a lack of purpose, motivation or ability. Never been a problem with me. I've had so much fun being Jack O'Green that I haven't had time to be bored. In fact, it's only been in the last three hundred years that it's even been necessary for me to slow down a little to prevent drama. Since you naked bipeds invented the internet, every geek with a cell phone is out there, trying to get famous. One bad night, and I'm the glow-in-the-dark sewer monster on Utube. We don't like that kind of thing. Believe me.

Life was easier for us before the electric light, European explorers and the insistence on naming things and nailing things down. "It's Australia, so it's wazza-wazza miles away. It must be, because the earth is this big, and it's a sphere, and pi, math, space and time. It's reality, don't you know? Gravity sucks, the wind blows, ice is cold and blah, blah, blah-de-fuckety-blah."

You changed the fabric of existence with all your labels, and the rest of us get to figure out how to live within your little bubble.

Like you people have any real concept about the nature of 'reality.' You get to be my age, and you find some things out about 'reality.' Space and time don't exist, for one. They're imaginary constructs that the human mind learns to make because it can't perceive everything, everywhere happening all at once. Your senses give you what information the little knuckle of lizard meat behind your eyes can handle, and they lie to you constantly.

Ennui has never been a problem. Not that there aren't problems with being Fae: there are. Most notably keeping a straight face. Part of that's our fault. We can't help it. We see you capering tree-apes making all kinds of silly hooting noises about something, and it wakens something malign in us.

One of my favorite scams works like this: you find some beautiful, tormented jerk; one of those dick-heads with the curly hair and the smoldering eyes. If he's nobility, that's tops, and it works even better if he's got an addiction. You wrap yourself in thirty-seven layers of glamour and then you go whisper nonsense in his ears for a week or two. A month later a feverish manuscript about Kublai Khan's palace will land on a desk somewhere, and this wild-eyed, romantic, liar will go down in legend.

I still laugh when I read Coleridge's work. Or better yet, we wreath melodramatic, pouting frowns on our faces and 'Merchant Of Venice' all over the place at you while trying not to giggle.

"If you prick us, do we not bleed?"

But I digress. I'm a liar, and I'm proud of it. Remember that.

***

Molly gave a harsh laugh at what I said. "A 'god' huh? You don't look much like a 'god'."

I lay on my back, cigarette held in my fingers. I put it to my lips and took a deep drag, letting the cherry light my eyes. It was her first real look at my eyes and she shrank back.

"Really?" I said, "sooo . . . you've had a lot of coffee with gods, then? Been around them, know what they're like, that sort of thing?"

Molly didn't want to concede the point, but the evidence was beginning to weigh against her common sense. Besides, the silvery vapor trails of my magic were winding their way ever tighter around her. Still, give the woman credit. She put up one helluva fight!

She looked at me and then turned away, determination firming her backbone and a closed, hard mask settling over her face. I should've been paying more attention at that point. She didn't actually shake my magic off, but she was fighting it and winning. She was far more resistant to it than she had any right to be. You live and you learn, I guess.

"Jack, this has been most interesting, and I appreciate the . . ." she waved my expensive cigarette in her fingers at me. "I appreciate whatever this is, but I've gotta go home."

She dusted her skirt free of debris. I closed my eyes, feeling my natural cruelty slide to the surface.

"Molly."

It was only her name, but my tone and my delivery were enough to freeze her. It's you people who insist that a name makes a thing what it is; as if a tree were any less a tree for being called a 'tree.' Names give the namer, not the named, power. The named already knows who and what it is.

I put my cigarette in my mouth and my hands behind my head. My eyes were closed, but I could see every beautiful line of her. I was enjoying myself.

In a quiet, non-threatening tone that forced her to listen, I said, "Molly. You can get into that faggy jeep of yours and you can drive away. Or you can come with me to get a cup of coffee. The decision is yours. I can promise you, though, that if you choose to drive away, you'll regret it for the rest of your life."

She whimpered once and I felt her start to shiver. "Is that a threat?"

I sighed. "Yeah, I suppose it is. But not because I'm threatening you; not really. What I'm doing is confronting you with future truth. If you turn me down, for the rest of your life you'll wonder every single day, 'What if I had taken a chance and gone for coffee with Jack?' I'm giving you the option to take the road to mystery, kid. It's a once-in-a-lifetime opportunity. If you get in the jeep, you've blown it."

We always give you an out. It's one of the rules. You may not recognize it, but it's always offered.

"I have a request."

My eyes popped open in response and I looked at her, my interest piqued.

"All right. That's allowed."

"You're not a 'god.' I don't know who or what you are, but I know you're not a 'god.' I go with you, you tell me. Deal?"

"What is it with you people and names? Does calling it 'the moon' change its intrinsic mooniness? I am what and who I am, and I'd like to have a cup of coffee with you, a beautiful chick that just happens to be called 'Molly.' If I spat a bunch of syllables at you in pig-Latin, you'd take it as gospel and write it down as a genus and species-"

"Whatever. But I know you're not a 'god.' So tell me . . .' Jack.' What are you? And who are you?"

I took a deep, long pull off my cigarette, letting the cherry light my pleased smile and cashing the thing out, all at once. I sat up, dusted my hands, and threw the butt away.

I had a couple of options here. I could challenge her to the riddle game and collect my prize if she lost or forfeited by not knowing how to play. I could keep lying to her and bury her in suffocating sheets of glamour.

I could tell the truth, but I hardly ever do that.

"All right, Molly. All right. Fair enough. A fair question, and fairly asked. It deserves a fair answer."

I waited, seeing if she'd catch on. She didn't disappoint.

"There were two questions, Jack: what and who."

"Ah. So there were. All right. I'll start with 'what' since I don't know that 'who' would mean a bit of anything to you. I think we can keep 'Jack'; it's close enough, anyway."

I took a deep, breath; as if what I had to say was cumbersome. I'm good at these games. I really am.

"In the closest approximation of the word, and that's stretching it as far as it'll go, believe me, in a tongue that's far older than anything spoken or written by man; that is, in a bastardized sort of way . . . you could call me a . . ." And I paused here. I took a slow, deep breath and exhaled it gustily, as if expelling the secret weight of ages. ". . . a . . . fairy."

It didn't have the effect I had hoped it would. Humanity has some really stupid ideas.

Molly's face broke open into a vacuous expression of wonder and delight. "Oh! Like Tinkerbell!"

"What?"

"Yeah! Tinkerbell! And Peter Pan! Like those little princesses with wings that live off flowers and sing songs, and dance and play!"

I stared at her with my mouth hanging open. She'd just associated The Strangers with a fucking greeting card illustration. I mean, I knew, in a roundabout way, that humanity had hit on this idea that we were lawn gnomes. I had even made something of a study of some of their goofier interpretations of us. But I had never actually had it expressed to me; especially not by a wide-eyed human. It was like she'd told me she liked having her boobs peeled off and turned into glue.

"Great-bloody-silver-stone, no! No! I don't mean little fucking princesses with stupid fucking wings that live off flowers, sing songs, dance and fucking play! I mean bloody-handed, coldly beautiful, lords and ladies of the night; stealing mortal children and leaving behind wrapped, empty husks. I mean hidden revels held under the moon where we guzzle blood like college kids pounding beer!

"I mean The Bright Ones, Molly. 'The Hunt,' the 'People Under the Earth,' the 'Harvest Kin,' the Strangers, the 'Children of the fucking Silvery Blade!' We're your monsters, your nightmares, your boogie men! We live in the dark and we eat the unwary! There's no flower fucking princesses!"

I watched her eyes widen as part of her caught up to what I was saying. It's hearing the lion roar in the jungle. You take a human from New York and you drop him in the jungle. He might've never been anywhere near a lion. But part of that lizard behind his eyes knows what that noise is, and it knows it's bad news. You hairless-tree-monkeys carry around a lot of shit that's been around since before the ice melted.

"Would you like to know what 'Leprechaun' means, Molly? What it means in the tongue of Errth? It means 'Dread Lord of Blackest Night and Tangled Briar.' And do you know why? It's because leprechauns live under ground and eats things that are dumb enough to walk over him. They're also called 'The Cobbler.' Would you like to know why, Molly? You people say it's because he helped the poor shoemaker. But it's because he likes to make shoes out of skin, Molly; out of the things he fucking eats.

I was working myself up into a good rant; pacing, throwing my hands around. It was pure theatre.

"I've heard it all before, Molly. You meat-socks are victims of some five-hundred years of politically correct, homogenized, pasteurized, Quakerized, storytelling."

I dropped a layer of glamour and lifted my hands to her, letting her see my nails. She gasped and stepped back.

"Me? I'm a Green Lord. I'm not a god, no. You were right about that. But I've eaten things that made some of the gods nervous."

I let my nails glisten in the dim light. "See these? I once used 'em to pull the still-beating heart of a man from his chest. You've heard the cliché', I'm sure, of holding it up before his eyes so he can see it beat before he dies. It sounds impressive, but it's not a tricky thing to do if you're quick. Hypoxia can kill you fast or slow. If you cut quickly and cleanly with your fingernails, ripping a beating heart out of a chest is as easy as licking a stamp. It beat for a good five, six seconds before it quit. I left his corpse in his bed for his family to find the next morning."

"That's awful!"

But something in her eyes looked back at me with approval. Whatever it was, it glowed from within her. She was even lovelier, if that were possible, and a ferocious hunger—something I'm still sure she was unaware of—blazed out at me like a blow torch.

I shook my head. I still wasn't paying as much attention to what was right in front of me as I should have been. "No, it just is. Like a lion pulling down a water buffalo. It's neither good nor bad; it just is, as part of its basic nature. We're not "wee, beautiful creatures that dance and sing and live on only the dew on flower petals." We're mean, we're cruel, we're petty, we're mind-blowingly beautiful, we're bloody small-minded, and if you piss us off, we'll eat your heart, fuck your skull and make a coat out of your skin. Calling me a 'fairy' is like calling a werewolf a puppy."

Her eyes were wide. I laid my hands down on the cool, dew-bedecked grass. I took a deep breath, and, when I exhaled it, I allowed my shoulders to slump, indicating that calm had returned. Yes, a bit over-blown, maybe, but we're dramatic. You would be, too. And while I'm a phenomenal liar, I'm an even better actor.

In a much softer, quieter tone, I said, "I'm a fairy. But you've no idea what that really means."

"But . . . but . . ." she sputtered.

I held up a hand in a warding gesture and looked her full in the face. I took down my hood, took off my cap, and removed my glamour. All of it. This was the point in the script for that to happen. I let her see my eyes and face in full for the first time.

My voice was gentle and pitched low. I looked her in the eyes and tried to talk to her heart. I've never learned the knack of that, though, and I've been forced to fall back on simple language.

My unglamoured eyes, I'm told, can be quite unnerving; especially at night. I've practiced in mirrors enough to know they look like glowing green eggs. They have no pupils, tend to reflect all light, and flicker as if lightning were dancing across their surfaces.

She stared at me. I stared back. She was so beautiful; dark, like smoked honey. Her eyes were like limitless pools, as shadowy as the rest of her. There was something lurking in those beautiful eyes; a fierce hardness with a hunger that could eat you alive. She looked at and you felt broken glass shifting around inside her. I couldn't wait to find out what that was all about. It was probably what drew me toward her.

Molly reached a finger towards my face. "May I?"

"Sure."

Her finger lightly traced one of my steel horns before tracing the other. It felt good.

I let her prick her fingers on the points, drawing thick blood, and then I stepped back, resuming my disguise. I ran a hand through my hair and replaced my ballcap.

I pulled my pocketknife out of my pocket and started cleaning my fingernails with it while Molly stared at me, her mouth open and her eyes wide.

It was a habit I picked up years ago to stifle further conversation. People get nervous around knives. Long years of caution have taught me to always carry a pocketknife. Yes, I'm an extraordinary magus. Yes, I can pull the arms off an orangutan. And yes, most of the people I hang out with aren't bothered by steel, cold or otherwise, despite what you may have heard. But it's been my experience that if you stick several inches of well-sharpened metal into somebody's lung, I can guarantee you've got their undivided attention.

My knife's special. It's seven inches long, folded, fourteen inches long, unfolded. The whole thing weighs less than eight ounces, and I can slide the blade between light and shadow. It was made for me by Hephaestus out of thirteen different kinds of metal. He sharpened it on the song of night, and it won't break. I once used it to cut a hole into a bank-vault. I could drill through the center of the sun with it if I wanted to, but mostly I use it to clip and clean my fingernails.

I felt Molly's eyes drift to the knife. "Is your name really 'Jack'?"

I cleaned my nails for a moment longer before answering. "Of course not. It's fucking Rumplestiltskin. Didn't I tell you that? Or . . . ooh! Yeah! Puddintame! I've got ID. Ask me again, and I'll tell you-"

"Okay, Jack," she said, interrupting me, yet again, with what I considered to be an appalling lack of manners.

I grinned. She was fun.

"No, Molly. It's not 'Jack.' But to pronounce my name, you'd need a third set of vocal chords, less teeth, and the ability to hear sounds above what a dog can hear. 'Jack' works, though, and it means the same thing anyway."

I put my pocketknife away, extended my hand, palm outward, and waited.

After a very brief, very tense pause. She took it.

"Good. Now. Let's go get a cup of coffee! I could eat the grounds at this point."

Chapter Nine

We walked in silence for a while, and I began to shift us through the realms. I had a hankering for walking through the fields I know. The field we started in, for example, probably didn't have trioliths in it. I like trioliths. I'm particularly fond of a couple in a big field in England. They're an object lesson in how easy it is to get a lot of humans to commit themselves, their families and everything they own to a pointless endeavor for generations.

Molly looked around her as the moon rose. The Wee Ones, masquerading as fireflies in hopes of dinner, brightened in response. They rose in a glittering, chiming shower from every flower and blade of grass around us. Molly laughed.

A thick perfume danced on the air, and we heard the distant sound of hoof beats.

I wanted to kiss Molly, suddenly. Just grab her, wrap my arms around her, bury my fingers in her hair and tongue-wrestle. There was no reason for this sudden desire. I thought at the time that it was just an immediate fancy brought on by the pheromones The Wee Ones give off when they're hunting. If I'd been paying more attention, I could've stopped things then. But magic is subtle, and when it's being cast on you, by someone smarter than you, sometimes you just miss it.

I pulled out my smokes and lit one. The smell of cassia and cedar drifted away from us as we walked.

"Jack, where are we?"

I smiled, took a drag off my smoke. "Where do you think?"

She looked over at me, the moon lighting her like a spotlight, and the glittering dance of The Wee Ones surrounding her like diamonds on a queen's dress. They tinkled and chimed, spiraling upwards around her in the perfumed breeze. She spread her arms, lay her head back, and closed her eyes.

I stuck my cigarette in between my lips. Any minute now . . .

The Wee Ones slowly flew toward Molly. One gave me a knowing, smirking wink from its oddly human face. Molly still had her eyes closed. I caught the little fucker, squeezed it until it popped and threw the dripping remains as far as I could into the night. The entire herd flew off to feed, chiming and twinkling as they went.

Molly opened her eyes, still smiling and looked over at me as I wiped my hand off on the be-dewed grass.

"Jack! That was beautiful! What were they?"

"A flight of The Wee Ones, Molly."

"Are they fairies?"

"Yeah, but we've already talked about that. They aren't your diaper-wearing, flower children. We don't do the "hiding in the night, waiting for delight," thing. The Wee Ones are something like a swamp mosquito with magic, a bit of personality, and a bigger appetite."

Her smile faded and there was no more talk for a while.

I broke the silence. "Have you ever been in love, Molly?"

I pretended not to notice her sudden stiffening, and reached out for some honeysuckle from a low-hanging vine. For the last few moments I'd been shifting us toward a verdant wood filled with the stuff. What can I say? I like honeysuckle. Doesn't everybody?

Her voice, when it came, was quiet. "Why do you ask, Jack?"

I handed her the flower with one of my glamour-soaked smiles, spread my hands wide, taking in the magnificence of the night, the thrum of crickets and frogs in love, and the twinkling of majestic stars above us. "It seemed apropos."

Molly nodded. She gave a strange, hurt-sounding laugh.

"Yes, Jack. I've been in love. In fact, you might say I've been in love for twenty years."

She stopped then and pulled the left shoulder of her blouse down off a well rounded, honey-colored shoulder. She took my left hand and put it on her shoulder, spreading my fingers in a way that I'd imagine a Braille-reading person would recognize. I could just feel a heart with some writing inside it. I looked in her eyes. Her face was still, but I could see tears threatening. And the hidden knife-wielding maniac back there was waving at me, too.

"He's got one just like it. I carved a heart and my initials in his shoulder, he did mine. I bled for three days and cried like a little girl."

I nodded and took my hand back.

She pulled her blouse back over her shoulder. "Aren't you going to ask me?"

I took a drag, considering. Finally, I shrugged. "Your story, dude."

She looked at me for a long moment with those tear-spilling eyes and still face. Finally, she lowered her eyes and gave that hurt laugh of hers again. She shook her head and said, "You really are just a perfect bastard, Jack. You know that?"

I shrugged. "Comes with the territory, darlin'. We've got a bit of a walk ahead of us, though, so why don't you unload yourself? I mean, you can stand here all night calling me names if you want, but it won't get anything done, and I've heard it all before, anyway. I'll listen to whatever you have to tell me. Honest. Your dear ol' Uncle Jack promises to listen to every word and to keep his fucking mouth shut."

She looked at the ground for a moment more, and then looked up at me, wiping her eyes as she did so. "Deal."

I spit on my right hand and held it out to her. She smiled, spat on her own, and shook.

"Done."

"Okay. Molly's Heartbreaking Love Story, as told by the author, herself."

We walked, the grass swishing under our steps and the night taking on solemn meaning. When she spoke, her voice seemed quiet and scared; as if she were ready for an approaching emotional summit and emerging from the caverns of her hurt; lost sounding.

"It was one of those, "Hi. I love you. Give me babies!" kind of deals. I laid eyes on him, and that was it. I was done. I belonged to him: heart, mind, body and soul. He just didn't know it yet.

"You know how it is, right, Jack? Maybe once in your life, you meet this person; just this amazing, life and world-changing person. And it's this instant, like, karmic connection, on a level that has nothing to do with your mind and everything to do with your heart. 'From that moment on, everything changes, and you've got no say at all."

What do I know from love? But I kept my mouth shut.

"He was beautiful, Jack. I mean, Apollonic. You know? Like, there are statues in museums that . . ." Her eyes glazed. She licked her lips. There was a very heavy, very pregnant pause there, between the two of us. She took a deep breath and shook herself before continuing. "Let's just leave it at that. He was beautiful, Jack. Okay? I mean, just gorgeous. He had this golden hair and amazing blue eyes. His smile was enough to get me hot. I mean it. He had the kind of smile that started at like, his belly button, and just worked its way up his face until it blew up all over. His smile made a girl's knees all weak and trembly. His smile was like . . . was like . . . an orgasm, Jack. He'd talk to me, and he'd hit me with that smile, and I'd just die. I'd stammer and grin and stutter like an idiot."

She closed her eyes and was silent. We walked on.

"I was young, and naive. Didn't know anything from anything about anything. And here was this amazing, wonderful, beautiful, golden-boy, all-American, wholesome-white-bread-apple-pie-Boy-Scout, and he wanted me, Jack! Me!"

She sniffled a bit and wiped at her face. I stuck my cigarette in between my lips and pulled a lace handkerchief from nowhere. She nodded her thanks and dabbed at her eyes and nose with my handkerchief. She shook her head again and that flowing mane of coffee-colored hair danced around her face.

"We started out as friends, Jack. You know, "Hey! Howsit goin'! I was thinkin' of you." We'd double-date, and we'd talk on the phone for hours on end. And I loved him, Jack. I loved him fierce and hard and hurting. He was just . . . he was just . . . everything. You know?"

She fell silent after that for the longest time. We walked in a spreading cone of her spiritual need. The weeds and wildflowers around us turned sympathetic heads toward her heart's ache.

"He wasn't too tall, his hair was blonde, his eyes were blue, his body was perfectly formed. I could talk to him about anything, and I respected and admired him for being him. I gave him everything I had, and he believed he gave me everything he could. We'd have these like, marathon love-making sessions, and then we'd just lie there in each other's arms, talking. We'd hold each other, late at night, and whisper things like, "forever love" and all that kind of sweet, lover's pabulum in each other's ears. You know? There was the rest of the world, and there was us, and that was fine. It was hot, and it was sweet, and it was so very good and then the dumb stuff started.

"We stopped talking. It was like, this wall of silence suddenly went up between us. I keep telling myself it wasn't my fault. I'd try to talk to him, but as far as he was concerned, there was no need to. We still had great sex, but the . . . the . . . love, I guess, wasn't there anymore.

"We started fighting about little things: money, whose responsibility it was to clean house, the toilet seat's position, whatever. And I kept saying to myself, "Hang on. It'll improve. It's just a downturn, that's all." And it never did. It just kept getting worse."

I looked up, the question unasked but obviously visible.

"No. He never hit me. That was your next question, wasn't it?"

I nodded.

"No, he never put his hands on me in anger. Not that. It was just . . . dumb stuff. I mean, we were the type of couple that would carve each other's names on each other, and get silly, ill-advised tattoos, and all the other things you do to prove you love somebody. Like . . . I don't know, joining the Army or something. You know?

"And then he started coming home late. There was always a reason, or an excuse, but he didn't feel the need to explain beyond "I was out." And maybe he had reason. Maybe I was clingy, or possessive or whatever. Maybe he needed some space. I don't know. But it just kept happening. He'd come home late, smelling like a brewery, or like sex. And I'd ask, "Where you been? I've been worried." And he'd grunt some monosyllabic explanation at me, and my heart would die a little.

"I started drinking. It was easier than trying to understand what was happening. I mean, I'd given this guy my soul! And here he was dragging it through an emotional sewer! You know? Like, "Call the cops; there's murderin' to be done!"

I kept silent, waiting. There's always more.

She laughed, and the noise was sad, painful. "We had our own song. You know? Like, every time it came on we had to stop what we were doing and like, dance with each other. And it was the stupidest song, too."

She crooned words I couldn't hear in a dirge-like melody.

"It got to a point where I started hurting myself. I'd take a knife or something, and cut myself deep enough to draw blood. Once I tried to carve our initials into my right forearm. I was drunk, horny and angry. I drank this bottle of wine, looked at it and just broke it over the living room table. I sat there for a minute, staring at the broken shards, and then I picked one and just started carving on my forearm with it. I passed out before I could finish. Woke up in a pool of my own blood and broken glass. I'd tried to carve our initials into my arm with a broken wine bottle, Jack. I mean, how damaged do you have to be when that seems like a good idea?"

She paused in her story, stopped walking and looked over at me. "Don't misunderstand me. I'm not a pity whore. These were never suicide gestures or anything. I didn't want to kill myself, I just wanted to die. There's a difference. I drank because I hurt, and I cut myself because the drinking didn't help. I told myself it was a quick, temporary release from the way my heart ached, Jack. And I wanted to work it out, and I couldn't. He wouldn't or couldn't talk to me about it, and I just kept spiraling down. The only thing I could do was tell him, over and over, "I love you. I love you in a way that makes my heart hurt, my hands sweat, and my head swim. I want you, I need you, and I'd spend every waking moment of the rest of my life doing what I could to make you happy if you'd just agree to be mine and mine alone forever and ever and ever." And if I live to be a thousand years old, I'll never forget the way I felt when I came home and found he had gone. The way I was relieved. Like, 'The absolute worst has happened. Nothing in your life will ever hurt as much as this does right now'."

She turned away from me. In slow motion, she gently collapsed at the knees and sat on the ground, hugging herself. She sobbed, just once. She sat there like that for a slow count of twenty. Then she stood up, wiped her eyes and turned to look at me.

"Pretty pathetic, huh?"

"What? That you got "forever" tattoos? Yeah. That's a fucking cliché', right there."

She laughed. It sounded weak and forced to me, but it was better than her breaking down in the middle of Fae.

We continued.

"You know what's even worse? Every so often I'll think about finding him and telling him, "I love you." I'll fantasize about maybe working up the courage to tell him how I felt, how I still feel. And then a hard, cold part will push it all down into a deep crevice within me."

For just a second the steel that lay buried deep within Molly shone out of her eyes. I could see it there, wanting to cut something and taste hot blood. Molly was operating under the weight of my magic, and it was making her garrulous. I was hearing secrets I think she kept from herself. "I don't want him to hurt. I think I want me to hurt; to punish myself for trusting and loving him. It's almost like I need to hurt, Jack. Like, this pain has become part of who I am. You know? I mean, this all happened years ago! And I still find myself wanting to cry when I think of him. There've been others. Lots of others. But there's always and ever only really been him. Every time a man would touch me I'd see his face and burn for his touch. Every time a man would whisper things into my ear, I'd hear his voice. Every time a man would make love to me, I'd imagine it was his body I was clinging to. And I wanted it to be him, Jack! I want to be loved and wanted by one man so much that I just give myself away to any man that makes the slightest effort. I've been making needy, sweaty, wanting love to the same man in my heart every time I touched any man. And it hurts, Jack. It hurts right down to the bone."

She sighed into the night a sound that sounded like twenty years of pain, rolled into one exhalation. "Have I been in love, Jack? Yes. I've been in love. I'll most likely die in love.

"I'll never have him. The heart doesn't care. The heart just loves him. Forever. And I think that if I can keep my lonely bed warm for the rest of my life with the simple idea, the simple fantasy of him, then I will be content. Not happy; no never that, but content."

The night was spread out before us like a jeweler's velvet. There was nothing to say. She'd squeezed some of the poison from her wound. If it made her feel better to vent those years of pent-up spleen all over me, then okay. Her question, when it came, shook me from a rather pleasant reverie. "What about you, Jack? Have you ever been in love?"

I laughed. "Love, Molly? I dunno. Maybe. Maybe once, a long time ago. We're incapable of love."

She snorted, and I smiled in response.

"No, I don't know that I've ever been in love, Molly, but I suppose it's possible, maybe. Been in lust, though. Been in lust more times than I care to count or remember. Powerful motivator, lust is."

I grinned at her, letting the moon glint off my semi-feral smile. "But I won't demean you by telling one of those stories. They're not fit for the ears of a genteel lady." I smiled wider and growled once, roguishly, low, deep in my throat.

Her answering smile was pale and wan. Fuck, what do I know from making a woman feel better? Time to get things moving again. "Hey. You hungry, Molly?"

"Starving. Emotional housecleaning really takes it out of a gal."

"Feel like a slice of cherry pie?"

"A real one, or was that some clumsily disguised bit of innuendo?"

I laughed. She'd snuck one past me!

"Molly scores with the two! No, as enjoyable as I'm sure that'd be, I mean real cherry pie."

She grinned and gave me a clumsy little curtsy. "Yes, Jack. I'd give my left thumb for some good cherry pie."

I smiled and exerted my will on the non-fabric of space and time. It wasn't as hard as it might've been. Diners are pretty much everywhere. The one I was looking for was a little, non-descript place I frequent. It was just a diner. The kind of place you go to after drinking all night long for a plate of bacon and eggs and some strong coffee. The sort of place one enters for a hamburger and a cup of coffee and one exits with greasy fingers, a touch of salmonella, and the lingering taste of dirty-dishwater. The air is always heavy with generations of uncirculated cigarette smoke, the smell of hash browns, and the ghosts of beef that's been cooked until it's deliciously carcinogenic.

No James Dean or Marilyn Monroe lounging carelessly against the counter, drinking terrific coffee from art deco cups. Nothing special about this place at all . . . to all casual observation, that is.

The thing to remember: We Are Everywhere. We lurk, we blend, we hide in plain sight. You might sense us, but I doubt you'll notice us. And we like diners as much as you do. Some of them we've claimed without doing anything as gauche as putting a fucking sign out front saying "No Mortals."

A really sensitive, empathic mortal walking into my little diner—somebody in touch with the universe, themselves and all that good shit—would maybe sense an odd vibe; a chill. Most of you wouldn't notice or see anything. They wouldn't see, for example, the hag drinking a cup of coffee and reading a newspaper in one corner. The cook, looming over his counter, his eye-patch and his glamour making you see what you thought you should see, wouldn't register either. You might think it odd that he kept adjusting his eye-patch, but you'd justify that somehow. "Maybe his face itches." or "He's probably really self-conscious about it." Granted, the eye-patch and his massive height are both unnecessary. He could make you think he was a four foot tall woman with five eyes if he wanted, but like anybody else, we can be vain. Many immortals find it too hard to let go of some things. Cyclops are known for holding on, and immortality makes for a level of stubbornness bordering on perfection.

Vampires, werewolves and zombies are the least of it. Everything you've ever thought might be true, is. Story is the strongest of all the seven magics we can cast, and every story starts somewhere, gaining truth as it's told. Giants, goblins, kobolds: you just never see us. We don't connect in your brain as what we are. You bump into us on a daily basis, work with and for us, babysit our fucking kids, and you still don't see us. We're real and we exist. You just never notice. It's better than invisibility. "That can't exist, so it doesn't."

And we're subtle. Survival requires it. Never mind keeping a low profile. There's bigger, badder and meaner shit out there than us, and it likes to eat too. You learn subtlety quick. Then you learn magic. And then you learn subtle magic.

Subtle magic, woven by a master, plays on the things you know; your perceptions and opinions on the nature of reality. It deftly wraps its way around your brain and tells you things are what they aren't, and you believe it.

Any third-rate magician can pull a rabbit out of a hat. A better magician will make you think he's going to pull the rabbit out, and further, that he should. A really good magician can make the rabbit want to co-operate, but a subtle magician can hold a living, kicking rabbit up in front of you by the scruff of its neck and make you wonder why he's holding a bag of potatoes and grinning.

So we like diners for a variety of reasons. Not least of which is that a diner's a great place to prey. Lots of us have developed a taste for meat over the millennia. It gets a little sophisticated, sometimes. Some of us like fear and fatigue poisons, so we get the prey all worked up before going in for a sandwich. But some of us are tired of hunting, and we just want the food to come to us. Diners are good for that. Your guards are relaxed and you're too busy shoveling food down your throat to notice the subtle machinations of the arcane. It's always really nice to be waited on by you, too. Kinda reminds us of home. So long as our waitress is a mortal and we're subtle about it, we can keep a diner solvent for decades with just the occasional mortal disappeared. Ask me how often policing agents get bent out of shape over a missing, minimum-wage soup jockey.

****

The diner's lights beckoned to us from the field and we walked in. Molly looked around and a large, matronly waitress greeted us with a smile.

"Mornin', ya'll." she said, through that maple-syrup grin they all learn. "Ya'll make yourselves at home, an' we'll be with ya', soon's we can."

Quiet conversation rolled without touching us. In one corner a juke box played the Turkish Sonata.

We found a table and another waitress bustled busily over.

"Help you, sugar?"

"I'll have a cup of coffee. No, make it a pitcher, and bring me two cups. Black as the devil's heart and sweet as an angel's kiss. Follow that with a big ol' slab o' foot-high cherry pie, please."

She nodded, ignoring my charm and looked at Molly. "Hun?"

“The same, please. Thank you.” Molly gave the waitress a smile. The waitress winked in response, and bustled busily off.

I kissed my fingers, reached across the table and laid my fingers against Molly’s cheek. ”Pardon me, my love, but I fear I must bid you, however temporarily, adieu.”

“Wow. That was some loaded stuff right there, Jack.”

“Yeah, yeah. Fuck you. A guy tries to be charming and this is what he gets.”

She laughed. “Where you going?”

“I’ve run out of smokes.” I slid out from our table.

“I’m going to go check out the juke-box,” she said. I nodded and waltzed over to the counter.

“Pack of smokes please,” I said to the Cyclops cooking hamburgers. We weren’t friends, but I come in here enough for us to be familiar with each other. I’ve even brought a date or two here.

He nodded, and reaching one massive paw under the counter said, “New bit of ass?”

His tone was conversational, but his voice sounded like rocks rolling against each other in some deep hole. I smiled and pulled out some money to cover the cost of my smokes.

“Something like that.” I said, more to be polite than because I cared. I haven’t got a lot of use for giants. Good cooks, though.

He handed me my cigarettes and my change.

When I returned to our table, Molly asked me, “Have you got any quarters? The juke has a song on it I really want to hear.”

I sighed and dug through my pockets, while muttering about “fucking gold-diggin’ bitches,” just loud enough for her to hear.

Molly waited with palm raised. I gave her a fistful of quarters, and she took them with a grin, running over to the juke.

That was a little odd, and probably should have told me a thing or two, but I was hungry. I wasn't paying a lot of attention to smaller details and it bit me in the ass later. I opened my cigarettes, shook one free, and our waitress returned. She placed my pitcher of coffee, my two cups, and our plates of foot-high slices of cheery pie down with a grin, and said, "Mug of motor oil, heavy syrup, and bleedin' eyeball pie. Kinda sounds like the ingredients for a spell, doedn't it?"

Fumbling for my lighter, my cigarette perched in one corner of my mouth, I replied, "You have no idea, darlin'."

She grunted and bustled away. A group of young people had wandered in, glassy-eyed with whatever drug they'd been taking. They were loud, obnoxious, and smelled vaguely of sex and the unwashed carpets on the inside of a van.

I lit my cigarette and took my first, satisfying pull, the purplish smoke wreathing around my face. I like to sometimes have a smoke I didn't make, summon, roll or otherwise have anything to do with.

After sitting a moment in pleased silence, the oily, somewhat obnoxious tones of an 80's hair-band god began to bleed from the juke like pus from a wound. The song was all about the prettiest snakes being the most poisonous. It was a less-than-clever song he wrote about a woman who cheated on him. I really hated it. I hate most of the glam-band, make-up-wearing faggots who poisoned the music scene in the eighties. But I particularly hate this song. It was a power-ballad; all about masculine emancipation and the way things are always hurting the poor tortured poet. He's got a couple of lines about the way kittens have sharp teeth and claws, and the prettiest flowers poke you the hardest. So he gets hard, and he tells her not to cry anymore 'cause he's not buying it, and they break up. I don't have to have a reason, but if I ever meet the guy who wrote Tear Drowning, I'm going to eat his lungs.

"Your kiiiiiises make me bleeeeeeeeeed and I'm droooooooooooowniiiiiing in your seeeeeeeea of teeeeeeeears, but it's your teeeeeeeeth I fear!"

The group of stoned youngsters groaned and jeered in response. Molly sat down, her grin wide.

"That thing's great! It's got all these cheesy songs from the eighties on it! We're gonna be listening to Hair-Rock for an hour!"

I groaned from down below my balls. "Oh, come on! Seriously? You bought that one? I fucking hate this song! I'm unplugging the juke!" I stood up, ready to put word to deed, and Molly grabbed my arm.

"Let it play. Please?"

I stared down at her, looking carefully at her eyes. Even then, with her hands on me, and her eyes looking into mine, I couldn't feel her spells or sense them. It hurt my pride a lot to realize she fooled me so easily, later.

I sighed and sat down. "This is the song, isn't it? Your and his?"

She didn't say anything. Her hand on my arm was gentle.

"I hate you, Molly."

She laughed, but it was a painful noise. I played it up.

"Don't laugh! You're gonna pay for this. Eat your pie, Molly. And try not to sing along, will ya'?"

Our pies are the best there are. Anywhere. This is not an exaggeration. Our cooks cheat. We load our baked goods with ingredients not available to mortals. The stories told by feckless losers who've trespassed on our banquets are only the very mildest exaggerations. If anything, they were limited by the scope of language. There aren't words in any human tongue for 'The meat tasted like the creature lived on winds and moonlight.'

Our aforementioned pie really was a foot high. It gave off a steaming, fragrant odor of freshly baked crust and syrupy, crushed cherries. Looking at this pie, you knew that the crust would flake delightfully under your fork and the cherries would partially evaporate on your tongue like good brandy. It would be just chewy enough to convince you that the cherries had been picked this morning. When they were baked into this pie, they gently exploded, one by one, giving off a sweet musical tone—sad but resigned—as they did. They'd break open on the tongue like a heart delivering its secrets. You'd take a single bite, and your taste buds would sing. You'd wince at the way they'd nova through your mouth. It would be pleasure bordering on pain.

I poured her a cup of coffee, and sat watching as she exclaimed in open-mouthed, drooling, delight over the pie.

It really is good pie. My people call it 'Gypsy Pie.'

We ate in companionable silence. I smoked my cigarette. I watched as Molly inhaled her piece.

"Tell me a joke, Molly." I said after she had finished and settled back into her seat.

"Oh, no. I can't tell a joke to save my life. You tell me one. If you know any. Do you know any good jokes?"

"Hundreds. Let me tell you my favorite."

She settled back into her seat, a smile on her lips. She has such nice lips, does our Molly. She has the kind of lips you wish you could fall asleep on.

"Knock, knock."

"Seriously, Jack?"

"Seriously. Molly."

"Okaaaaaaay. I'll bite. Who's there?"

"Nobody."

"Nobody, who?"

And I sat there, staring at her, while the juke sang to us about motorcycle-riding cowboys.

She shook her head and scraped some of the cherry pie from her plate.

****

"Molly."

"What?"

"I imagine you're wondering why I've brought you here."

She snorted. "It's not for the pie, or the delight of my company? Or maybe to inflict me with more bad jokes?"

I smirked at her and she laughed.

"It is good pie, your company is delightful, and if you weren't so indoctrinated about modes of humor, you'd see my jokes for the masterpieces they are. But I have other business with you as well." I took a drag off my cigarette and stubbed it out. She sat back and looked at me.

"Dramatic, Jack."

"I know, right? I practiced that little scene in a mirror before I hit you with it."

She laughed and looked at her plate. Her face slowly turned serious. "Jack, we just met. What possible "business" could you have with me? No, no, don't tell me. Gonna sell me a condo? Maybe get me to shave my head and play a tambourine at an airport?"

My answering smile seemed to be chilly enough to cool her levity. I infused a weave of magic directly into her cerebral cortex. It was nothing major, but I didn't hide it at all. I looked in her eyes, making her sit up, listen and pay attention. She gasped and her eyes widened even further when it hit. I let her feel the connection to me for a long moment, let her see what it was and where it was coming from. It was the first time she'd actually felt the hand of my magic, and I was not gentle.

"No, Molly. No condos, no radical hair-dos. I am going to do the very worst thing I can think of to you, but not just yet. Tell me: do you know anything at all about magic?" I lit another smoke, looked away, and broke the weave between us.

She shook her head as the magic ebbed away. I could hear her heart from where I sat and I could smell her fear hormones. I had to fight not to flare my nostrils in hungry response.

And the sharp-edged beastie in her eyes was back, capering and gesturing at me. 'Want a piece of this, Faeire? I'll fuck you up!'

"No, Jack."

"So you're unaware that sometimes powerful magic requires ritual? Sometimes it's a profound thing requiring priests and dancers and sacrifices made under the moon. But sometimes the ritual can be as simple as like, saaaaaay, the sharing of a consecrated smoke between two people who've never met or the acceptance of an invitation. Maybe a stranger will meet you in a parking lot and offer you a cigarette. Maybe the same stranger will invite you to have some coffee and pie, and all you have to do to take part in the ritual is accept the invitation; drink the coffee and pie. There's long boring stories about why you should never eat or drink in Fae. Most of it is shit I made up, but some of it is relevant."

"What exactly are you saying, Jack? Did you cast some kind of a spell on me?"

"No. I cast a fucking boatload of spells on you, Molly, and I've started to cast the big one. But see, it's like this. Sometimes one of my kind gets to a place in his . . . well, for lack of a better word . . . his 'life,' where he's ready to move on to the next stage of his existence. We don't die and we don't fade away. We move along a steady path from first to last. But in order to go from this stage to the next, there has to be transference."

The lies were coming slick and easy to my lips, and Molly looked like she was eating them up.

She swallowed once, her throat clicking. Her eyes were wounded in a pale face and streaked with fresh tears. "Transference of what, Jack?"

I didn't answer.

"So this is what this has been about, huh?"

"Yeah. But you know, after watching you, a weak, whiny part of me has grown fond of you. You and your 'tornado-red' jeep and your pathetic, hopeless life, and your overblown, dramatic wants and romantic needs. Hell, girl. I think I might even love you."

With her eyes wide and now leaking tears, her lips barely moving, she replied. "Jack, you don't know anything about women, do you? Ever thought about flowers or chocolates? Maybe reading some Shakespeare or some of the other old romance masters? Anything'd be better than this!"

I looked down at the table-top, and traced a puddle of grease with one finger, playing it up for all I was worth.

She shook her head, trying to digest what I was telling her and what I wasn't. I rolled over the top of her confusion, stampeding my way ever onward. "Darlin', I could finish the spell and you'd have no choice in the matter. In fact, you as you would . . . well, you'd be something else. But I like you, sweetie. Genuinely. And against my better judgment, I've decided to give you a once-in-a-lifetime choice. Complete this spell with me, Molly, and you'll spend all the rest of your forever tasting the infinite experiences the universe has to offer. I'll live out the rest of your life, and die when you would've. You'll have all of creation to choose from. The magic of the spheres! The music of the cosmos! Would you like to drink wine with the Pharaohs, Molly? Would you like to dance in the nursery of the stars? All of this—every bit of it—will I give you if you'll just give me what I want."

She looked at me for a very long time. What looked like concern creased her face, almost in spite of herself, I thought, and in a different voice, asked, "You're dying, aren't you, Jack?"

I looked at her. Said nothing.

"What are you dying of?"

I turned what I like to think of as my "tired, weather-beaten grin" on her, and I let all my many, many winters wash over her. I let her shiver her way through Ice-Ages, the Stone Age, the Flood, and the coming of White Man to the shores of the New World. I let her see just a portion of my personal infinity, and then I looked down at my puddle of grease.

"Apathy."

She took a deep breath, and looked down at the table herself. "I want something in return, Jack."

My interest was piqued and I looked up at her in surprise. I hadn't expected that at all. "All right. What? I mean, in addition to the fact that I'm offering to make you immortal."

She looked up at me and it was my turn to gasp. The little beastie was fucking eating Molly's eyes and shining out at me from the diminishing brown of Molly's gaze with naked desire. "I want your story."

Chapter Ten

The hunt's more enjoyable when your prey does something surprising, isn't it? I mean, who wants to go running through the woods after a hare that runs in a straight line?

I sat back in the booth. Not one of them had ever asked me for my story. I applied my very best poker face, shook a smoke free, and chain-lit it from the one already in my mouth.

"Fucking things'll kill me," I said, as I stubbed the old one out, stalling for time.

Molly sat at her side of the booth, the strange and intense look in her eyes.

I blew a smoke ring toward the ceiling. It shimmered in the blue air. I found, to my befuddlement, that I wanted to tell her my story. Why not? Tell her and let her deal with it. The real problem here wasn't that I was reluctant to tell her the story. The problem was how.

How do you tell someone who's never lived without electricity about the way constellations she'd never seen shone under a desert moon? How do you tell someone who's never been more than twenty feet from central air and heating about living underneath an animal hide? How do you tell a modern American woman, with her sense of entitlement, about the rights of a king and his nobles? How do you tell Molly that back then it wasn't rape? How do you tell someone—someone like our dear, sweet, Molly fer fuck's sake—about the Pit? It's like trying to explain sunburn to a mole.

There were other ways, of course, but how open did I want to be with her? What would it cost me? Sure, I could Storyweave, but did I want to do that with her?

I shrugged. Fuck it.

"Are you familiar with the Bible at all, Molly?"

"Sure."

"How familiar?"

"I read it every day, Jack."

"Okay. So if I start spraying you with Scripture, you're not going to be looking at me like a stoned chimp, right?"

"No more than I usually do."

"Funny. Okay. My story begins with Scripture. You ready?"

"Anytime you are."

I reached over and took her hand. Some stories can be told, some have to be experienced. I opened the vault of my heart to her and began speaking.

Her eyes glazed and lost their intensity as the magic stormed through her. I took a deep breath, and began.

"'So Cain went out from the Lord's presence and lived in the land of Nod, east of Eden'."

****

The wind never stopped blowing here. It was dry and cutting; carrying voices on its breast; desiccating everything it touched. Lies and stories, black as poisoned night, whispered on it and cut holes in the soul and skin. It was the first noise you heard, just below the threshold of hearing when you were born, and the last thing as the light in your eyes failed and the eternal night of forever fell.

The sun blistered everything. The people waited for death, ulcerated in the sun, and dreamed black and midnight dreams with the voice of the wind whispering, whispering, whispering.

He missed Mother. He missed the way she smiled, so tired, but with love shining from her eyes. He missed her smell of sweat and rare, costly ointments. He missed the way her skin felt when she held him close as they slept in her closet. He missed the way her bangles and jewelry had jingled in the warm, comforting dark.

There were times she was required to wait on the king's pleasure, and she would whisper, "Be as still and as quiet as you can, my love. I will return soon."

And she always did. The king used her in ways that left her weak and battered, but she always returned to him. Sometimes she had bruises and sometimes she smelled of spilled wine, sweat, musk and other, baser odors, but she always came back to him, always kissed away his tears. She fed him with the food and drink she could sneak from the king's table and crooned gently in his ears until he slept again.

He missed her voice lulling him to sleep.

She'd been holding him, singing softly in his ear after being gone for three long days. The king had been cruel to her, leaving livid bruises and rips on her skin and causing her lips and eyes to swell. Her hands were mangled and torn, her fingers misshapen. They were wrapped in oozing bandages. She'd groaned as he climbed into her arms, and then she gently held him and sang softly into his ear.

"Sleep, sleep. All is well. Sleep, sleep, mother's boy. Close your eyes, rest your head. All is well."

It was nonsense, but it was soothing nonsense. And for a small boy, lost and confused by his strange world, it was the voice of love.

Then the soldiers came.

They tore him from her arms. She'd shrieked in fear and anguish, grasping at him, and tearing at the soldiers with her ripped and bloody hands. One of them hit her across the face with a mailed fist, knocking her down.

She spat a tooth, and crawled to him, begging and pleading.

He'd laughed. "On your feet, bitch. He calls for you."

Wrapping a hand in her hair, he started dragging her away, and she pled with them to spare her son, her only son.

The soldier laughed again. "Don't worry. His majesty has plans for your precious boy."

Her scream still woke him up some nights, echoing down through the years and shivering its way across his burned and bloody soul.

One of the soldiers targeted him specifically, kicking him and abusing him with insults and more words he didn't understand.

The soldiers dragged the pair of them, crying and begging to the king. He was cuffed and kicked, battered and beaten, and blood was dripping from his nose and lips as he stood there, shivering and sniveling before the man who was his lord and master. One of the soldiers put a hand like a claw on the back of his neck, squeezing and pushing him down on his face.

The room they were brought to was small, much like the closet he slept in with his mother. Light trickled in from somewhere and the air was hot and stuffy. Shadows covered every wall, moving sluggishly under their own power. A smell, like decomposing meat, or unwashed bodies, filled the room. A bed, a basin of dirty water, a cupboard and a small box, sitting on the bed, were the room's only fixtures.

"Who did this?"

The voice was so close to the sound of the wind that he thought it was the wind itself speaking to him.

He looked up. Those high, dead, crazy eyes—like two badly cooked eggs—were staring at him. He remembered the way the swirling circle, like a fingerprint, on his black skin, so like his beloved mother's, had glinted in the light. The burns covering the king's skin were red; raw and livid, twisting like scorched ropes over the entire surface of his body.

The soldier's hand on his neck began to tremble.

"I did, my lord. I thought-"

The king struck. Blood showered down, covering his head and blinding him. The hand's pressure increased, unbearably, for a fraction of a second, and then it fell away. He heard a noise like a sack of meat hitting a damp wall.

Turning, he saw his tormentor lying on his back. Most of his face was missing and he was gurgling through a torn hole that had once been his mouth. Blood was drenching his robes and beginning to pool on the floor. Even as he watched, the soldier died.

The king wiped a hand on his robe, leaving a smear of blood and meat.

"I didn't ask you to think," he said, his voice not rising above a pained, gravelly whisper.

The king put his hands on him, one of them still stained with warm blood. Those repellent hands, the same ones that had left so many marks on his Mother's fair skin, settled on his shoulders. He felt the king's breath, like the warmth of a snake in a close place.

"This is he, woman? This is the child you bore to that creature?"

The king's voice sounded like bones squeaking and grinding together. He never changed his tone, or raised his voice above a slight whisper, but that was enough to drive a man mad. The king's hands were gentle as they lay on his shoulders. A smell, like wine mixed with sweat and fear rose from them, tickling the nose.

His Mother lay on her face, sobbing. The king smiled, drew back a sandaled foot and kicked her in the ribs hard enough to flip her over on her back.

"I asked you a question, woman." His voice had never changed. Not one bit.

"Pl-Please, My Lord, he is but a baby. How can he threaten you? He cannot be blamed for the sins of his father!"

"And who are you, woman, to tell me what to do? Who are you, woman, to tell me of the affairs in my own house?"

His Mother lay where she'd been kicked. She gasped and sobbed. He'd tried to go to her, but the king's hands had squeezed his shoulder with paralyzing force.

"The favors of your body, daughter or no, earn you no leniency here. You force my hand, woman."

The king handed him to a soldier. Walking with a limp, he moved to the box resting on the bed and opened it. The box's lid resisted him, opening with a dusty creak. The king reached inside and took out a velvet bag, the size, shape and weight of one of the melons that sometimes grew wild on the palace's walls.

"You are not my son, boy. You are the son of another. But my blood flows in your veins. Your mother," he spat the word like a curse, "couldn't keep her legs closed. I told her there would be consequences, even for one of my blood, but she didn't listen."

He fondled the bag as he spoke, caressing it and touching it like a man with a beloved pet. "And so here we are: father, faithless daughter, and son, ready to spill the secrets of the ages. You are not my son, boy. But you are my seed, and you must know from whence you come. You must feel a taste of the power I wield. And then, in the time of my choosing, then you must die."

The king opened the bag, pulling out a severed head. The skin was gray and stretched across the skull. There were no eyes, no lips, ears or tongue. The jaw moved, once or twice, and seemed to be trying to say something. Teeth, like jagged razors, pierced the upper and lower jaw, clashing and grinding against each other with a squeaking noise. The skull was covered in a shining patina, like grease. The little boy whimpered in shock and fear.

"Oh, yes. Yes, my little bastard. It lives, but not as we live. It has lived so for many, many thousands of years. And it has secrets to tell.

"I spent ten years searching for it. Stories have been handed down to us, and there are legends. But where the timid feared, I sought. And though it cost me gallons of blood, life and treasures untold, I found what I sought. I found the evidences of the kingdoms that were before. Great castles, reduced to little more than piles of random rubble, covered over by seas, lava flows and great caverns. Time, boy. Time kills everything."

The king lifted the head to the side of his own neck. The head bit a hole, and began to feed on the blood running with sluggish force from the neck.

"It is dead, but it still whispers secrets to me, my son. It still has gifts to bestow."

With a casual gesture, the king ripped the ancient skull from his neck and returned it to its velvet bag, the jaw still working and blood leaking from the hole where a spinal bone still protruded like a broken thumb.

The king turned to the boy. "This your blood, boy. Now come. I must feed."

And the king pulled him toward his face, with elongating teeth and red-rimming eyes, with implacable, unstoppable force. He'd screamed in fear and shock, his mother keening like a lost soul. He felt the teeth biting, drawing his blood from him and chewing a hole into the side of his neck. The pain was unbearable and endured for more time than he could remember.

The king drank and threw him on the floor. From his place, he saw—even as consciousness faded—the king taking a sword from a soldier and moving toward his mother. Just before the world washed away into white, he heard the king say, in a voice that might've been used to order a plate of figs and a glass of wine, "Throw him into the Pit."

****

Molly ripped her hand out of mine with a gasp and ran out of the diner. I went after her.

She sat on her hands and knees, a puddle of vomit in front of her. She groaned and sobbed at me when I pulled her hair back from her face.

I rubbed her back and whispered meaningless endearments to her until she'd settled down. After a few more stomach-emptying noises she settled back on her butt on the curb and moaned liquidly with her head between her knees.

I sat, rubbing her back and whispering. She sat up and leaned against the diner wall. I offered her a snot rag that she took with a teary-eyed smile.

"He was Cain, wasn't he? The king? The very first murderer?"

I sighed. I'd met Cain later. Much later. He was a bad-ass motherfucker, and not somebody I personally wanted to fuck with. I'm not scared of him, but I'm not suicidal either.

"Yeah."

"Jack . . ."

She lifted a hand to my face, looking at me.

This was really getting complicated for a slice of hot ass.

"Molly, this story just gets worse. You sure you're up to it?"

She nodded.

We went back into the diner to find the waitress bustling over with a cool rag and a glass of water. Molly took both with a grateful smile.

The waitress said something we didn't pay the least bit of attention to, bustled away, and Molly wiped her mouth clean. She looked up at me.

"Who was your father?"

I shook another smoke free and lit it.

"'The sons of God saw that the daughters of men were beautiful, and they married any of them they chose'."

"Genesis chapter six, verse two, Jack."

"Right again, Molly."

"So what are you telling me, Jack?" Molly reached a hand across the table at me.

I ignored it. Took a drag off my smoke and looked back at her.

"It's all part of the story, Molly."

I took hold of her hand then and rose with her into the flaming tide of Story.

****

He dreamed for a thousand years. He was kicked and beaten, but his body, already surfing on the changes wrought on him by his careless grand-sire, defended itself as his mind dreamed. The pain was exquisite and touched every part of him, even as he twisted in his dark world of personal misery.

When the voice came, it came like a small beacon in a world of darkness.

"Hold on, boy. Hold on."

And hands, gentle but strong, held him, pouring warmth, light and strength into a body small and beaten. Consciousness came and went, like a light flickering in a dark room.

His body kept changing, but he was still weak in a world that hunted him.

Moving away into the darkness, his mind slept while his body survived.

****

Molly wept openly.

I let go of her hand for a moment to light another cigarette. It's best if this is taken in small doses. The pain can be pretty intense.

And there's nothing you can do about the smell. By the time I got there, the Pit had been used for nearly a hundred years as an abattoir, a sewer and a breeding ground for tens of thousands of criminals, slaves and others like me.

The waitress bustled over, refilled our coffee cups, and Molly wiped her eyes. She took a deep breath and a sip of coffee.

The juke started playing a song I thought I recognized; heavy melodics and a syrupy guitar feel.

"I criiiiiiied for you on the day you diiiiiied, but not when they buried yoooouuuu ten years laaaaater . . ."

I took a drag off my cigarette and reached for Molly's hand again.

****

The Pit was all of the world. A long abandoned copper mine, surrounded on all sides by a steep wall made of glass. Criminals and "enemies of the state"—anyone who had earned Cain's displeasure—were thrown in to die. They were not fed, and they were given no water. All of the necessities for survival came from the other inhabitants of the Pit, or scrounged from what one could find in the many tunnels and holes.

It was not a place for the weak or the slow. Survival in the Pit relied on being able to move faster than you could think. If you sat still for too long, roving gangs of the strong would come find you.

Day and night were indistinguishable and time passed in increments of sleep and hunger. His body fed on what he could find while his mind raced and coursed, dreaming. He wept frustrated tears of pain and rage and kept the circling predators at bay with strength he could not control or understand.

"Psst! Boy!"

The voice caught him unaware. He'd had no problem seeing the man in the grave-like darkness of the Pit. The perfection of his face was marred only by the way his eyes glinted dull silver. They shone with a light that spoke not of evil but of madness. He grinned at the boy, his teeth perfect and strong in that handsome face.

He was sitting on his haunches, his back against a wall. He was dressed in a long, black cloak of a shimmery material. The space around him was clear.

"I been watching you, boy. You want out of here?"

His voice was like music and it stroked the boy in a way that only his Mother's had before. He didn't answer. If his strange and confused time here had taught him anything, it was 'Don't. Trust. Anybody.'

The man reached beneath the cloak and pulled out a roasted leg of meat. He could smell it from where he stood, some six feet away, could see the juice running clear. The man pulled a strip free of the bone, and put it in his mouth.

The boy groaned with an inarticulate, animal longing.

"Looks good, don't it?" the man said, his eyes shining.

The boy nodded and stepped closer. The man tossed the meat at his feet, and the boy fell on it.

"Yeah. You're strong enough, anyway."

The man laid a hand on the boy's head while he feasted, and Jack opened his eyes.

****

Jack swam slowly back to the world of life and light. Something had just happened, and he didn't quite know what it had been. The strange man had been kind to him; had fed him, and put his hand on him.

And then . . .

And then the whole world had flashed white, Jack felt like he was falling into a pool of dark, wandering stars, and sleep crashed over him like a flood. He stared at the ceiling, not comprehending who he was, or what he was doing there.

A warm, strong hand touched him gently on the shoulder.

"It's your birthright, boy: the First Gift a father gives his Faeling. I woke your mind, soul and body to the powers lying dormant in you. You're Fae, and you have a lot to learn. Fortunately, we're not going anywhere for a while, so we might as well use the time wisely."

His voice was smooth and gentle, with rough edges that Jack found soothing. He sat up, looking around him. The man he'd met stepped out of a deeper pool of shadow, and smiled down at him.

"Hello, Jack. I'm Tam Lin. Tam Lin Bird-feather, and as much as it pains me to admit it, I'm your father. I've come for you."

Jack stared.

Tam Lin laughed, and it was a rich, melodic sound; so alien in the fusty, stuffed darkness of the Pit. Something in a further corner moaned in misery.

"Caerdy got your tongue?" he said, still smiling at Jack.

"Wh-who?"

"Caerdy. A cat spirit that enjoys dressing up like a woman and invading the dreams of men. She goes out in such a way as to leave most men speechless. She feeds sometimes, but not greedily, and the sucker mortals have a dream to look back on when they're old, dry and twisted. Myself, I'm of the opinion she learned that kind of trick from her momma, Lilith, but I imagine that's not for me to say one way or the other. Are you going to lie on your back all day, or are you going to get up and greet your father?"

Jack stood up and stared at the man.

"That's better, boy. Never let them see you on the ground. They can get a talon in and rip your innards out."

Jack looked around at the darkness and shivered at something he couldn't see. He'd heard it moving just beyond the corner with a furtive, slithering step. "Can we leave here?"

"How, boy?"

Jack pointed a hand at the grille far above them. "Pull it out. We'll run away."

"Oh, yes? Well, try it."

"I can't reach."

"Neither can I. Can you fly?

Jack stared.

"So that answers that, doesn't it?"

"Can't you . . ." He waved a hand in futile expression, trying to fit words around concepts that were completely new to him. The sparkling motes of his new-born magic fizzed, popped and gently bubbled in his veins, but he hadn't the slightest idea what to do with it, or how to go about using it.

Tam laughed again. "What? Magic it away? Sure. I could ask Earth to open for us, to part around the grille, or even to transport us out of here. I could do that. The bargain of Earth and Fae would cover the two of us quite nicely, I think. We'll be out of here in a trice. You ready? I'll just go do that. Or maybe I'll re-write the fabric of reality so the grille isn't there anymore. Then I'll ask Earth to create a rising wave to lift us up there. And then, when Cain comes riding on his pale horse of fiery death to investigate, why, I'll just waggle my fingers at him. Is that what you meant?"

Jack stared at Tam, who sighed. "Boy, we're here for a reason. There's much you have to learn. Travelling, the bargain of Earth-"

"Earth?"

"Earth, boy. Earth." Tam waved a hand around him at the cavern walls. "Earth. The planet. She's alive, boy. Alive, breathing, and listening. And we of the Fae have the birthright of the bargain. In certain small ways we can control how she behaves. Oh, it's a fine sight, watching rolling waves of dirt smothering your enemies! And the best part is that the bargain of Earth is something Cain can't touch. Earth won't go near Cain. He's poison; tainted; diseased. He marked her once, and she's never forgiven him. But we'll come to that in time. Bide, boy. Time will pass and you still have a long way to go. There is much you need to learn and this is as good a place as any to teach you. We'll leave here when you come into the fullness of your power. I'd hate to think I've wasted a trip."

He sighed, and the darkness around them seemed to grow fuller. "You've got a sorry wind to fly, my son. Cain's grandson is no person to be, I'm thinking. But Cain's grandson is not all you are, and his wee skull can't erase what you've gotten from me. You need to learn what you're becoming, and instead of erasing you in madness and pain, like your grand-pappy wanted to, I can tell you about the rest of who you are; the legacy you got from me, your Daddy. For it's not a sorry gift to give a boy, Peership of the Wyld. You're a Child of the Harvest, my boy; Of the Green. These are mighty titles and mighty gifts. But you have to learn to use them. Are ya' willing?" And Tam held a hand out. It glowed with light, like lightning dancing on the moon. Jack stared at it in naked wonder.

"Magic, boy. Yours for the taking, if you can learn how to use it."

The hand hadn't moved. Jack reached toward it and felt, for the first time, the magnificent power of the First Magic, Story. It filled him with light and song, and he gasped at the unfettered majesty of it.

"Don't fight it, boy. Ride the waves and let it become part of you," Tam said.

Jack lowered himself into the weave and felt it spinning him away. The Story carried him.

He saw a seed, naked and alone, waiting in fertile earth. The rains came, the sun warmed the earth, and the seed split into two equal parts. In the one half a seedling, that of a tree, green as a snake and strong as time, began pushing through the earth to the warm sky above, ready to take its place in the pathways of life. In the other half was an infant. Its skin was green, its hair was wheat, and its fingers and toes were the small branches of a tiny tree. Its eyes were flowers and its teeth were rocks. It cried, lonely and alone in its place under the Earth.

"Our first mother, boy. We call her 'Aliulu.' It means 'First Woman.'" Tam Lin's voice was soothing, and somehow part of the images flashing through Jack's head; integral to the story. He noted the words without commenting on them.

Earth, hearing the cries, nourished it, comforted it, and made it its own. Earth pushed it toward the sun, gently encouraging the infant to grow, to spread wide its arms and embrace all of the Wyld, the Green. Earth had no daughter of her own, so she made Aliulu her own, and gave her the gifts she had held for herself. For Aliulu, the Earth was responsive, aware. She grew fruit, flowers, grass and tree in response to Aliulu's wants and needs and protected and served her as best it could. The elements, tied as they were to Earth, responded in their kind to Aliulu as well.

And so the infant grew, growing and flowering. In time, it fruited, and all the children of Fae grew from the fruit.

And from that time to this, the Fae have been of the Green, and Earth has been their mother.

"This is only part of who you are, boy." Tam's voice echoed in the disembodied caverns of his head. "There's another part of your story, given to you by Cain's wee vampire. We go to where the Last Father began and we hear his story, told in your changed, cursed blood. This is where you begin to learn who you are now, and this is where you will need to return to finish becoming."

Jack dropped fully into the Story, wrapping himself in the glowing weaves and wearing it like a skin.

Chapter Eleven

Consciousness returned slowly, like blood returning to a limb. There was light and pain. That struck him the hardest as he came back to the light and life. Pain. How long had it been since he had felt pain? For the first time since he'd been infected, Lord Phalen Tornagow, Ducal Seat of the Empire; Dark Scourge of the Middle Wastes; Empire's Scion to the Blood Throne; Prince Of The Thorn March; Duke of the Black Marshes et cetera, et cetera, et al, woke slowly and sluggishly and in pain.

His limbs, normally surging with the untamed power of the elder vampire, were limp and flaccid; hanging from his torso. His eyes were hard to open and felt thick, glutinous, as if something had glued them shut. His thinking was dull. He knew hunger; the ravening blood hunger that comes from long deprivation. Ducal Lords did not know hunger. Food came to them, docile and meek, with washed necks, and chaste, lowered eyes. To feel this fatigue, this weakness, was alarming.

His thinking was muddled. His last clear memory was of the royal ball, held at the palace. Lord Phalen had been invited by the queen herself. They were occasional lovers, as time and circumstance brought them together.

Lord Phalen Tornagow was tall and lean, with a dancer's grace. He was famed for his strength, coming as it did from his sire, Lord Tornagow. His features were hard and peaked, as if chiseled from ice. His cheekbones had the wild edge of the wolf. His jaw was long and lean, and his teeth were as wide as a dagger's blade. His eyes were the narrow, black pits so favored by the ladies of the court. He never wanted for company.

The feast had been an amusing affair. The king had trapped several of the ferals who still lived beyond the realm of the kingdom, and had shipped them to the capital, for the enjoyment of the queen and her hand-selected guests.

It had degenerated, as most royal feasts did, into an orgiastic debauch. One fine, squeaking creature—a plump, young thing of perhaps twelve summers—had made a merry chase of it; running from Phalen's slavering jaws and getting his predatory excitement up to levels he hadn't reached in several hundred years. The chase had taken them into the benighted halls, and there had been . .

What?

Something.

Something large?

Try as hard as he could, he couldn't remember. There was an impression of size, and then one of pain, but beyond that, nothing.

He lifted a hand to wipe at his face, and that's when he felt the first stirrings of alarm. Something was dripping on his face; something warm; something wet. He wiped a hand across his jaw and felt something hot and viscous come away on his fingers. He lifted the hand to his eyes and tried to focus on it. It was too much. The effort caused the last meal he'd eaten to pound in the vessels in his head. He squeezed his eyes shut against the pain. The viscous fluid was unpleasant on his fingers and Phalen made to wipe it off on his doublet.

His fingers touched the bare skin of his chest and Phalen's eyes flew open.

He looked down toward his feet. He hung upside down, naked, from a ceiling that looked like stone. His feet were held by a thick, grey substance that immobilized them from just below the knee. As he watched, part of it dripped away and hit him, with a warm splatter, on the chin. It looked like clear, chunky snot.

Phalen strained against the lock on his legs and could not move. He tried to pull himself upright, to swing at the substance with a fist, but found he was too weak to do so.

As he swung back to an ungainly vertical, his eyes fell on the pyramid. It sat in the middle of the floor. The pyramid was enormous, rising well into the shadows filling this space. It appeared to be constructed of symmetrical, round rocks. Some of the rocks had a multi-colored growth on them. He tried to see more in the tricky light, but his over-worked, fatigued eyes ran with blood, and he was forced to shut them and blink them clear.

"What is the meaning of this?" he called. His voice was a weak, whispering squeak; far below his usual, commanding baritone.

The reply, when it came, was in a voice that was hard and deep. It shook Phalen's bones with strange resonances. Phalen knew, without any doubt, that he did not want to see the possessor of that voice. It spoke a single word.

"JUSTICE."

****

The sound of the water was soothing somehow.

The Beast sat on the edge of his underground lake, on the stone that had eroded into the shape of his brooding body, and listened to the 'plink,' 'plink,' 'plink' of the falling water.

They had come here. They had come here, before . . .

But he couldn't remember it. He had forgotten so much. He had pursued his single-minded purpose for so long, he had become the purpose. There was so much about himself that was no longer important. There was no room within him for anything but the purpose.

He didn't know his name any more. If he still had it within him to weep, he would've wept over the loss. A man should never forget his name.

He wondered, sometimes, if there were anyone alive who could tell him his name; anyone who still remembered who he was or where he had come from. He wondered if the woman who'd given birth to him would see the features of her son in his ravaged face. Or if she, like so many had, would scream and run back to the slavery of the maggots.

He shook his head; matted, filthy hair swinging wildly.

It did no good to dwell on the past. There was life and there was the purpose. What more was needed? Listen to the water; watch the stone grow; feel the changes taking place around you and pursue, pursue, pursue.

The water was cool and it tasted of stone. He wondered, given time and world enough, if the pyramid would eventually become stone; one with the earth it sat upon; if the eyes would forever close under a fluid cataract of the white stone. It was a reasonable question. The eyes could blink, and the lips mouthed curses and pleas for mercy, but the heads could not move. Eventually, he felt that the cleansing waters would pool and collect, purifying the world of the vampire taint forever.

If he could only collect enough; if he only had time enough!

Some of the older ones, the ones at the base of his pyramid, had a bleak and empty look in their eyes. The heads grew hair for many years, sometimes growing a thick mat over the heads they sat upon. It took decades for the hair to stop growing.

He assumed the heads on the bottom had absorbed enough of the water falling from above them to kill the hair. Some of the heads had grown together from the stone-forming water falling on them. Those eyes no longer moved. Those lips no longer pled empty-mouthed for mercy. If it were within him to feel it, he'd feel elation at that. As it was, the strongest emotion he felt when he looked in those bleak, mad, dead eyes was a surge of satisfaction; a sense of a job well done. He hoped they looked upon the madness of eternity.

He'd sit, sometimes for days, listening to the 'plink,' 'plink,' 'plink' of the falling water and watching the heads as they refused to decay. He hoped it gave her some peace.

That wish for her peace was one of the very few things he managed to hold onto underneath the overwhelming psychic weight of the purpose.

He had turned it into a litany; something he said as he sat upon the stone and listened to the falling water: 'Take the head. Take the head for her. There is no room for grief. There is no room for mourning. There is life, and there is the purpose. What else does a man need? Take the head. Take the head for her.'

He mouthed it, over and over and over, and he kept himself from remembering.

He remembered her name, though. If he didn't allow himself to look upon those images of his long forgotten past, he let the sound of her name beat within the walls of his heart.

It drove him, and it drove the purpose. He took their heads, their filthy, blood-sucking heads, for her. He brought them here and he laid them upon her grave.

How many heads had there been? How many years had he hunted the lords of the vampire empire? How many times had he . . .

But, no. The newest maggot had to be taught how things stood.

He surged to his feet and walked to where it hung from the ceiling. He peeled an eyelid back with thumb and forefinger, taking no care to prevent injury to the eye.

As he thought. The pupil was slitted and knife-edged. It wouldn't be long now.

****

The predator awoke. It did not know where it was, nor did it know that it went by the name Lord Phalen Tornagow in better times. It only knew its hunger.

Something lumbered gracelessly toward it. It moved in the slow-motion, time-compressed way that the predator saw everything in. Whatever this graceless, lumbering monstrosity was, it had a beating heart. The predator could hear it.

The thing touched the predator's face and opened its eye. It stared into the predator's eye (not yet not yet not yet notyet notyet notyetnotyetnotyet) for a long moment, and then withdrew.

As it took its hand away from the predator's face, the predator struck.

****

The maggot, secured as it was from its hole in the ceiling, lashed out with claws and teeth at him. It was faster than many. It managed to get a couple of its claws inside him; drawing hot, thin lines of pain across his right arm. The maggot doubled over on itself and lunged upward at him, its jaws opening wide.

He locked eyes with the vampire. He wondered what it saw with those knife-edged, red-rimmed eyes like black holes in the world. The saw-toothed muzzle coming at him fit within the palm of his hand. His fingers were as big around as the vampire's legs, and he cupped them—gently, like a parent would around a babbling child's lips—on the vampire's lower face. His thumb was on the chin, his index finger was on the vampire's upper jaw. The vampire's mouth closed on its own tongue.

"MUSN'T BITE, MAGGOT." He said, as he pinched his finger and thumb shut.

He wondered what it felt like to try and scream through broken teeth, a severed tongue and a mouth held shut.

There wasn't much blood, as the vampire had not fed in some time. The vampire would heal. The pain would go as well. But the vampire would remember, and it would recognize its place.

This wasn't about pain, even though he enjoyed hurting them—and he knew so many wonderful ways to hurt them: the twisting, ripping and breaking of joints that could heal in moments; the collapsing of organs under probing fingers; the crushing of eyes, skull, and other softer parts. This was about justice.

He let go of the vampire's mouth. It cursed at him in its thick, glottal tongue. He ignored it and ran a hand over the scratches the vampire had inflicted on him; wiping his fingers through the thin lines of blood. He grabbed the vampire by the back of the head and wiped these fingers across it mouth.

It tried to bite the fingers. He broke off one of its fangs.

"I TOLD YOU, MAGGOT. YOU MUSN'T BITE."

The vampire gargled and choked and swallowed. It spit the broken remnants of its tongue and the fragments of its teeth clear of its mouth.

****

Phalen returned from the wild edges where the predator lived. He felt the return of awareness and with it an icy, knife-slice of fear.

He still hung from the ceiling, and he was still naked. His face was aching, although that was going away.

Something must've fed him, but-

He looked up to see a face as large as all the world. The eyes were a foot across and as empty of emotion as a reflection.

The fear widened into an axe blade and drove a wedge into the dead meat of his heart.

"I demand to be released!"

The face ignored this outburst and turned Lord Phalen, like a hanging carcass, to his right. Lord Phalen felt both of his legs splinter above and below the knee. He shrieked in pain.

"Do you hear me?" Lord Phalen shouted, when the pain subsided enough for normal speech. "I will have you fed to the pit dogs-"

His voice broke off as his eyes fell on the pyramid. He could make out the individual 'rocks' it was built of.

They were heads; still living vampire heads; thousands of them. He could see the lips mouthing words no one would ever hear. He could see the mad eyes and the glint of fangs. The ones on the bottom had been there long enough for a thin film of stone to cover them. They were growing together, like some obscene, humped and rounded stalactite. There were heads he recognized among the pile; friends of his, relatives!

Vampires often went long periods without seeing each other. A month was negligible. A decade was nothing when placed against the eternity of a vampire's lifetime. But now Phalen suspected that these missing friends and relatives had not been enjoying the previous years.

Phalen slowly mastered his fear and began to take in the details around him. He looked at his captor, trying to take the true measure of him.

In shape, it was human: arms and legs, hands and fingers and toes. The thing was far too big to be a human, though, out-sizing one by ten or twenty times. It was easily nine feet tall, and almost as wide. The eyes were a disconcerting silver color that spoke of a life spent underground. The hair that grew from its head was a filthy mat. Things crawled in it; large, biting insects, and even a rodent or two. Save for the hair, the brute went about naked.

It walked in such a way as to make the air shudder in Phalen's ears. He felt every footstep. Yet, for all its size, it moved with a sure-footed grace and agility. But its strength! Phalen had never conceived of something that could be as strong as whatever this was. It made his massive, vampire-born power a puny, whinging thing.

Phalen watched as the thing moved to another one of its captives. He saw dozens, perhaps hundreds of them; all hanging from the ceiling by the same gooey substance.

The vampire the brute was regarding was far gone into the predator. Its body was neuter, having cannibalized all gender features in its search for food. The vampire slept in the healing, hibernative coma all vampires fell into when times were lean.

The fangs protruded from the lower jaw, thick and twisted. The ears were pointed, and the vampire was hairless.

The brute regarded the vampire for a moment. Then it lifted its hand and slapped the vampire across its jaw. The vampire snapped awake and attacked the brute, raking vicious claws at its arms and naked chest. The brute turned and looked at Phalen.

Their eyes met. The brute's were almost sad.

The feral vampire continued to rake at the brute, and the brute stood there, taking it, looking at Phalen with empty, emotionless eyes. The brute stood there for perhaps a minute, and then he grasped the vampire by its throat with one hand. With the other, he wiped fingers through some of the blood running down his chest. He then wiped these fingers across the vampire's lips.

Phalen closed his eyes in disgust at the pathetic, mewling noises the vampire made. This was no way for a lord of creation to behave! He looked at the other captives. Something told him he might need to revise his thinking.

The brute moved to a vampire who hung bonelessly from his bonds. The brute slapped the vampire. The vampire did not twitch. The brute slapped it again, hard enough to rotate the vampire ninety degrees. Phalen heard the noise of bone breaking.

The vampire whimpered softly, but did not react in any other way. The brute lifted a hand, and in much the same way as a man elsewhere would force his finger through the skin of an orange to tear at the meat inside, the brute forced his finger through the abdominal skin of the vampire. He ripped a swath of flesh, a foot long and several inches wide, from the vampire's belly. The vampire did not move or bleed. Its eyes opened, but they were empty; dead.

The brute put the flesh in his mouth and began to chew. He chewed slowly, mashing and tearing the skin between his strong jaws. He chewed the skin into a thick, dull, grey paste. He took the mixture from his mouth and smeared it over the bonds of the vampire that had just attacked him.

The hulking thing went about its business with a workman's clinical detachment. The blood from the many scratches on its arms and chest soon stopped flowing, and Phalen watched as the wounds themselves closed.

Phalen had never heard of a creature that resembled this thing. It represented an evolution.

In all the long eons of his existence, Lord Phalen Tornagow had been many things. He'd been born a lowly guttersnipe—seventh of twelve—to a drunken slattern and her heavy-handed husband. Phalen's Father was a tanner; enslaved by the vampire empire at their tannery. Phalen had forgotten his father's name or even what he looked like. Given his Mother's sexual predilections, there was doubt as to who his father—or even 'fathers'—had been.

Phalen didn't remember what his name had been as a mortal. It'd no doubt been the first thing his father had grunted as soon as he'd seen that he had yet another mouth to feed. Life was not good as a slave of the vampire empire, and being seventh of twelve children didn't help. His father had all twelve children working in the tannery by the age of seven. This was convenient as he could instruct them to pull smaller bits of unprepared hide from the wash and sneak them home for dinner. There was often little or no difference between the meals they ate and the hides they prepared. If he lived a thousand years more, Phalen would never, never forget the taste and texture of rotten horsehide.

By twelve, he was a thief, taking whatever he could from whoever he could. He wasn't all that talented, but he did not hesitate to gut a mark when it was necessary, and this was viewed as being exemplary.

At thirteen he was a semi-professional murderer, taking what jobs came his way with a detached mien.

In the hard-living world of a vampire slave, maturity came fast or not at all. By the time Phalen turned fifteen, he'd reached his majority. He cut the fine figure of a man. His features were dark, brooding, dangerous. The ladies of Hamfist, like cats in heat, were quick to lift their skirts for him and he was all too happy to take whatever they gave.

They knew better—after one brainless slut had been found with the contents of her skull spread across the walls of an entire block of Hamfist—than to bring any progeny to him, expecting support.

He'd managed to catch the eye of a vampiress by the name of Lady Jaquwina Tornagow. She was as black as midnight in the jungle and as small as a child. Her teeth had glinted whitely in the night and her skin had felt like marble. Phalen shuddered every time he remembered her cold, wet kiss. She'd taught him so much about life and he'd worshipped her.

He'd jumped at the chance of turning and then used his new found power to kill his father, his mother, and every single one of his siblings; tearing their throats out and leaving the freshly-drained bodies in the tannery's wash.

Squeamish had never been a part of his makeup. He'd been killing since before he could shave. Fear had never gotten a strong hold on him; but this . . .

It wasn't so much the naked horror of the event itself. Phalen didn't care if other vampires died, just as those vampires wouldn't care if he did. It was the shock that something that dwarfed the power of every vampire everywhere, was doing this!

Phalen watched as the brute tore another swath from the vampire's abdomen. The sound was horrible. It was like the slow ripping of skin from a dead mule; a stack of parchment being torn in half by a lazy hand; the violent rupturing of a bladder.

The vampire hung from its bonds, making only an occasional whimpering noise as this great hulk tore chunks of skin from it.

Phalen watched as his captor began to eat the still-living vampire, beginning with the abdominal cavity. He was meticulous in his approach. He pulled the meat off in great swatches; probing a finger into the skin and then pulling away.

He ate every last bit, every tiny scrap of the vampire's skin. Then he moved to the organs, eating them with an unhurried deliberation that horrified Phalen. The grey loops of intestine were inserted into the great mouth and chewed, inch by inch. The hulk would suck up a bit more, like a man elsewhere would spaghetti noodles, and continue his grim feast.

Livers, pancreas, bladder, lungs, heart; each in its turn was slowly torn from the body cavity, thoroughly chewed, and then swallowed. When something fell with a wet splat upon the cold stone, the brute stopped and retrieved it.

There was not much blood, but the body's fluids are not limited to blood. The brute was soon dripping in ichors and enzymes that made Phalen's heightened olfactory senses recoil in absolute terror. His nose was telling his brain 'You're dying! You're dying! You're dying!'

Phalen closed his eyes when the hulk began to skeletonize the vampire, tearing the muscles off the bones with muted 'popping' noises. Phalen was hit by a bit of severed tendon and he gave a whimper.

At last the chewing noises stopped. Phalen opened his eyes. The vampire was making no noise, as it had no vocal cords or lungs to move air over them. It still had a face and its eyes were whirring madly in their orbits. The mouth was opening and closing in a shocked, desperate way.

The brute grasped the head between finger and thumb and broke it away from the spine with a sickening cracking noise. It put the head in its mouth and worked tongue and teeth over it for a moment, cleaning up any spare bits of flesh or fluid. It was very careful with the head, handling it like a cat does her kittens. Then it put the head on top of the pyramid.

"FOR YOU, MY LOVE," it said.

It stood there for a long time.

The mouth opened and shut. Slime was coagulating on the vampire's mouth. It was thick, viscous, and had a rubbery, elastic quality. He watched the slime drool over the vampire's lips. A bubble formed and burst with the frantic opening and closing of the vampire's mouth. The brute just stood there, watching it and waiting.

Phalen felt sick. He'd just watched an enemy of the state dispatch its victim in a perfect way: starve the vampire into the hibernative coma to slow its regenerative powers then eat the body with the head still attached before decapitating it, separating it from the head forever. Any vampire so treated would be powerless. The head would have no body with which to reconnect and the body itself was gone. Or was it? If the head was still alive, wouldn't that indicate that the body still lived as well? Something about that was niggling at him; something he should know or realize. He groped at it as a man does for a candle in the dark, but it remained just out of sight.

He looked his captor over, noting the physical characteristics he hadn't had time to when he first emerged from the predator state. It was standing in front of the pyramid, staring at the various heads.

At first glance, it was easy to assume his captor was a 'he.' It bore none of the gender characteristics of any female creature, mortal or otherwise. It had no facial hair, other than the thick mat on its head, and it had that deep, basso profundo voice.

He thought about the thing's regenerative powers; about its apparent, natural ability to bind what should be unbindable.

Phalen began to wonder about that. Was this a natural thing? Was this unbridled power something his captor had been born with? He didn't think so. If something had the might to so threaten the vampire empire as this thing did, there'd surely have been tales of them, wouldn't there? If this thing had been born this way, then it stood to reason that there were more of them about somewhere; breeding and eating vampires, but he'd never heard of it. Why would they hide when nothing on earth could threaten them? If a hundred vampires, bound together through blood oath and dark magic, tried to take one of these things on, Phalen suspected the vampire population would shortly decrease by a hundred.

Phalen had never seen one, had never heard of one, had never heard of anyone who had and he suspected that this creature had been born a mortal. The changes wrought in its body were related to what appeared to be the sole component of its diet: vampire.

Whatever it was, it had evolved, through its own form of natural selection, to be the perfect vampire predator. It represented, within itself, within its own existence, thousands of years of evolution for this one grim purpose.

And even if it were not as fast as the vampire, so what? It was far stronger and could absorb so much pain! So much damage! It would need to only grasp the vampire once. Phalen suspected that was the point of the brute's illustration of letting the predatory vampire attack.

Up until now, Phalen had believed that a predatory vampire was the most fearful thing in creation. Other vampires feared it. Vampire families who made war upon each other would often starve certain members of their family until they went predator, keeping them in steel coffin several feet thick, and then release them upon their enemies.

This thing didn't fear the predatory. This thing taunted it into attacking and stood there, taking it.

A realization was bubbling up from within him. It seemed to start in his livers; roiling and coiling, foaming and breaking against his insides. It moved its way up his throat and emerged as a dreadful, fearful moan.

The bodies of the brute's many victims were not gone. They had regenerated! They had regenerated within the brute, lending it their power, their strength!

Lord Phalen looked around him at the dozens of vampire bodies hanging from the ceiling; the thousands of heads stacked in the pyramid.

How do you stop such a thing? Fighting it was out of the question. The thing would mow through a regiment of standing vampires like water through smoke. A one-on-one combat was foolishness not to be considered. This thing could fight the tides and win!

Poisons were out as well. If it had eaten the livers of every vampire it had conquered—two, three, sometimes more, per vampire—then there was no way any toxin could take hold. It would have the purest blood of anything that'd ever existed!

Phalen suspected that the frailties of most mortals: breathing, starvation, extremes of heat and cold, were no longer an issue, either. A vampire had no care for the weather; it ate blood, and it didn't need to breathe. So how mighty was the predator that preyed on the predators?

****

She came, as she always did. She drifted from the center of his pyramid of justice. She wore a sad, sweet, smile that spoke of ten-thousand years of happiness deferred.

He looked at her and whispered her name; one of the few memories the purpose allowed him.

"ALLELE."

He saw her as she had been on the day of her death: young, vibrant, alive. There had been music, dancing, singing. She had laughed and sang, tumbled and twirled. He sang his song, watching her smile at him. How beautiful she had been! How gay! Then the maggots had come; those dead feeders upon the dead, and they had- But no. That was not for now. She was here now and she didn't want to see his grief.

He smiled back at her.

He ran a scarred, heavily pitted tongue over his many sharp teeth; rows of them, extending from his lips to the back of his head, lined up like soldiers in his mouth. Each tooth was three inches long, and just as wide. He picked at wayward bits of flesh while he smiled at her.

There'd been things she'd said that he couldn't remember; a name she'd called him. She looked at him sometimes now and mouthed that word up at him, her eyes shining with love and sadness. But he couldn't make it out. He couldn't see the words being formed by her lips anymore.

She was smoke and dust; a ghost given form by his love and his will. She reached for his hand, as she always did, and smiled that same sad smile.

"NOT YET," he said, whispering the words. "THERE ARE MORE OF THEM AND THEY MUST SUFFER."

She smiled. Her mouth worked, and he looked, and he saw nothing; knowing somehow that this was the core importance of his entire existence. And if he should make the maggots suffer for all eternity, it was as nothing when compared to the tens-of-thousands of years he'd spent, trying to remember her words; trying to remember what she'd called him. Trying to remember her as more than a ghost.

He did not sleep. He had not slept since that day, thousands of years ago, when everything had been taken from him, and he had assumed the grim yoke of the purpose.

His eyes had changed, along with the rest of him, and they were now protected by a thick coating of tissue; something like a nictating membrane, but harder.

But if he did not sleep, he still dreamt from time to time, as wayward wisps of memory weaseled out from under the smothering weight of the purpose.

He did not sleep. His eyes were open, watching her pale ghost, and he dreamt.

****

Phalen swam in a vast reservoir of hot blood. The smell, far finer than any exotic perfume, filled his nostrils. He lowered his face to drink.

With a vast noise, like the gurgling of some immense throat, the blood drained away. He stood in a desert with the lingering smell of blood clinging to him.

"No blood for you, Phalen."

He turned around to see the speaker and regarded a pale, thin, vicious version of himself.

"Who are you? Where am I?"

The thing grinned, ripping dead lips over thick, twisted teeth.

"You know who I am, Phalen Tornagow. You've known me for a thousand years or more. You've known me since before you were infected. I lived in the center of you even then. I drove you to become the man you are. I drank the sweet wine of your family's blood."

The doppelganger lifted an inch-long, dark, red talon to its mouth and picked absently at its teeth. It gouged huge holes in the top of its mouth, setting the blood to flowing. It looked around the desert.

"Dry here, isn't it?"

"Where am I?"

"Well, that's sort of a difficult question. First off, you're in trouble. Deep trouble."

It waved a hand and a window opened in the sky.

Phalen saw his captor, standing in front of his pyramid of skulls.

"Not a pretty way to go, I shouldn't think." It waved its hand and the window closed. "So. Are you going to let that happen to you?"

"What choice do I have?" Phalen screamed.

"There's always a choice, my sweet. Sometimes they're hard choices, but there's always a choice. Do you want to spend all of eternity as another building block in that thing's sad pyramid?"

"Of course not! But how can I stop it?"

The mad creature who'd lived in Phalen his entire life; that separate part of him that had made the whole everything it now was smiled a cruel, slow smile.

"Well, Phalen, I guess you need to leave that to me, don't you?"

****

The dream was the same.

She'd danced and sang and played her tambour, and all the crowd had watched her, and they had all loved her.

"If we starve, we starve! Let us make merry while we may!"

And they had danced with her; the merry dance of life being lived instead of waiting for death's sure hand.

Then the vampire had come.

"Where is my tithe? Where is my sweet angel that warms my cold bed?"

He'd tried to hide her, but the vampire, that fat, slow, maggot had smelled her out.

"NO!"

He put his face in his hands and turned away from her; turned away from the dream. He tasted the currents of air that washed over his skin: vampire, stone, cold, water. He stood there for a long moment, breathing it all in and reminding himself where he was.

The dream was the past. This was now. All that mattered now was the purpose.

Even as he thought it, it began to whisper its song in his head. He went back to work, burying his dreams and memories under the suffocating weight of the purpose. He worked for hours, smearing the slime over bonds; checking and double-checking that his captives were held; harvesting heads that were ready for it. And all the while he kept his mind closed while his lips repeated the purpose. "TAKE THE HEAD. TAKE THE HEAD FOR HER. TAKE THE HEAD. TAKE THE HEAD FOR HER."

It happened every so often, usually just after the collection of a fresh maggot. The safe walls he kept around his dangerous memories would crack. Light and air would fall on the sleeping, dead dreams he carried around with him. They would rush to the surface, growing faster than any cancer, and demand to be seen. It weakened him when it happened. It stole his strength and denied the purpose for weeks afterwards as he cascaded through his guilt. So he worked, burying it. And it was good. It was justice. It was right. It was retribution for what they had done to him. For what they had done to . . . done to . . .

"DONE TO HER," he said, in the wall-shaking tones of his enormous grief.

And just like that, the crack widened and he was gone.

There had been music . . .

***

Phalen looked at the diseased, thin version of himself. The creature smiled its cracked-lip smile at Phalen. It reached a hand over and pinched his cheek. It felt as if the thing was trying to tear a hole in Phalen's face.

"In answer to your unasked question, Phalen, I'm not the predator; the living symbiotic-thing that makes us vampires so much better than we deserve to be. No. I'm something much worse."

The creature smiled, and its lips spread in a horrible parody of merriment. "I'm you. I'm the you you've always been. I'm your true self. Now listen up, 'cause this is how we're going to do this."

The creature waved a hand and that magic window opened again. Phalen turned toward it and saw the brute on its knees, rocking back and forth and sobbing.

"What's wrong with it?" Phalen asked.

"Who cares? Look at the pyramid. Tell me what you see."

"What am I supposed to see? There's just a bunch of heads stacked on top of each other!"

The creature slapped him across the face hard enough to rock his head around. Its long, sharp claws drew four perfect lines of white-hot pain across Phalen's face, just under his left eye. Phalen felt those humiliating furrows seeping.

"If you want to stay here, keep being an idiot. If you want to escape this, look."

Phalen looked. At first he saw nothing but the heads and the way they seemed to have grown together.

"Look closer, you fool."

Phalen looked. The heads were covered in the thin sheen of clear fluid, something that came from the brute's preparation of them. He saw nothing else about the heads. They were almost pristine. In fact, save for that sheen of slime, and where the heads were covered in their film of stone, they were-

"Clean. They're clean?"

"Yesssssssss," the creature said, drawing the last syllable out with tongue between teeth. "They're clean. Washed within the confines of that thing's mouth. And do you know why?"

Phalen lifted a hand to his cheek, fingering the scars already healing there. He thought about it for a long moment.

"It's the blood, isn't it? He's careful to keep the heads from being contaminated with the blood!"

"Exactly. What do you suppose will happen if a small stream of blood were to be dribbled over those heads?"

"I have no idea."

"Would you like to find out?"

****

They had lived at the water's edge, taking what they could from the river, and keeping their numbers small so as to avoid the notice of the vampires. There were only ten of them. He was their hetman.

For generations, they had bred within smaller and smaller circles. The people of the towns were not fit to marry, and the 'Weyashagah,' or 'Wild Ones' were dying out. The children who were born to them were strange, twisted creatures; abominations, usually left at the water's edge as sacrifices to the vampires' never-sated hunger.

In the last five years, no new children had been born to their tribe.

Then had come his little Allell; his teeny angel. She'd been so much smaller than any Weyashagah had ever been, being barely larger than his two cupped hands. But she'd been perfect. She never grew tall, but there was strength in her smallness and a lithe quickness that dazzled the eye. She soon took her rightful place in the tribe, as was proper. A young man of their tribe, Dayahstock, a brave and noble hunter, had asked for permission from him to carry his Allell to the breeding tent.

He'd spoken to Allell about it and she'd had no objections. She'd even blushed.

There had been a famine in the land, a long one. The river ran low and the fish no longer swam in their waters. They had discussed the possibility of moving, of relocating somewhere more vibrant.

'The vampires do not know we are here,' he said, in the recess of his memory, to the circle of tribesmen and their children. He could not see himself, but he felt strange; lighter somehow. His voice was higher, and there was a difference in the way he walked.

They'd discussed moving to the north. Then one of his tribal elders had asked about the upcoming marriage.

'Will we feast, hetman?'

He had looked at the ground, ashamed of his inability to provide his beautiful Allell with the feast she deserved.

Allell stood from the circle and taken his hand. 'If we starve, we starve. If we must move, we must move. For now, let us make merry, for today, I become a woman!'

They'd made what feast they could, and Allell had taken his hand and danced with him, her feet moving so fast he could barely see them. She moved like the quicksilver that the storms brought. Her laughter had been music in his ears.

And they had danced. And they had sang. And the threw their axes at one another, diving at the last instant to prove their bravery.

There was music, and singing, and Dayahstock had run into the circle of flame, his face fierce in his wedding day make-up, and he had thrown Allell over his shoulder, and growled fierce threats of retribution against any who followed.

Allell's screams of panic were full of healthy giggles, and he could not help but smile.

Then they heard the growls . . .

****

"You know what this will require?"

Phalen, in his very deepest heart, a coward, looked away.

His twin stalked to him. Phalen could smell the dead things festering on its breath.

"Oh. I see. I was under the impression that you were not interested in spending the next few thousand years as a memento to some freak's grief." It walked around Phalen, gesturing with its hands. "I guess you enjoy hanging from the ceiling, like some diseased rodent, in a thick wad of snot."

Phalen spun around, his hands balled into fists. "Shut up. "

"I could, Phalen. I could shut up and leave you here to fend for yourself. Of course, that'd mean the end of me too, but I'm willing to do that if you insist."

Phalen sighed. "Can't you think of a better way?" he whined.

"Well, sure, Phalen! I mean, I've got a couple of years to play with! It should only take a decade or so for things to come about just right. We've got the time, don't we?"

"I can't!"

It reached over and grabbed Phalen's lower lip. It pulled. Phalen's eyes ran fresh tears of blood and he made weak, mewling noises. "You can, Phalen, and you will," the twin hissed through clenched teeth. "You will. Because if you don't, you'll be stuck here, for eternity, with me."

Phalen met its eyes for a fraction of a second. The promises of violence he saw there decided him.

" . . . alright . . ."

"Goooood." the creature murmured. It let go of Phalen's bottom lip and stroked the back of Phalen's head with its other hand in much the same way a contented lover would. "Now listen carefully, Phalen, because this will take all of your will . . ."

****

The noises of joy had changed to screams of terror.

And with a rising horror, he realized he would hear, again, the words his Allell had been saying to him for the last few thousand years. He would hear them in the recess of his memory, flavored, as it was, by her panic and her pain.

He fought to push this dream-thing away; to set it under the suffocating weight of the purpose and bury it forever as he had thousands of times before, under the weight of cool, grey slime.

He heard the shrieks and growls, as he had so many times before, and he heard his Allell saying the word he never allowed himself to see or hear. He heard her calling for him, calling for him by his name. He heard the word she said when she appeared from her pyramid of justice. That precious, loving word, came boiling out of his throat.

His head fell back on his neck while tears of pain and outrage fell down his face. He screamed the word with all his strength at the cold stone and the hanging maggots. He screamed it and felt his heart break into a thousand tiny pieces.

He screamed it and he felt his eternal life tear neatly in half.

"MOTHER!"

He was helpless under the weight of combined memory. Ten-thousand, thousand years had not sufficed to wipe away so much as a single eyelash of that horrible day. He could still smell the burning, singeing furs; the spilled blood of his tribe mates; the tangy smell of burning meat.

They'd fought the vampires, of course, fought them as best they were able. But the vampires were moving too fast for the stone axes of the tribesmen. Their furs were no defense against the spear-like teeth and knife-like claws of the vampires.

The Weyashagah were no more after that terrible night.

He could still hear, with perfect clarity, the panic-stricken screams of precious Allell, and the horrific, snapping, gurgling sounds that were Dayahstock last life song.

He cowered on his knees, surrounded by the now fitful, hanging carcasses of his many captives, and watched as he jumped over the fire, ax in hand, and rushed toward the breeding tent.

The beast watched his hands—as they had been then: slim, but strong; a warrior chieftain's; a mother's; a woman's hands—pull back the laced flaps, now tattered and torn of the breeding tent. A vampire's face was clamped over Dayahstock's, completely obliterating his features under the grinding teeth. He could hear the horrible things those teeth were doing to Dayahstock's eyes, his nose, his lips. She could not see anything of his face below the chin, or above the eyebrows. It had disappeared into the gaping, toothed maw of the vampire's muzzle.

She saw the red, red eyes of the vampire, narrowed to hungry slits, small and hard as river pebbles, just above its frantically working teeth. Dayahstock's life flowed down its gullet, over its lips, down its chest. Dayahstock twitched and shuddered in the vampire's arms. Even as she watched, the tan life-color of his skin was drained to a sick and pale white.

He watched, helpless to move, or react, or even think, as the vampire, moving faster than anything possibly could, casually broke Dayahstock's neck with one hand, discarding the corpse with its red ruin for a face, and reached for the screaming Allell.

The vampire struck her with that reaching hand, knocking Allell sprawling. She heard the sound of something within Allell snap like the breaking of a wet arrow. The noise of it drove right through him like a bolt of lightning. Then the vampire turned to regard her. Her reflection shone in the vampire's eyes. He could see the long, flowing hair; the healthy, muscular breasts; the womanly form. It looked her over, lust firing its features into something even worse. The red fury of the feeding drained from the vampire's eyes.

"Well, well, well, my priiiiiiizzzzzzzze," the vampire drawled, running a blood-stained, elongated tongue over teeth pitted, sharp, and serrated. "Come to join our little party?"

The vampire reached out a lightning quick hand, and she moved even faster, striking the offending hand off at the wrist.

"Oh, ho, HO!" the Vampire said, grinning at her, blood splashing everywhere. "My little prize has spirit! I like to see th-"

Whatever he'd been about to say was forever left unfinished. Even as the vampire's hand had still been falling to earth, she'd turned the stone-axe back around in a killing swipe that caught the vampire just under the chin. The axe hewed through the vampire's neck with very little resistance.

She'd caught the head before it had fallen away from the fountain of blood spurting from the severed neck. The body collapsed, onto its front, and fell onto the fire in the breeding tent. She looked at the eyes of the vampire and saw the naked, spinning panic there.

She knelt for the briefest possible goodbye. She'd placed a blood-stained hand on Allell's cheek, and then run off into the night, carrying her grim trophy with her.

She'd spent the rest of that night holed up in a running creek. The water had been cold, and she'd held the maggot's head under the water, fearful that it would begin to cry out to its companions.

When she'd finally worked up the courage to return, there was nothing left of the Weyashagah. They'd been eaten or driven off, and only the trampled and destroyed remnants of the breeding tent remained to show they'd ever been there.

The vampires had found the slain body of their tribe mate and they'd left it where it had fallen. Next to it they'd left Allell's head stuck on a stone spear.

The maggots had pulled her head from the corpse. The skin of her neck was stretched and ripped. She'd wept bitter tears over her and tenderly removed the head from the spear for later burial.

The roasted, still incorruptible body of the maggot, she ignored.

She stayed there for a week, grieving and slowly starving. The vampire's head blew panicked bubbles of blood and ichor. Its eyes rolled in its sockets and an occasional blood tear ran down its ashen cheek.

After a time, steeling herself for the inevitable, she'd examined the body, curiously, her stomach roiling within her. And then she'd given in to her hunger and eaten what there was to eat. She took a perverse pleasure in making the vampire watch as she dribbled bits and pieces of its flesh into her mouth.

That night, the first of the changes had manifested itself, setting her on her immortal journey of justice.

****

"Yesssssss, Phalen. Yessss," his dark twin said, still stroking the back of Phalen's head and watching along with him. "You see? It's half mad anyway. This'll almost be easy!"

"What if it doesn't work?"

"Then it won't work, Phalen, and we're both going to die. Won't that be nice?"

It dragged a talon across Phalen's scalp. "But it will work, Phalen. It'll work just fine."

Phalen closed his eyes. "Let's do it," he whispered.

His twin smiled and took Phalen into its arms. The gesture was tender, almost loving. It stroked the side of Phalen's face and tore a hole in his throat with its jagged, pitted teeth.

****

He was too lost in the wash of memory to see the maggot revert with supernatural quickness into the predatory state. The maggot's ears lengthened to sharp points. Its muzzle sprouted from its normally human face and grew thick, twisted, spear-like teeth and hair. The nostrils recessed into slits, high on the muzzle. The eyes narrowed and lengthened, spreading out across the face until they met—left, knife-like point to right, knife-like point—directly over the muzzle.

He did not see the feral, crimson gleam as the eyes opened again.

He was weeping pale blood when the fingers, the hands, the arms, lengthened and grew thick, gnarled talons. He did not see the way the legs shrunk into mere twigs.

The beast watched as he was re-born. He watched as he/it-who-had-been-she began the long, slow descent into the creature he was now.

Her body tried desperately to purge the flesh of the first vampire; to vomit it out, to defecate it forth, but she clamped down on it and held it inside her with an act of will. Her body fought her for three days.

She found a hole in the river bank and curled inside it, holding her arms around her middle. She bit bloody holes in her lips, holding the cries in, knowing there were more vampires in the woods, no doubt looking for her or others like her.

The changes were slow and painful; one change after another, after another, after another, and so on.

First, she no longer grew tired, nor felt the urge to sleep, to eat. Those concerns of the flesh were no longer hers. Next, her senses grew more acute. She could smell things that her brain insisted were "pain," "lust," and "hate." The smells came from the city of the vampires, several miles away.

Her eye sight sharpened and she found she could track the invisible. She saw a fly moving in her hole, at night, and she saw the individual movement of its wings. She lifted a hand and caught the fly between finger and thumb.

She felt the manic beat of its heart in her fingertips, smelled its insect confusion and fear.

So far as she knew, she still lived, still walked among the living, but she no longer gave those signs of life common to the living.

Her teeth felt sharper; harder; longer; wider. They felt as if they were straining within her mouth, trying to burst free of her lips.

And the hunger! Not for food or water, that her body rejected out of hand. No, she hungered for paler flesh. The hunger raged through her like lighting bred fire through a dry prairie. She could not stop the overwhelming desire, the insatiable drive, to sink her teeth into the pale, liquid flesh of the vampire. She hunted the remaining vampires for the next week, taking them one at a time as they sought their pleasures. This was made easier for her as the vampires often hunted alone and thought nothing of it when one of their number did not return to their common camp. After all, what was there that could challenge the might of the vampire?

She took them, one by one, and ate every last scrap of flesh on their bones, save the flesh of their face. Some of them fought her, of course, and they fought viciously. And while she could not move as fast as they could, she was, somehow, far stronger.

They slapped and clawed and bit and tore at her. Her blood no longer provided them with anything remotely like food, and she accepted what she had to until she could lay a hand on them. When she did, she always broke something: here an arm, there a leg, a back; a neck. Even a vampire could not heal broken bones as fast as she could heal the rips in her flesh.

And with each vampire eaten, she grew stronger and stronger.

She soon had consumed the entire hunting party. The last three had opened drunken, blood-sotted eyes to see her massive, twisted form looming above them. They were so bloated and overfed that their movements were sluggish, torpid and dull; like a snake that's eaten something much too large for it.

She'd pulled their heads off. Slowly. With two fingers. It was not long after eating those bodies that she decided to rid the world of the vampires once and for all.

She'd curled into her hole to think and had licked her lips, trying to clear her mouth of an unpleasant taste. She wiped a thick, scarred hand across them and it had come away sticky and covered in grey slime.

The idea that had become the purpose began to tickle inside her at that point.

****

The dark twin had a far more intimate knowledge of what their shared body was capable of. It knew how to shift things. It knew how to change the shape of Phalen's body into something that would fit their purposes. It required a titanic effort and an enormous act of will. It took a deep breath, settling itself for the coming conflict, and began to change.

It concentrated its energies on their shared legs. It pushed its will into the cracked and pained bones; the throbbing, flaccid tendons; the strained ligaments. The pain was about what it expected, and at first, it enjoyed the sensation. It was a bit like riding an electrical wire, or being pushed through a very small hole by an unstoppable force. After a time, the pain became inconvenient, so it pushed it off on Phalen. His panicked, blood-filled shrieks of agony in the space of their shared head were most enjoyable and served as background music for what the dark twin was trying to do.

It redoubled its efforts. Tripled. Quadrupled. Phalen screamed himself hoarse and the creature could hear tints of madness breaking into their voice. It was beginning to feel some of the agony itself by this point, and realized it would have to succeed in one final push or kill them both trying.

It pushed with everything the two of them had against the stubborn flesh of their legs.

It almost didn't hear the subtle shifting noises of flesh changing shape below the high-pitched screams of black, insane agony the two of them made, and blacked out for just a moment . . . not regaining consciousness until it hit the ground with a wet, sodden thump.

The grey slime that had held Phalen's thicker legs was not nearly enough to hold their newly thin, stick-like legs. A still-damp shower of the stuff rained down and Phalen was making weak, mewling, whimpering noises in the back of their head. It would do no good to get free only to be glued to the floor.

"Shut up, Phalen." Phalen's noises subsided to whispered grunts. The dark twin hissed through compressed lips and surged to its feet. It tottered for a moment while their shared body re-learned the equilibrium necessary for balance, flapping its arm-membranes to and fro. It dragged them away from the pool of wet slime, and sank, with a grateful sigh, into the cold waters of the cave lake. They'd managed to escape the ceiling, but now they had to free themselves from the brute.

The dark twin closed their eyes and began to push their legs back into shape to the delightful chorus of Phalen's mental screams. With a loud popping, grinding noise that filled the entire universe, the eternity of crushing pressures and black, insane pain ended. The twin worked their shared legs; bending at the knee and rotating the ankles. It felt like a dull knife was being leveraged in between the joints, but they were in their proper shape.

Phalen's voice came spiraling up from the darkness of their head like a ghost's down some impossibly deep well. His words were barely coherent, slurred and mangled. They sounded as if they were melted together, like burned flesh; like fat dripping down a stone wall.

I t drooled upward in one long skein of nonsensical pain and complaint: "Nooomorrre pleeeeeeease nooomooore oh bloodanskin anpleeeeeeease noplease noooomorrrrre plllllleeeeease no-"

The twin snarled. Phalen's mental voice trailed off to whimpering mutters and garbled slurs of pain. It ignored him. It was time to get out of this hellhole and maybe get some payback on the way out.

The brute, for its part, was still sitting on its knees, keening and sobbing. The dark twin stared at it with a measuring eye.

"Wonder if its blood tastes the same?"

Phalen whimpered.

****

Even captive as he was, in the millennia long wash of memory, part of him knew what was happening. Part of him was trapped in the cycle of killing and eating, grieving all over for Allell and their lost people. Part of him was listening and even watching Phalen escape.

It had no name, this silent watcher; even beyond the forgotten namelessness of the whole. It had no purpose, other than keeping the whole alive. It had no real intelligence, other than the wild, unrestrained drive to survive at all costs. It did whatever was necessary to keep the entirety of the entity alive. It had grown stronger and changed, along with the whole, with each vampire eaten. The two of them could now communicate after a fashion. It was nothing like Phalen and his inner twin, with their threats and their philosophical arguments, but it was communication. A chemical would be released and perhaps the whole would act on it. Perhaps the whole would not.

The thing was the size and shape of the average human brain, but denser, and hard; throbbing with blood. He felt it sitting there sometimes, inside his skull, just atop his spine. He felt the heat of it burning under his mind like some magmic tumor.

When it released chemicals, he heard the action of valves opening and the quicksilver spurting of those chemicals down various vessels within him. It sounded the way web spinning from a spider's belly must to the fly. It watched and listened; collated data and recognized threats, muttering silent warnings to the rest of him. Muscles twitched. Adrenalins, cortisones, acids, proteins, fats; antibodies that resembled nothing so much as microscopic sharks; amino acids, and millions of other hormones and blood by-products surged hotly through his blood vessels and bodily byways whenever that symbiotic knot atop his spine decided they needed to.

The knot atop his spine decided Phalen was a threat. It flooded his system with fight hormones. The arteries on his neck stood out a full three inches. His hands changed color and twitched, idly. He would not be caught by Phalen unaware.

The hot knot atop his spine watched Phalen change himself. It watched him fall from his bonds and land on the cold stone.

It fed all these warning messages to the rest and was shocked—within its capacity to be so—to receive the return message from the higher consciousness within their shared head.

That hot muscle atop his spine didn't know that the whole it nurtured and protected had been watching his precious Allell die again. It didn't know that he'd realized that he'd watched this same scene before, and he'd watch it again.

The knob of red tissue didn't feel the twisting ache in his heart when he saw that perfect, heart-shaped face atop the stone spear. It couldn't feel the splash of tears or the ache of knowing that no matter how many of the maggots you killed, you'd never kill enough to bring back Allell.
'He' who had been 'Her' watched his Allell die under the hands of a vampire for the millionth time and he listened as the survival drive within him warned him of the maggot's approach.

He heard the snapping of Allell's neck. He never wanted to hear it again. He wanted to see her dance, to hear her sing.

'Yes. Good. Let him come.'

****

The twin moved to the kneeling brute, picking its target. It could see a blood vessel throbbing against the side of the thing's face. It was a little closer to the thing's tightly closed eye then the twin would like, but it was also a target too tempting to resist.

It flew through the air like a bolt from a crossbow; talons extended and mouth agape. It hit the brute on the side of the face and locked onto that throbbing vessel. With a guttural snarl, it tore the vessel open and rejoiced in the wash of hot blood across its shared face.

It drank the thing's blood, gorging on it like hot wine.

****

"ALLELL," he whispered, and the stones around him shivered with the noise.

He lifted a hand and clamped it to the back of the maggot's head, holding it to the side of his face.

****

The dark twin felt something on the back of its head but it was too busy feasting. Such blood! The taste of it was foreign, exciting and somehow forbidden. And there was so much of it!

It felt itself falling within Phalen's mind. It was being subsumed by the hunger-lust of the vampire. He could hear the growling, ripping, snarling noises of the true predator within Phalen struggling to take its share of blood.

It grinned a final, feral grin, and said 'Have at him, my boy,' before sinking into the depths.

****

It held the maggot against the blood vessel, feeling the action of those saw-like teeth; the grinding, ripping motion it made as it sought to have even more blood.

It gorged, drinking itself full, and then drinking more.

"ALLELL!"

He lifted his other hand to the dancing, swirling, laughing child he could see, his precious Allell, reaching for him . . . just beyond his fingertips.

There was one last thing to do.

He gripped the maggot by the back of its head, ripped its teeth from his face, and cradled it—still snarling, and ripping at him—to his chest with arms like ten-thousand tons of forged steel. He walked toward his precious Allell. He reached a calloused, scarred, and impossibly heavy hand out to her.

He felt the briefest touch of her fingertips . . .

****

When Lord Phalen Tornagow, Ducal Lord of the vampire empire, regained consciousness, he wondered why his eyes would not open. It took him several long moments to realize they were gummed shut with dried blood.

He was crushed beneath something heavy and he could not move. Not so much as the merest millimeter.

He worked his eyelids, squinting and pulling at them with his facial muscles until he was able to pry them open. The first sight to meet his eyes was the horrific vision of the brute's serrated, pitted teeth, inches from his face. He screamed; a tinny, helpless sound.

The brute did not move.

Phalen realized he could not feel any signs of life from the immense weight atop him. The brute's eyes were open; staring, but unseeing. He tried to move again, to wiggle out from under the beast. Nothing budged. The brute had wrapped him tightly up in its arms and then fallen on its face, smashing the two of them into the stone.

He panicked, trying to tear at his captor with his teeth. He opened long furrows in the skin near his mouth, but this accomplished little. Blood, long pooled, tepid and foul, poured over his lips and mouth with a syrupy consistency that made him struggle not to vomit.

Nothing he did was of any use. He could move nothing below his mouth. He could not nod his head. He was smashed to the stone like a bug in amber.

He tried to get free for a very long time long after he realized the truth.

****

Life continues. It perseveres. It digs its horny toenails in and continues in the unlikeliest of places. Empires rise and fall, the world continues to spin in its orbit around the sun, and life, in all its fulsome glory, continues. Sometimes life is slow. It takes a while to kindle in the stubborn womb. Sometimes the tree shoot dies before it truly sprouts. Sometimes the spirit of the infant never awakens in the body. Sometimes the mother eats her pups.

And sometimes life is microscopic and lives in the very rarest of environments. Phalen could feel it happening. The stone was cold, but his heightened vampire senses gave him a blow-by-blow of the process. He wondered if perhaps his spine had been misaligned, and then healed, without the proper alignment necessary for motor control.

He wondered at so many different things while he screamed and cursed and wept bloody tears and the stone resolutely grew, and the brute above him remained dead, unchanged and unchangeable. The brute's body did not decompose. It sat atop him like a planet, crushing him into the stone, growing hard and cold. He screamed until he felt something within his throat tear. It did no good. Not even the beast that lived within him heard. The water dripped down from the ceiling, into the pool in the cave, and atop the body of the brute. It was cold, that water; full of ice melt from some hidden reservoir far above them. It was also full of hungry bacteria. The process was slow, but it was a determined, unstoppable force. The laden water fell from the ceiling one slow drop at a time, atop the combined body mass of the brute and Phalen, leaving behind the white snail-trail-stains of calcium and limestone.

The cave was in a remote area of the world, far underground, where it is dark and cool. Nothing came to disturb what had become Phalen's grave.

Years passed. Decades. Centuries. The brute's body took a very long time to cover completely, but it soon had a microscopically thick white shroud of cool stone on its legs, its back, its shoulders. The life in the water could find nothing to sustain it there. The same things that had made the beast what it was and incorruptible in death made it unfit for life.

Then the first few drops of water made their slow, drizzling way downward, toward the front of the brute's body and the trapped Phalen underneath. The hungry bacteria in the water found Phalen's body and the mind trapped within it. Here was something the bacteria could eat! Here was something on which life could thrive!

Phalen Tornagow knew nothing of life. He was a creature of darkness and death, a paladin of the antithesis of life. He stood for all things cold and dark and decayed. But in his second death, he learned how resolute life could be. He learned of the small teeth and tiny bites of bacteria. He learned what it meant to be consumed in a process far more awful than anything he could comprehend. The bacteria were hungry, but the meal was so large! And the water took so very long to pool. There were only so many places it could reach. Phalen's body was an endless feast for a billion billons of their generations. They fed, bred, defecated, lived and died in tiny pools on Phalen's corpse, leaving behind the white, translucent stone of an enormous, misshapen stalagmite behind.

There was no blood, of course, merely the running of clear fluids from Phalen's small wounds. But there were mountains, oceans, galaxies of pain. One of Phalen's toenails lasted nine hundred years. The pinkie finger on his right hand took the bacteria thirteen hundred years to eat. And he felt every second of it. He lived every bite. He was aware of every tiny mouthful. He screamed his lungs out as his body was slowly, and ever so painfully dissolved and covered over with thin, translucent, white stone.

The bacteria took a long time. In a bizarre twist of fate, it left Phalen's head alone. Phalen's eyes were not covered by the thin veil of stone and they rolled wildly in their sockets. His mouth opened and closed, opened and closed.

The world changed shape several times over before it was done, and Phalen Tornagow, death's champion, had many thousands of years to appreciate life in the shattered fragments his mind became.

The stalagmite became one with its companion stalactite and eventually became an enormous column of stone.

The stone continued to grow, obliterating all traces of what had once been. The bacteria moved on to other pastures. Soon even the stone forgot.

It took another thousand years for Cain to find the place and to free Phalen from his matrix of stone. But somewhere, out beyond the furthest stars, a Mother was reunited forever with her perfect Daughter. Somewhere, out beyond the silence of the void of eternity, they danced to the music of drum and tambourine.

Chapter Twelve

Jack came back to himself, retching.

"Not very nice, is it?" Tam Lin said.

Wiping his mouth, Jack sat back on his heels and moaned.

"We're not sure what they were or where they came from. All anyone really knows is that about a hundred-thousand years ago, when man was still finding his way after Eden, there were three Vampire Empires. They drank blood, they lived so long people believed they were immortal, and they were part beast.

"All the rest of the information we have is stories; legends; tales handed down, person by person. Personally, I'm of the opinion that they were a part of the human family that didn't work out so well. They were like the creatures up north that live in caves and have the pronounced eye ridges. They look like humans, act like humans, and breed with humans, but aren't. Not really. They are a different branch of the human family tree, and I think they will end up dying out completely. The smaller, weaker humans will kill them.

"It's about duality, son. You're part Fae. You get that from me. Fae is beyond the farthest stars and as close as a breath, just this side of hell and above the grave.

"But that's a small part of who you are. You're part of the first Creation; a direct descendent of one who bore the marks of the Creator's fingers. You saw the mark on Cain's skin?"

Jack nodded.

"That's part of you, now. You're the great-grandson of Adam; of the line of Eve. If you're lucky, you'll take after one of them, and not your grandfather.

"But you're also part Vampire. The original Vampires, not the pale recreations handed down to mortality. I'm talking about the creatures that fed and feasted at the beginning of time and walked on worlds that have long since been bled into twisted cinders of hate. Your grandsire was Cain. Cain bit you, changing you yet more, and Cain was himself sired from the Last Father. The Last Father, the head in the bag Cain was bitten by, was changed by the strange blood of the one we call the Feasting Beast. The Last Father was really two creatures in one body, as was the Feasting Beast. Altogether, that makes you the sum of six parts. You are utterly unique in the history of creation. You're a Leprechaun; neither all of one thing, nor all of another, but an agglomeration of many different things, all of them powerful."

He smiled at Jack. His eyes were sad. "The first lesson you have to learn? Adapt. Survive. Change when you need to. Evolve. Learn. Grow. Change or die, my son. Change as often as you need to, adapt when you have to and survive. Change or die. I can only imagine that once you find yourself, the lands will tremble beneath your feet. You're almost pure Story, and you're not even ten years old. That's who you are, but only you can decide who you will eventually be."

****

I let go of Molly's hand for a moment to light another cigarette. I was proud of the "Leprechaun." It had that touch of plausibility a good lie required.

"I spent . . . I dunno. Maybe the next several years there, at the bottom of the Pit, growing stronger and learning from Tam Lin. I never knew his story. He appeared one day, told me my story, told me he was my father, and led me into becoming who and what I am. I never knew much about him. It's been the greatest mystery of my life. I started calling him father, and that was good enough for the two of us. He taught me magic, and he taught me about Fae.

"One night he took me by the hand. "I figure you're as ready as you're ever going to be. It's time to go, boy." And we asked Earth to open a hole for us. Just like that. We crawled through, and left. Tam Lin didn't say good-bye. He laid his right hand on my head and I felt a warm glow coming from it.

He smiled at me. "I give you the one thing I can give you, my son. I give you yourself. You are, forever and always, Jack."

"He turned his back to me, dropped his clothes, and disappeared into the night. I never saw him again. My first encounter with other Fae came several years later. It made me what I am now: a creature of moonlight and dew."

I pulled my pocketknife out and cleaned my fingernails with it. I find it's as useful a prop as my stupid cigarettes are. It gives your hands something to do and most people get really nervous and quiet around a sharp knife. Mine's a beauty. Made by good ol' Heph, and it's so sharp the edge glows in dim light. I could sharpen it on a baby's breath.

"Decades later, I came back and razed the city of Lantia. Cain had left by then and his sons were no match for me. I filled the Pit in with the bones of the city's dead and then had the ground sown with salt. I've never been back."

There was silence from Molly. She sat back and wiped the tears from her eyes.

"How long ago was this, Jack?"

"I dunno, Molly. I wasn't keeping track for the first couple of centuries. If I had to guess, I'd say it was some fifty, sixty-thousand years before you people crawled out of the trees. The continents were in different shapes. Mountain ranges were seas."

"How could that be? Were the people in the city of . . . of . . ."

"Lantia."

"Lantia. Right. Were they human beings?"

"Yep."

"But human history doesn't go back that far."

"Seriously? That's what you're fixating on? I tell you a story about vampiric heads, Cain and a man who may or may not be some kind of a bird and you're worried about history?"

I could feel her grinning. "Okay. A very long time, then."

"Yeah. You could say that."

I took another drag off my cigarette. I don't know why I smoke the damn things, other than for effect. It's not like my body absorbs nicotine. I looked over at Molly while she took a sip of her water.

"Does knowing any of this help? Does it like . . . I dunno; make you understand me better, or something?"

She looked up at me. "I don't know, Jack. I don't think you answered any of my questions, and you left me with more than when I began. Carrying that around for the last couple of millennia must've been a real burden."

"So now you're a therapist?"

She gave me a smile.

I finished my coffee off at a draught, sighed and gently put the cup back in the saucer. "Molly. Do you want to get out of here?"

She looked deep into my eyes, looking for what, I don't know. Now that the moment of decision was upon her, I found myself half hoping she'd refuse. I needed Molly, but I don't think I wanted her anymore.

After what seemed to me to be enough time for the sun to burn out and the universe to sink back in on itself, she nodded.

We rose, paid the check, and left that place.

****

The closest I've ever seen any mortal language come to being able to mimic the musical, lyrical, rollicking syllables of Fae is probably Icelandic. The language spoken now in Iceland is remarkably close to the language spoken in Iceland a thousand years ago. There's so little variation that many of the literary works written then can be read with little, if any, loss of meaning, now. And there are remarkable similarities between their language and Fae. Those Vikings knew what they were doing.

In their language 'Due Dareaga' would be translated as 'Du Draga,' or 'To Draw.' That's not quite right, but it's close enough for me to finish telling this story. In Fae the word means 'The Dragon.'

Everything has a name; a proper, 'This is my identity, and it applies to no one and nothing else,' name; a tag that covers it and its individual soul/kismet. You people don't understand that names, along with the real force that can be language, is a magic in its own right. For example: 'tree.'

A mental image flashes across the mind, right? Probably looks like something vaguely tree-like, with a green triangle atop a long, brown part. There may be minor variations from person to person, but the overall effect is the same.

Now take that feeble mental image, and try to apply it to a 'towering Forest Lord, road to many different worlds, worshipped as a god in certain cultures.'

Yggdrasil is the name—the tag, if you will—that gives the namee its power; its soul; its identity. 'Tree' is, at best, an ignorant label. And every tree, everywhere, has its very own name. Calling an individual tree a 'tree' is like taking a full color, three-dimensional photograph of a tree, and then asking a child to draw it with a stick in wet mud. Every language on earth has this limitation. Words don't do the justice of names. They are childish scribblings in wet mud; moronic drawings on a bathroom wall. So you'll appreciate that what I'm trying to explain is something well beyond the barking, clicking squeaks of language.

'Due Dareaga'—or 'The Drawing', for purposes of convenience—is glamour, spell, ritual and effect, all rolled into one neat little package. It's a noun, as in "the creature who partakes in the 'Drawing.'" It's a verb, as in "the process of 'Drawing.'" And it's an adjective. As in, "the way life and spirit spirals forth when 'Drawn.'"

It's a living part of me; a symbiosis. It remains quiescent until released, and emerges for one reason and one reason only: Due Dareaga.

It's a heady experience, far more potent than sex, or childbirth, or most anything else you little shit-monkeys do. It's a mingling of life forces, a consummation, an interweaving, a devotional devouring. It's singular: emotional, exhilarating, and exhaustive. Imagine feeling the very apex of every emotion you've ever had, all at once. It's not uncommon for me to be left, by turns, weepy and lethargic, manic and giggly for weeks after a vivid drawing. It is Due Dareaga. It is my birthright; part of my twisted genealogy. It is Due Dareaga, and it is my right.

Got all that? Okay. Now add to that the fact that I really am part Vampire. And when I was sired, it changed me all the way up and all the way down, touching every single part of me, including Due Dareaga. The other Fae, they feed too, with something a lot like Due Dareaga, but they let go. When I feed, I feed completely; absorbing and consuming until nothing is left.

And, yes. I'm supposed to be a lot smarter than I was. I let my guard down, however briefly. I got overconfident. You live to be eighty-thousand-something-odd years old, kicking ass all over the entirety of creation, and you'll be cocky too. Besides, I mean, Molly? Our dear, sweet Molly? Who'd've guessed, right?

****

The night was brisk, and the moon was shining high above us when we stepped from the smoky embrace of the diner. It was a spell-weaving moon, a full, pregnant moon. It was bright and delirious and wonderful. I raised my face to her and bathed in that spill of clear, white light. I could taste the salty cold of the moonbeams dancing on my tongue. I smiled and closed my eyes.

You people have a word. It's 'lunatic.' It's one of the few times that you've managed to get close to the absolute truth of something. If you chased the etymology of 'lunatic' far back enough, you'll find it literally means 'follower of the moon.' If you could feel the moon the way we do, you'd be a lunatic, too.

From my right hand, Molly spoke in a dazed sort of whisper. "She's gorgeous tonight, isn't she?"

"She's beautiful every night, Molly."

I reached for her hand. She took it. We smiled stupidly at each other and walked off into that cold, clear, wonderful light.

We walked for about a mile that way, our hands laced together, a comfortable silence between us. There was no need for words. We were content to just be. We walked, and we were. I like to think it was the first time in her life that Molly existed in the single space of moment to moment. Our feet were soon wet and chill from the dew, and I began to look for a dry spot to stop. We found a large, flat stone that was big enough for us to sit on. The Fields of Fae are sensitive and respondent to the desire of a deft weaver. The stone was brilliantly lit by that glorious moon and as dry as could be wished. Taking this as sign, omen, and convenient-foot-drying-place, I smiled over at Molly and we climbed up together on its wide, flat, face.

We sat, listening to the night.

Molly sighed and lay back. When she did speak again, I could tell she still had her eyes closed.

"Jack?"

I took out my smokes, shook one free, and lit it before answering.

"Molly?"

"You're dying of apathy and you can do this," a flung hand indicated the night around us, "anytime you want? What's the catch, kid?"

That last in a Cagney sort of drawl. I snorted at her, drew deep and blew a smoke ring into the moonlight. "You ever know anybody who had an inoperable cancer?"

"No."

"Well, then, this analogy will probably stink, Molly, but pay attention, anyway. People with inoperable cancers come in a couple of different types. You've got the 'I'm-not-gonna-let-this-beat-me!' optimists, who rail against the dying of the light, et cetera, et cetera, et cetera."

Draw, drag, smoke ring.

"Then you've got the 'Why-is-this-happening-to-me-God?' types who sometimes fall into this morose, unending depression that kills them faster than the cancer does. And sometimes you'll meet what I like to call 'the resolved.' They're the ones who say, 'Okay. I've got a cancer and it's gonna kill me. People die. Everybody dies of something, sooner or later. For me it's cancer.' And they have this . . . this, emotion around them. It's like, this sense of relief, almost. Like, instead of worrying about everything, they're like, living until that cancer kills them. You know? They're not railing against an unfair fate and they're not despondent and broken. It's almost as if they're saying, 'What've I got to lose? I'm dead soon anyway.' and they just don't worry. And I tell you, Molly. The very happiest, most content people I've ever met in a long, long, long lifetime are these people. You just don't know what real, perfect contentment is until you're looking your day of reckoning in the eye . . . and not spending any time or effort worrying about it."

"I'm sorry, Jack."

I shrugged. "It happens, kid."

I lay back upon the stone next to her. I felt Due Dareaga rising within me, seeking release.

'Soon,' I told it. 'Soon.'

"So what now? Do you cast a spell, or what?"

I blew another smoke ring into the night before answering. I didn't want to seem too eager. "Are you accepting my offer?"

She touched my hand with hers. The feel was warm and gentle.

"I think I want to help you."

Despite myself, I was touched. "We've got time. Lay here with me for a minute. See the stars?" I flung a hand upward, and the moon backed off enough for us to see the constellations of Fae.

Everything about Fae is wild. Everything about Fae is unrestrained. Everything about Fae is Magic. Our constellations are no exception to this rule. Our stars burn like gems in the jeweler's velvet of our sky: blue, aquamarine, incarnadine, the colors are enough to take your breath away. They're also much closer. They look as though they are the size of a large man's fist as opposed to your weak little pinpoints. But combine them into pictures, and they are inexpressible.

We lay there on that stone and the stars revealed themselves to Molly.

"Oh, wow!" she said, and I doubt she knew it. One by one, the stars winked into being. We watched as they began to spin in place, their fires spiraling outward.

Then her mind began to put them together into their attendant constellations. "It really looks like a dragon, Jack!"

And with that, the Dragon woke up. I grinned as The Dragon, that enormous star-creature that eats up half the horizon, slowly turned its glittering, violet eyes and regarded us. Those flaming, spiraling, twinkling eyes held neither malice nor love, only a dull sort of interest. Molly gasped, and her hand again found mine.

The Turtle, even slower, but no less majestically, followed suit shortly thereafter.

"You have got to be kidding me . . ." Molly breathed.

I lay there, grinning. This was fun!

One by one, every constellation in that sky turned their endless, regal gaze upon us. It's impossible for me to describe this scene to you. It's impossible for me to describe the feeling of those gazes; like we were being weighed in the balances of some cosmic scales.

After an eternity of this, the constellations turned away. The celestial hierarchy of Fae had seen us. The bugs had been noticed.

Molly turned to me, her eyes wide and bright.

"Jack. Swear to me you had nothing to do with that."

I lay there on the stone and laughed until I felt my bladder spasm.

****

"Jack."

"Molly?"

"What's eternity really like?"

I smoked for a moment and thought about the best way to answer. "When I was a kid, the moon was different. You people, you look up, when you bother to, and you see this big, round white thing in the sky, and go, 'Oh. The moon's out. How nice.'

"You have these vague, romantic notions you inherited from somewhere, and you get all misty-eyed and romantic.

"When I was a kid, the moon was this enormous, blood-red eye staring us down from the sky; the devil watching us from hell with one eye. See, at that point, it hadn't quite quit cooling. Lava, as dark and red as blood covered it. We didn't know it was lava, of course. We just thought it was blood, or the spilled wine of the god of war, or some equally stupid shit.

"When we looked up, the moon was right there, Molly. Directly overhead. Forget about occasionally seeing it in the daytime. You could see it whenever you looked up. You could watch the tides of those lava oceans crossing its face three times a day. It was the biggest thing in the world, bigger than the sun, bigger than our lives and it hung overhead, just . . . looming.

"You could feel it, too. You'd be walking somewhere and it was like being tugged along by something invisible. Like, the fucking iron in your bones was being drawn toward the sky. You couldn't see the stars. Ever. The moon made the nights too red, too bright. Night time when I was a kid was a time of blood. You could operate at night as easily as you could in the day time; and daylight was mostly red instead of blue.

"Our tides were miles high, miles long and miles deep. Forget about living near the ocean. You lived twenty miles inland and you still got fucking fish in your doorstep every night.

"The moon was worshipped as a god, Molly. Not because we loved it, or thought it was really cool, but because we looked up at that great, big, bleeding eye in the sky and we could feel the end of the world every fucking night.

"That's what eternity is like. Eternity is watching something you feared fade, cool and shrink into something romantic and chilly. Eternity is a tunnel. A tunnel that climbs, descends, bends, twists and turns, never allowing you to see the vanishing point on the horizon. You walk down it, expecting, eventually hoping, to see some kind of an end. Any kind of end, but every day it's just more tunnel.

"You know the Flood?"

"What? Like, with Noah and the ark?"

"Yeah."

"Okay, sure. What about it?"

"I lived through the Flood, Molly. And that was eternity. There was no dry land. The entire world was covered in water."

"I thought-"

"Yeah, yeah. I'm sure you did. I'm sure you've got all kinds of theories and stuff. But I was there, okay? All that water, and all you could do was swim or sink."

"What did you do?"

And there was the question. There were words, but how to reach through those words to touch the truth of it. I tried not to think about it, but it kept me awake at nights sometimes . . .

You ran. You ran because the world was drowning. You walked, and Travelled and you kept going. Surely there was somewhere that was safe, somewhere that was dry, somewhere that the sun still shone with warmth and invitation. But no. The World Ocean was flooded. There was no place to go, no place to walk to that was dry. Water covered all of the dry land. Every inch of creation was covered in water. All of it. The Fountains of the Deep had been opened and the water flowed from every cave, every hole, every torn place in the ground. Every volcano, everywhere, burst open; every geyser, every well, every source overflowed and flowed some more. Then the rain started.

At first, people thought that if they went high enough they'd be safe. They climbed trees, they climbed hills, and then they climbed the mountains, and the water kept coming. They climbed until they died of asphyxia and still the water kept coming. They climbed until the sun was shining below them, and the water just kept coming, forming pools of ice in the void before outer space. They climbed and they died, and the water was full of the ripe lush stink of the drowned. Man, woman, child, animal, everything that moved on the surface of the earth drowned.

And if you were an immortal? Someone who didn't need to breathe? You could swim for a good long time. And when fatigue caught even you, you rested on the bodies of the dead for as long as they floated. But the time came when there was nothing left but to sink into the cold, eternal darkness. You felt the cold. You felt the skin shrink from your fingers and toes, and you felt it rotting from your face in that omnipresent, freezing wet.

And still you sank. The pressure squeezed you and your bones changed shape. The darkness reached for you and your eyes changed. You adapted. It was what you did. But it was so cold, so dark, so brutal.

There was no bottom, no final resting place. The water flowed and it kept flowing. It kept getting darker and colder and the pressure kept climbing, and you kept changing, because it was change or die. But you wanted to die. You wanted so badly to die.

Everything has a hell. Everything that lives has a forbidding place of eternal torment. The Deep was the hell of the World Ocean. The hell of All Who Swim, and those . . . Things, those lost, mad, eternal Things swam around you. Hells a thousand layers thick clustered around the Maw of the Deep, and all of it was swimming around in that faceless, crushing dark. You were touched by fin and claw, fist and hammer-tongued toe.

The World Ocean had been polluted. The creatures that lived in The Deep were swimming in the warmer waters of life. You sank, and you fought off what you could. You lost your softer bits to those sharp, biting teeth and ripping claws, but you held on despite wanting so much to let go and to die.

And then came the point when everything was fighting to get away from you, to swim in every direction but the one you were falling in. Because every hell has princes and every hell has a king.

The pressure changed first, as even the water was pushed ahead of it. And the darkness swelled and swirled, twisting like smoke, and the cold climbed until you could feel the ice forming inside your bones.

And then it rose from the depths. Eyes: cold and eternal; gleaming in the darkness. A million eyes; eyes like knives on a face as large as worlds and mad as the bottom of night. It swam toward you, face working, and eyes swirling with the promise of your cold, painful death. And you knew that the time had come for you to swim, to swim against the impossible pressure, far worse than the bottom of a black hole, and you knew, you knew, you knew, that no matter how hard you swam, or how far you climbed toward the light, no matter how long you held on to the gasping, fading thread of life, you knew that it would find you, that it would consume you, and you would forever be a part of its torment.

Leviathan. World Smasher, Star Consumer, Lord of The Deep, and coming on every beating pulse of its star-sized flukes, coming for you.

Forever and ever and ever and ever-

****

There are some places that I don't like to go. When the waters dried up, I swore I'd never go to an ocean ever again. And I've kept that promise. I looked at Molly, shaken from my little PTSD episode, and choked out a response.

"I sank, Molly. Some places go everywhere. And I sank into that everywhere. You could only swim for so long until you had no choice but to sink. I sank to the bottom of the world, and I swam against the Maw of the Deep. I looked into the deepest, darkest abyss there is anywhere; home of Leviathan and the Creatures who Sleep. I waded through the mud, the muck and the mire, and I touched the banished darkness that lives there. It was cold, it was crushing and it was wet. Every second I spent down there took a million years. I watched the dead float by and I thought I'd never again see the light of the sun. Once you got down far enough, you couldn't swim back up. Not under your own power. The only choice I had was to fucking walk across the bottom, looking for dry land. It was hell, Molly. An eternal hell.

"You want to know what eternity is like? Try living it, Molly."

Silence. Long and thoughtful.

When she spoke again, Molly's voice was quiet, subdued. "That's not much of a selling point, Jack."

I laughed.

"Jack?"

"Yes, Molly?"

"There's something I'd like to do. Something I've been dying to do since we first met."

"Oh? What's that?"

I rolled over on my side, cradled my head on my arm and looked into her eyes. She has amazing eyes, does our Molly. They're dark, slow, somehow entrancing with glints of green and hazel that made the eyes of the constellation The Dragon look like the end of a guttering match. And there's that maddening something dancing around in the dark in there, always just beyond the horizon of sight and touch. You feel like it might be close enough for you to get to, and it dances away again, hiding.

Molly's eyes belonged in the sky.

I smiled, using only the natural charms God made me with.

She smiled back at me. "I'd like a kiss, Jack."

Those glorious eyes went somehow coy and shy, and color rose in her cheeks. She licked her bottom lip, and rolled over onto her side, facing me. She opened her arms to me, her color rising even more. I nuzzled into her embrace, and she lowered her mouth to mine.

Her lips felt like watered silk; like the essence of a rose petal. She tasted of smoke and fire, jasmine and pearl. Her mouth opened above mine like a flower to the heat of the sun. Her tongue shyly crept from her mouth into mine. She rolled it over my lips, playing with them in that same nervous fashion. She explored the warmth of my mouth like a well-behaved child in a candy store. She gave a little noise of what I took to be desire, and ran a hand through the hair at the back of my head. Her hand ended cupping my face like a mother holding an infant.

I've never been more aroused.

She settled her arms around me, drawing me further into her embrace, and I wrapped my arms around her in turn. I rolled over onto my back, pulling her partly atop me, and she gave another inarticulate noise of approval and desire.

Due Dareaga beat within my chest like a restive locomotive. I gripped it firmly in my mind exactly as a man yanking on the collar of a large dog. 'Wait. Not yet,' I told it. It snarled in response and lurched forward, dragging me with it. I growled deep in my throat and chest. Molly laughed and drew her head back.

"Liked that, huh?" she asked me, her eyes smiling.

Seeing her smile like that broke something loose within me. Due Dareaga broke free of my hold and rushed forth, taking full control. I cupped Molly's face in my hands. They had already assumed the muted, soothing, blue glow that is Due Dareaga's coming. Molly's eyes rolled back into her head at the touch of my hands and her body spasmed slowly.

The blue light, shining forth from my hands, my eyes, and my mouth, enveloped us both. Due Dareaga held her face inches away from my open mouth. It took a deep breath, drawing at Molly.

A wispy, brilliantly glowing mote emerged and drifted, like a firefly, between us. Due Dareaga growled in hunger when it saw this small portion of her coalesced life—her kismet—given form. It drew the mote into my mouth with another deep breath. My eyes closed in bliss as the mote melted delectably against my tongue.

With another wordless growl, Due Dareaga drew hungrily against Molly.

I could do nothing but watch. The Drawing had begun. My hands gripped Molly's face. The blue glow brightened in intensity, limning the area with a neon-like blaze. Due Dareaga drew deep, pulling her life force into me. It's not unlike the sweet taste of oxygen after drowning. You pull hard, with your belly muscles, drawing at that which keeps you alive.

If Due Dareaga had a face, and wasn't an invisible hunger, it'd be one madly staring eye and a tooth-lined, slobbering mouth. Due Dareaga is famine. It doesn't care about feelings or colors or creed or age. It doesn't care if you're educated or dumb as a box of used hammers. It has no higher motivations, no higher emotions, and no morals. The only thing it feels is its unreasoning, screaming hunger, and brief satiation for a time after it has fed. It exists for one reason and one reason only: to feed. It is the ultimate predator. Due Dareaga stalks its prey, letting us use whatever we have to use in order to get close. I find that the 'apathy' story works wonderfully. "Oooh. Lookit me. I'm a poor tormented immortal. Please save me! Love me!" I like to call it the Interview With A Vampire effect. You people can't resist trying to heal our 'poor, tormented souls.' I've been using it since that movie came out and it's never failed.

When Due Dareaga pounces, it consumes the prey. Mine goes for the life-force, the body, and anything else it needs to. It's not uncommon for me to get indigestion as a result of trying to pass blue jeans and belt buckles. I had a belly ache for six months after eating a pair of combat boots, laces and all. I try to get you people naked to avoid this and that's not hard to do. You people will jump at any opportunity to fuck.

It's not a perfect system. Due Dareaga is helpless until it begins to feed, and if it were somehow interrupted, it wouldn't be able to defend itself. That's what I'm for. Still, I've been doing this for a very long time, and the glamours I cast over Molly should've been enough.

I watched as Due Dareaga shifted position in order to Draw harder. So long as I don't interrupt the process of feeding, I am free to watch or do whatever I like within the confines of mind. Hell, I could balance my checkbook if I wanted to . . . if I had a checkbook. Due Dareaga doesn't care if we watch. Once it starts to feed, Due Dareaga doesn't care about anything. Its blind, mad, groping mouth latches on and sucks the victim dry.

Vampires usually come to mind about this point, and that's close, but not exactly right. Normally, the other Fae don't kill their victims. Due Dareaga is where you get your Rip Van Winkle stories from. Victims will stumble around for a few months; weak, confused, disoriented and feeble, and eventually they'll be fine. Me, I kill. When I'm done, there's nothing left. Plus, Due Dareaga has some rather interesting side effects. Like the memory show. And no vampire I've ever met has ever said anything about the memory show.

There's a low muttering of voices during Due Dareaga. I believe this to be the collection of the victim's memories swirling into Due Dareaga's maw. Nobody knows for sure, but it makes sense. It's like a radio playing every one of its stations at once at a very low volume. It's white noise: agreeable, but unimportant.

Every so often Due Dareaga will choose a victim who's got bright, hard, glittery memories. Some are the victim's most recent experiences. Others are important events in the victim's life. They sit in the surface of mind like rocks in a still pond. The Drawing will pull those memories free to eddy between us for a time and they become plainly visible. It's not like watching a movie, as a recollection is really a series of images that are tied together in a person's brain, but we call it 'the memory show.' It's like flipping through the channels on a TV with the sound turned all the way up.

Think about looking at someone. Then think about looking back at yourself through their eyes, with their facial features in the way, and their body hanging from your skull. Then try to add the emotions they're feeling as they look at you. Add the small, surface thoughts they're thinking, as well as the gargantuan ones taking place in their undermind. Layer on top of that all the subliminal cues and chemical effects that take place in your bodies, and all the things your mind notices that you don't. And all of that takes place in a fragment of a second.

Due Dareaga Drew on Molly, and a low, hungry moan escaped my lips. A memory stone, consolidated from several smaller fragments, floated across the void into my mind's eye. I watched from Molly's skull as she maced a stocky, cap wearing individual who was nonchalantly smoking a cigarette near her jeep. I felt her emotions surge and splash. I felt her fear, her confusion and her curiosity. I smiled as I felt her belly gurgle, and a bit of a crick developed in her left elbow. She was hungry! No wonder she'd murdered that slice of pie!

Due Dareaga thundered on.

More stones floated across, and I watched each curiously.

Molly graded a stack of papers, her mind running on auto-pilot. Molly watched a movie that had her weeping, remembering her love. Molly was sleeping, and her belly was gurgling again! I chuckled to myself. 'Kid must've been starving herself,' I thought.

Due Dareaga paused to take a deep, settling breath, like it was chewing a tough morsel of beef and then taking a sip of wine. It rolled over on top of Molly, pinning her to the stone so that it could Draw every last bit of her life force free. My pocketknife was poking me in the leg. I wanted to move it, but Due Dareaga could care less about my discomfort. I sighed. It wouldn't be much longer, and I'd put up with more pain than this.

Due Dareaga gave a low growl, like a dog seeing a hand approach its food. I settled back, trying to ignore my discomfort. It stared at me for a moment, and then went back to its meal.

A memory stone glided into my head from Molly's past. She was making love to her man. I felt her nails pierce his back; I felt his blood run over my fingers. I shuddered in time to Molly's physical rapture, and I felt her hunger. Her nostrils flared when she smelled her lover's blood. She was enjoying it. I sat up, paying attention, but the memory stone floated free.

Due Dareaga had no eyes for anything but the bright motes of life force floating all around us. I watched as, beneath me, Molly juddered and shook, experiencing the ecstasy and agony of Due Dareaga. She was giving off enormous amounts of pheromones as her body spiraled its way to death and she was making all kinds of noises. She was groaning and panting for breath. This is very normal, but I could swear I could also hear her stomach growling, and that's not.

Before I could do more than notice it, another memory stone floated free, and it was awful.

The smell of blood was heavy on the air. Molly was feeling a pant's-wetting fear and an unbearable sorrow. I watched as, from her perspective, a man drove a spear or a lance of some kind, over and over and over into some sort of a creature. The man looked like a peasant and he was shouting something that sounded like scripture. There was a shrieking noise that reminded me of a pig being slaughtered, and I realized it was coming from both the creature and Molly's mind. Molly kept whimpering, and her mind kept screaming 'Mother! No, Mother!'

The stone floated free, and I felt tears on my cheeks.

Due Dareaga roared on.

I looked at Molly. Her cheeks were beginning to sink into her face. She was becoming wan and pale. Something was tickling at the very edge of my mind. Something I had missed. I looked at Molly again, trying to figure it out. Molly was fully under thc thrall of Due Dareaga and fading fast.

Molly's stomach growled.

The stone, when it hit my mind, hit with the power of a bullet. It was a little like the one of the man driving the spear or the lance, but more detailed. It must've been a core memory of Molly's; something that she thought about several times a day, every day. The memory stone was clear and defined. It left me staggered, gasping and in shock:

. . . sex and blood and stone and urine and musk and the scrape and slither of scales against the floor of the den the comforting darkness surrounds her as her mother rumbles contentedly, purring; above her the taste of her mother's teat is hot and good in her mouth the feel of the scales pleasant against her tongue and the blood-tinged milk flows freely into her body while she nurses whimpering softly in her hunger she's always hungry the animal smell of her mother and her litter sisters surrounds her the sweet musky tang filling her senses her litter sisters scramble and crawl over her each trying to find the preferred teat and her mother's rumbling almost seems to be laughter her face is the only face she sees the only face she knows the only face she loves her eyes her mother's eyes are wide amber gems with black slits in the scale-armored carapace that is her face when she nips her mother that face appears above her the eyes soften and the rough, raspy forked tongue that can pull meat from the bone strokes her gently admonishing not with clumsy words no never that but the smell changes and she understands clearly enough 'Not so hard, little one, there's plenty' and she sighs and nestles closer to the furnace heat of her mother's body the smell is the smell of 'warm' of 'safe' it is the smell of a beast's den sex and blood and stone and urine and she feels so safe so warm so happy so loved until the men come and drive the iron lance into her mother's body and drag her away to bleed and char and smoke under the light of the horrible sun . . .

I had just enough time to recoil in shock. And even though I knew it wouldn't do a bit of good, I screamed in the shared hall of our head at Due Dareaga.

"Lamia! Lamia!"

But Due Dareaga wasn't listening. It Drew fiercely at Molly's life force, and I lunged at it, thinking that if I could somehow stop this before it was too late . . .

And I got to watch as the final mote of Molly's life force floated into my mouth to be swallowed by the black hole that is Due Dareaga . . .

. . . and Molly—the real Molly; the undermind-Molly that let the soft, pink ticklish thing I'd been stalking run things while it hid in its cave, safe and protected from the world—opened her eyes.

Due Dareaga was caught by surprise as Molly lifted a hand and backhanded me across the face hard enough to loosen some teeth. I rolled, helpless, off the stone, and landed on my face, the various objects in my pockets tore holes in my legs, my pants. Due Dareaga was still firmly in control of my muscles, and it did not understand. I screamed at it. 'Lamia! LAMIA!'

The stupid thing turned its blind mouth back toward Molly, wondering where its meal went.

Her eyes were pale amber slits. They were wild and mad. A forked tongue emerged from her mouth and licked her face.

'I'm gonna die. I'm gonna die,' I thought as I watched the Molly-Lamia stride toward us, Due Dareaga was still stupidly reaching out to feed, still keeping me from doing anything.

"So here's how it works," Molly-Lamia hissed at me in a voice full of blood. It crouched down beside me in a fluid movement. "You spend all your time denying your inner nature, denying your inner hunger. You go through life, pretending everything's normal."

She picked me up with one hand and threw me. I flew through the air and landed four or five feet away on my stomach.

"Okay, so maybe you order a bloody raw steak every so often. Maybe you go to the pound once a week and you take home an animal nobody'll miss, because you crave the red meat! The hot pumping blood!"

She jumped to where I was, easily clearing the distance, drew her foot back and kicked me. I grunted as I slid across the damp grass. I felt a rib give. She stalked toward me and reached into my mouth. I watched, unbelieving, as Due Dareaga reached for her again!

Molly roughly rubbed her fingers against the blood that had pooled in my mouth and licked her fingers. She sucked noisily on her fingers and closed her eyes. When she looked back down at me, her face had assumed a feral look. I watched as scales began to march across her skin, popping up from beneath her like tombstones. She leaned over me.

"Then some filthy Faeling comes along, who should really know better. I mean, really Jack! Couldn't you hear the hunger? Or were you so impressed with your own Dirty. Little. Lies." She accentuated every word by punching me in the chest, "that you couldn't bring yourself to pay attention?"

Due Dareaga gave a whimper of pain and turned moronically toward me. Molly opened her eyes wider and the poison light of her hunger poured out from them, bathing me in its amber-green glow. Due Dareaga was silenced by the magic of the Lamia. It crept into the hole it lived in inside me. I was in control again.

My mind searched frantically for a way out. I was hurting. A Lamia's a doable opponent when it's right in front of you and you can see its hands. But on my stomach, with a broken rib and my defenses all out of wack, I just didn't know.

I felt warm blood running down my leg. I kept my mind carefully blank. When I made my move, it would have to be an ambush. If Molly saw it coming, I was well and truly fucked.

"I mean, who cares if your mom was a Lamia and your dad was mortal? Who even knows what a Lamia is anymore? We were safe, Jack! SAFE!" she screamed at me, tears scouring shiny tracks down her armored cheeks to land on my face with burning splashes of pain.

"We lived in the desolate places. The empty holes. And my mother wanted to go home, briefly for a visit. Just a 'breathe the air of Libya once more, my child, then we will return,' thing and some filthy Crusader comes along and sticks a spear in her!"

She kicked me again. Another rib went.

"So. You grow up. You walk away. You leave. You get a job, an education, and you try to blend in with them; you ignore the way the blood pounds in their veins, and you do pretty good! You go for months without needing it."

She took a deep breath, and stretched her body under the moon. "Then some stupid, cocky Faeling comes along, with his stories and his lies, and he reminds you of all that was; all that could still be. He makes his little offer and he tries to eat you, and you awaken as the man you've come to believe might be another friend is trying to destroy you.

"And you're so hungry, Jack. The last time you fed was a pale mortal who broke up with you. He learned, though. We never let anyone walk away and he wasn't much of a meal."

Her eyes flashed at me. They had flames dancing around them. Her lower body was disappearing into a sinewy, serpent-like form. "And it's been months, Jack. It's been long, hard months since I've fed."

She lowered her body and put her face close to mine. Her breath tasted like the grave. She whispered in a voice that was not meant to carry, "And I've never had a Faery."

And with that, she bit off my lower lip.

The hard part wasn't moving my hand to my pocket, nor was it surreptitiously pulling the thing out of my leg. No, the hard part was not screaming when she tore my lip off.

Molly reared back, her eyes closed, her confidence obviously supreme. Her stomach growled as it got some of the blood it clearly craved.

When I moved, I put all of my strength behind it. I lunged upward, faster than I've ever moved before, seven inches of bloody steel protruding from my fist. I buried it in her left side while she swallowed my bottom lip and blood poured down my chin. I heard several ribs crunch, and I realized that only some of them were mine. I twisted my hand savagely and fell back with a grunt of pain. Molly looked at me, her eyes wide and her face shocked. Then she screeched fit to shake the heavens. My hand opened and the broken handle of my pocketknife fell from it.

Molly kicked and screamed. From where I lay, I pitched my voice so she could hear me over her death throes; my voice distorted around what I suspected was a broken jaw and my missing lower lip.

"Yeah, okay. I got cocky. But you never, ever, go anywhere at all without a sharp pocketknife, Molly."

I stood up, holding my sides and tried not to weep.

"Besides," and with that, Molly's eyes locked on mine, and the hate there could've scored tracks in steel.

But I closed my eyes, denying her final attack with her death magic, and softly, slowly sang.

"Your kiiiiiiises make me bleeeeeeeeeed, I'm droooooooooooowniiiiiing in your seeeeeeeea of teeeeeeeears, but it's your teeeeeeeeth I fear!"

It took a long time for Molly to die. I sat and watched until the sun came up, and I felt her go just as the sun tipped the horizon. It burned her body away, leaving behind the now scorched, chipped remains of my blade. I sighed and picked it up.

"Hephaestus is gonna have a fit." I put it in my pocket along with the handle. It clinked against my lighter. I shook a cigarette free and lit it, blowing a smoke ring.

I heard the slithering long before I saw anything. It sounded like a snake sliding over loose rocks; gliding along with predatory purpose. I couldn't see her, but I could feel her, watching, waiting. The shadows grew long and cold. The sun, newborn on the eastern horizon, dimmed. She drew near, and I could smell her; like a rodent living in a wall, or the smell of billions of cockroaches, a drywall's thickness away. She smelled of musk, blood, sweat, sex and tears. She smelled of the death of infants. The heat of her body covered me in a dull, suffocating wave.

'What have you done, little fairy? What have you done to my precious little girl?'

The voice was a hiss. It sounded in my head and all around me. The shadows were growing longer still and the cold was searching for me like a grave opening.

"She started it."

A hiss. Louder than a thunder crack.

A shadow, deeper, fuller, taller and rounder than the rest, was forming over Molly's scorched remains. Two great drops, like tears, fell from that shadow and hit the burned corpse; sizzling and popping as they made contact with the sun-touched ground.

'You will pay for this, Faeling. Your blood will answer for the blood of my child.'

"Look, bitch. You wanna start something with me, let's do it. Let's do it here and now!" I was clenching my teeth around the words, trying to stay upright. The shivers were breaking my bones.

Her anger was like a sun flash; a slap across the face. I lifted my hand to my cheek and felt thin, running wounds. Blood stained my fingers.

'Bear my mark, Faeling. Wear my curse. I come for you in the time and place of my choosing. I come for you under dark skies. I will kill, eat and destroy. I come for you when you are weak and tired, when you are fearful, when you are alone. I come for you in hot blood and hate.'

The cold dissipated and the sun came back. The sound of slithering faded into the distance and I was left with the cooked blood smell of Molly's ashes in my nose and the poison feel of Lamia's claws on my face.

"Well, fuck."

I sketched a goodbye to the spot representing Molly's grave. Then I set my face to the sun and limped weakly away from that place.

Chapter Thirteen

Solly lit his pipe and smoked it for a time, saying nothing. When he spoke, he let his voice convey his feelings. "Was any of that true?"

Jack looked up at him with what Solly thought was an inscrutable look on his face. He smiled, and Solly saw the feral lie behind his eyes.

"You don't believe me?"

"Let's just say I'm skeptical."

"Okay. How's this: it probably wasn't all true before I told the story, but it is now. Storyweaving is about the truth of what is-"

"Yes, yes," Solly said, waving an impatient hand. "Let me see if I have this right. You told Molly you were a Stranger, before you killed her. And she was a daughter of Lamia-"

"Not a daughter! No! A grand-daughter. Her moms got killed, remember? Old boy stuck a spear in her."

"Ah. Forgive me. That does make it better, Jack. A beloved grand-daughter instead of a daughter."

"Dude. Who fucking knows, alright? Those feminazis fractal all over the place. Birth and death, blood and soil, moon and silver; they have more fucking aspects than I've eaten hot dinners."

"Alright. If you wish. You killed an aspect of femininity, no doubt getting the attention of every female power-"

"Oh, what? Like you never broke a rule to get some nooky?"

Solly rolled his eyes. "I never broke sacred oaths, no. And I never murdered favored daughters or grand-daughters of the gods, either. Nor did I tell people I intended to eat my life story, providing their avengers with a means of finding me right away. I don't go around pissing off aspects; especially female ones. I don't think I'd do that to get "some nooky," Jack. I respect the boundaries placed the way they are, and I don't go around thumbing my nose at devouring elementals from beyond the bloody walls of time!"

Jack said nothing for a moment before nodding in glum agreement. "Okay. That might've been a mistake. I get cocky sometimes, okay? It comes with being a bad-ass."

"Oh, but you aren't done, are you? You not only killed Molly, you brought the wrath of Lamia, and by extension, all her sisters, down on your bloody head."

Jack sighed. "Yeah. I've been pissing bitches off since the beginning of time. 'Pimps up, hos down!' isn't a philosophy, Solly. It's a lifestyle. And anyway, how the fuck was I supposed to know Molly was related to Lamia? I mean, it wasn't like she wore a label saying 'Hi! I'm one of the seven grand-daughters of an elder goddess. Don't fuck with me or my mom will rip your dick off.' How was I supposed to know? Who knows anything about Lamia, anyhow? Apparently she gets around with humankind. I guess that poet guy Keats and her were a thing for a minute. Maybe Molly came from-"

"Jack, I can't protect you from Lamia. I've got my own to take care of."

"Yeah, that's cool. The only problem is, the way I see it, you don't have a choice. I've been running since it happened, and this is pretty much the last place I can be. I've been chased out of everywhere else. See, Lamia and Titiana are like, best buds. And anything that pisses one off pisses the other off. I'm here. Lamia will be here soon, and she'll be piiiiiiiiiiiiiissed. That's bad. What's far worse is that Titiana might show up to help slap me around some. If one shows up there's gonna be a lot of corpses lying around. If both do . . ." Jach shuddered.

"I would not be worried about Titiana, Jack."

"Oh, right. 'Cause you laid the pipe to her sooooooo good, she's just gonna turn her back on a million years of sorority? Listen: you're not that good in the sack-"

Solly slowly turned a gaze on Jack that felt like roasting diamonds. Jack's mouth worked for a moment and then stopped. "Yes?" Solly said, his voice hard, cold, and full of dangerous edges. "There was something you wanted to say?"

Jack swallowed, rubbing his throat. "Nothin'. Nevermind. We'll . . . we'll just stick a pin in that issue. But. . .okay, I'm bound. Oath-Caged. I can't leave here unless— "

"Unless I release you."

Jack deflated. "Yeah. Yeah, that'd do it. But it seems to me I can help you. I think you want me fighting beside you with all my considerable ability. And if you protect me I'll tell you your True Name."

And there it was. Jack had beaten him. There was no way Solly'd allow the men under his command to die if he could help it. They were beset on all sides and Solly needed every advantage he could get. Even with the added threat of a rampaging goddess, Jack would be an asset. Solly turned to a solemn Jack. Jack broke the silence first, reassuming his accent. The time for casual camaraderie had ended, it seemed.

"I took yer oaths, Solly Mont, and I meant them right well, 'least as well as me kind's capable of. But I do swear to you by Sister Moon and by Those That Dance on Summer Stone, that I mean what I say. I came here for th' protection of a king, an' I came here under duress. I'm an asylum seeker who's walked a long an' lonely road for a time. I'm here, an' I'm ready ta' fight, but I need ta' know I'll not be fed to th' crows."

Solly gave a curt nod. He stood and put his right hand out. Jack cautiously took it. "So long as you keep your word, such as it is, you'll have a place here, Jack. As one of my own."

Jack's hand was warm and strong in his. He shook it, once, then nodded and walked out of the office. Solly watched him go, thinking of all the future might hold.

****

The days wore on under the endless sun.

All of the daily reports from the men now had one source: Jack O'Green.

"Sir! Th' crops are growin' at twice th' speed they usually do, an' what I'm gonna do with all these bleedin' cukicumblers, tomatalers an' radishers, I got no fookin' idear, savin' yer presence, sir."

Fergus also focused all his hate on Jack.

"Sir! 'e's a bloodthirsty, gutter-whore spawned, waif o' th' devil! Will ye stand by an' allow the men to be infected by such?"

"Sir! Jack's found a source o' water within th' walls o' th' fort! Th' water's clean and pure as any I've ever tasted!"

"'e won't wear boots, sir! By all tha's holy, how'm I expected ta maintain any order wiv such as tha' runnin' 'round loose?"

He put it all aside and focused on the attack he knew was coming. They were out there. He could feel their numbers and their ill-intent. If his men left off their guard for even a moment, the walls would be swarming with tribesmen.

Something was driving them. Some force was pushing them to be this aggressive, this organized. He felt it in his bones like a tidal-pull. There was nothing truly definitive: scouts reported seeing large numbers of tracks, and there was an increase in small skirmishes. But Solly knew. There was someone out there who wanted them all dead. And he or she was willing to use whoever they had to in order to accomplish it.

Solly feared for his men. He tripled the patrols around the fort, trying to stave off the inevitable for as long as he could.

It came late one night, under an oppressive, suffocating blanket of unrelenting heat.

Solly had decreed that every man was to keep his kit on him at all times, ready, when the attack came. He'd made a habit of inspecting the sentry walks every night, at a different hour, outfitted himself in full battle dress to train the men to be aware all night long.

This night was no different. He walked the walls, his eyes roving the dark night surrounding them; his ears straining to hear any noise out of place. He came to an empty sentry post. At first he assumed the man had stepped away for a moment and he prepared a long dressing-down for the sentry's laxness. He listened to the night.

He couldn't hear anything, and that wasn't right. He should have been able to hear the sentry coming back from wherever he'd snuck off to. His nerves jangled and he searched around in the darkness.

It didn't take him long to find the body and its murderer.

His first response was anger. It filled him like a hot wine.

A cloaked and muffled tribesmen, no doubt an overeager scout, was methodically looting the sentry. The stench of blood was high in the air. The man hadn't even bothered to pull his sword from the sentry before beginning his pillage.

Solly moved on soundless feet. He put one hand on the back of the raider's head and the other on his chin. The sound he made when he broke the man's neck was like a wet branch breaking.

"Get up, you sons-of-whores! They're on us! To arms! To arms!"

His voice shook the stones around him. Raiders began swarming the walls in a dark wave, completely unopposed. Those few sentries who had not been taken by the scouts were swarmed under in a sea of dust-covered madmen.

Within moments, the walls had fallen.

The raiders kept coming. The first opposition they met was Solly Mont. He stood tall, shouting to wake the dead, a cutlass in one fist and a pistol in the other.

A wave of tribesmen, twenty or thirty strong rushed him. The next few moments were busy ones for Solly Mont. His mind dropped away from him into the autonomous battle response of the warrior. A whirling flash of cutlass, a shot, and then those hammer-fist blows—indistinguishable from a sledgehammer—fell among the men around him. Tribesmen died as soon as they reached him. The smell of blood rode the night and Solly wore it like battle paint.

They kept coming over the walls. The smarter ones looked at Solly and realized that here was a rock; an obstacle to go around, not through. The fled his thundering fury, flowing around him and seeking easier targets.

Solly had no time for magic. Everything he could think of to do required a moment's time; a breath's space and concentration he couldn't spare. It was fighting at its most primal: slash, punch, club, and move; slash, punch, club and move.

Fergus appeared, chest bare; a musket in one hand, a pistol in the other. He shouted a hymn at the top of his voice and screamed blasphemous obscenities at the enemy.

"Come and get religion, ya' godless pig-fuckers!"

He shot indiscriminately. When both of his weapons had discharged, he charged the raiders and clubbed them to death, still bellowing his hymn and shouting imprecations. He took eight before he broke a sweat.

The men rallied and rushed the tribesmen with no sense of strategy or combat skill. The awaited attack had finally come, and like a surging storm, the men loosed all their pent up frustration and anxiety on their tormentors. Men disappeared into clusters of swinging arms and lightning-flash shots. Screams and blood sprayed the walls. The tribesmen cried out in their own tongue and kept pressing the men of Ft. Nowhere; pushing them back, and back, and still further back. Blood flowed in dark rivulets across the dusty stone. Solly moved like a machine. He used hard-won lessons learned on ten-thousand battlefields. Cold logic and harnessed reason worked hand-in-hand with hate-soaked fury. He stalked the slippery stones, killing everything he could reach. There was no finesse, no fine-tuned fighting here. It was a brutal struggle for survival, and Solly Mont had been doing that in one fashion or another for a very, very long time.

There was no time for anything but attacking and defending. The tribesmen renewed their attack and came at Solly in a black wall, targeting him as the commander. Solly even thought he heard one of them call his name as they rushed in.

His cutlass flashed and sang. Solly planted his feet, spread his stance and started yelling in chorus with Fergus; creating a sonic wall that provided the men with a point of reference to rally at.

His hands moved like windmills. He threshed the men in front of him; killing one per stroke, another on the return. The blood ran down his uniform and filled his boots, and still the tribesmen came.

He held his ground, fighting as only a man for the first time in far too long. Life was thinner than a spider's web here. He could feel the abyss yawing wide for him. One missed swing; one badly placed punch; one ill-timed return, and he would be lying on his back, seeing if death could take him or not.

He'd been surviving long enough to learn to divorce emotion from action, and he kept a center of cool deep within him while his hands went about their gruesome task.

Shouting at the top of his lungs, he took one small step forward, his hands moving too fast to be seen in the torch-lit darkness. The tribesmen were all around him, covering him like ants on a caterpillar.

Another step forward.

Two.

Three.

He had space to take two steps forward. Bellowing with renewed force, he slowly organized a center of defense. A tepid counter-attack started to form. Bit by bit, it began to whittle the mass of tribesmen off Solly. They were still a breath away from dying, but they were choking off the offense.

He fought through a dense knot of tribesmen, breaking bones with his fists, and feeling he calm center deep inside him whirling away under the awesome battle lust. His eyes were greying. Fatigue burned in his muscles. He re-doubled his efforts, killing the tribesmen three and four at a time; flinging them bodily away from his and smashing his fists through them as if they were eggs.

It took a million years. He went blind from the blood, deaf from the screaming and insane from the hate swirling all around him . . . and then he was through, clear space around him and the few men he'd drawn into his wake.

The men were fighting in tight knots all around them. Solly moved from one kill to another. Each fight he ended won him a trooper for his growing counter-offensive. He paused once to strip a scimitar from a tribesmen who'd raised hand against him a moment before and coughed his dying words out in freshets of blood.

He found Jack leaping and laughing about the enemy like a grasshopper; tossing them like pebbles to crash against the unyielding fort's walls.

The fight went on all night and well into the next day. In the end, it was a combination of Jack's laughter and Solly's untouchable reserve that broke the enemy. No-one could stand against them. Any that tried found a horny hand wrapped around their head or a sword cutting them in half. More men died under the flashing, laughing hands of Jack and the doom-soaked blows of Solly than all the rest of the swords, muskets and pistols combined.

The enemy's advance ground to a halt, as those still coming over the wall saw what waited for them. Those within the fort died, and those pressing so urgently for the fray a moment before began to run away. Some, possessed of their own brand of madness, fought on until death found them.

The remaining tribesmen, still outnumbering the men of Ft. Nowhere six to one, turned and ran just as a surly, blood-soaked sun sank beneath the horizon.

The men of Ft. Nowhere were left to greet the disaster of the falling night.

***

The respite was brief. Of his entire command, Solly was left with thirty men. Seventeen of those would soon join the dead. The rest, while not mortally wounded, were wearing bandages, slings, eye-patches and all the rest of the accoutrements of battle.

He ordered them to eat and drink, and to give what aid they could to their fallen and wounded comrades.

Jack ignored it all. He stood on the walls, looking off to the far horizon.

The report, when it came, was like a shot to the face. Jack's voice rang through the walls of the fort. "Fire on the horizon!"

Solly moved as quickly as he could to the walls. The horizon was indeed touched with fire: the hundreds of campfires of a still larger army of tribesmen.

The command counsel was grim. Fergus had fallen. Not surprisingly, with him had fallen much of the fighting spirit of the Fort. The men hated him, but he united them in their hate. When he wasn't there, pushing them forward into the meat grinder, they found their steps faltering. While Jack and Solly fought like devils themselves, there was something about Fergus' brand of fight that was . . . human. Solly and Jack fought on the side of the men, but they had been revealed as something 'other.'

Solly was surrounded by scared faces. He tried to rally their fighting spirit, but looking into those glum, fearful faces, he saw defeat. He sighed, dismissed them, and told them to prepare for the next wave as best they thought.

The men left and Solly collapsed against a wall.

He did not fear death. If Wisdom had decreed that here would be the place that he ended his millennial journey, then so be it. But the men, the helpless men . . . He had failed them by not protecting them. He had failed them by not preparing them better. He had failed them because he was their commander, and too many of them died.

It was against the principles he was slowly learning, but he swore a silent oath to make the foemen pay for every drop of blood spilled.

"Solly?"

The voice broke through his misery slowly, like a man rising through sleep. Jack stood above him, his face fixed in a smile. His eyes were deep, dark, serious pools. "You feel that?" he asked.

Solly stared at him, too tired to wonder what the man was talking about, when he felt something like water filling his ears. His ears popped and he felt his eyes begin to water. A smell, like rodents or cockroaches filled the air.

He pushed his consciousness out, searching for it. At first, his pain and fatigue got in the way. And then-

There. To the east. Blood and sex and stone. Like a bruise on his mind.

"Yeah." Jack said. "She's coming. Lamia."

Solly cursed. A fly, buzzing near to eat the blood on his face, died.

Jack smiled. "Niiiiiiiiiiice. Listen. I've got a plan. Sort of. I don't know that I like it, and it's got a price that's pretty steep and I'm sure I'm not ready to pay it, but fuck, dude. Everything's got a price."

Chapter Fourteen

"Okay. Lamia will be looking for me. Your fucking Oath-Cage painted a bullseye on my ass, but whatever. At this point she's wondering what's going on here and lying low. She's like a snake in that regard. She tends not to jump into a situation without flicking her tongue around. I'll take care of Lamia."

He stopped talking then and took Solly by the hand. The gesture was a strangely intimate one for Jack. "I'm not sure you're up to this, Solly Mont. But here we are. I need you and you need me. But listen: I know you know about the bargain of Earth."

Solly nodded. No-one knew much about it, but you heard things. The Fae had buried many of their enemies under Earth-granted falls of rock, ice, snow, lava, salt and ash. There were texts, some thousands of years old, that suggested Atlantis had offended the Fae, and they, in turn, had unleashed the Earth upon her.

"To some extent. Much of what I know is hearsay and legend-"

Jack interrupted him, his hand still holding Solly's. "Here it is in a nutshell, Solly. The planet is alive. Her name for herself is 'Errth.' That's where the word 'Earth' comes from. She's alive, just like you and me. She lives, breathes and bleeds. Eventually, she'll die. When you know how to speak her language, Errth will talk to you. Call her—this bright, blue, spinning ball of muck you live on—and she'll give you most anything you may desire, as long as it's in her power to give, and you ask nicely and in the proper way.

"What's free for us has a price tag for you people. Errth gives you nothing for free. She used to, but you people burned her, allllllll the way back in the fucking beginning of time. Adam forsook the three-way covenant, bringing the Curse of the Land down on you, and then Cain poured out his brother's blood without regret. Ever since then the land has been crying out against you. All of it. Everywhere. Every realm, every earthfield, every place there's fucking dirt is defiled to you, and Errth won't speak to man.

"You can't hear it, but Errth hates you people. The things you do to her . . . well, whatever. The point is, you're not allowed to ask her for anything anymore. You're only allowed to take what she gives you. Us, we get what we ask for, but if I'm asking on your behalf, it's gonna cost ya'.

"I can save your fort and the men remaining to you. The question you've got to answer is: are you willing to pay the price? It'll be you, Solly Mont, or whoever-the-fuck-you-are. You and you alone. I'll ask, but I have a feeling I won't be able to pay when this is all said and done. And if you don't pay the price . . ."

Jack swallowed. Solly saw something that looked like real fear crossing his face. "If you don't pay, just fucking kill each other now. It'd be faster."

Solly looked long and hard at the creature before him, weighing the question carefully, trying to see every angle through the poisons of fatigue and pain bleeding through him.

Solly reduced the question to a much simpler one: *could this save his men? Would anyone else have to die?*

"Jack, I will pay whatever price is demanded of me. Save my men."

Jack O'Green smiled and threw his head back and laughed long and loud.

"Right the fuck on, dude! Alright! Let's kick some ass! Okay. When you're ready for me to climb back down to where I can hear your True Name, you holler at me. Okay?"

Solly nodded. Jack let go of his hand and led Solly to the bare spot of earth where the dead had been moved. They lay in their winding sheets, their torn uniforms. They were covered in blood and gore; their bodies blasted, sliced, burned. Indistinguishable as individuals, Solly saw them as a mass of dead flesh. Nearly two hundred men, dead or as close to it as made no difference, lay strewn around, awaiting the burial promised them.

Jack picked a spot in the middle of the men, sighed and spread wide his arms. He closed his eyes. He tilted his head back until it was perpendicular with the ground and his forehead was actually touching his spine. His mouth fell open and a groaning sound began to emanate from him.

Solly watched, mystified, as a dark, gleaming cloud of sparkling motes, like a vast swarm of tiny locusts, began to rise from the ground, echoing the noise Jack was making. The motes swirled around them, touching them here and there, and tinkling gently like glass wind chimes in a small breeze.

Jack's groans deepened and spread further; like a boat signaling the shore with a horn in the fog. The motes echoed the sound, much higher up the register, and began flashing a green color. They settled on the dead. The chiming, tinkling noise they were making rose until Solly couldn't hear it anymore. The bones in his ears tickled and he could feel a tinny vibration in his sinuses.

The whole experience seemed later to Solly to have taken a thousand years: Jack standing there, his arms wide, his neck seemingly broken and that high-pitched, sub-audible buzzing all around them as the motes settled on the dead men.

Slowly, the men began to change. A green, like the color of a new spring leaf, shone through the motes. The green color of the motes began to sink into the flesh of the men before him like the underside of a leaf. Their hair looked like grass. The bright, sharp smell of a new mown field came from the men. The men picked themselves up off the ground with awkward, lumbering gestures; as if they were remembering how to make their bodies work and ignoring injuries that should've made movement impossible.

They assembled in a loose formation in front of Solly. Solly watched as one of his green troopers stuffed his torn green innards back into the hole they were falling from with a rough, careless gesture. The soldier bound his abdomen with his shirt.

They were a horrific sight: green, from head to toe, with green blood oozing from every wound. They made no sound. Their faces were blank, and their green eyes—the same color as Jack's—rolled uselessly in their sockets. Necks were left naked of severed head and lost limbs were ignored. Ghostly green appendages, like vines, grew in their places.

Jack's hands dropped to his sides.

"Ohhhhhhh, that shit'll kick your ass."

His voice was weak and he had gone very pale. He was sweating for the first time in their acquaintance.

"Are you alright?"

"Nope. I'm trying very hard not to puke my fucking guts up. But don't worry about it. The price, remember? Your own part will come soon enough, have no doubt. You be sure you pay what Errth demands."

****

The men were silent, and except for the swirl of dust at their feet, unmoving. Solly had positioned the green men in front of the walls. His remaining soldiers, the live ones, sat atop the wall, waiting.

Jack stood under a shading section of wall. He looked unconcerned, but Solly could see the strain on his face.

"You just watch. This'll work. The green doesn't tire, doesn't bleed, and you can't cut it with anything that isn't a fucking hoe or a plow. I doubt those ragheads out there are carrying anything even remotely like that. Their strength is the strength of Errth. The Harvest come to life."

The men watched the raiders until the moon rose. When it reached its zenith, the tribesmen lit a wall of torches and moved toward the fort in an undulating wave. "There will be no parley, men. No surrender!" Solly shouted, laughing manically. The men around him stared at him for a moment, and then responded with laughs of their own, and defiant curses.

"Come get poked inna ass, ya' sum-bitches!" Jack yelled, capering on the wall.

Solly saw horses running towards them and he wondered at the resources being squandered here; the needless hate of men who'd bring a horse to such a baking hell. There came on the wind, still quite distant, the sound of nearly ten-thousand men shouting in unison for their blood.

Solly stood tall and proud atop the wall, his musket raised in defiance. His men roared their approbation. Casting a spell, Solly caused the walls of the fort to glow with light. If they died here tonight, they would not die in darkness.

The horde screamed its bloody war cry and raced towards the walls. The men held their fire, waiting for better shots. The distance closed. Individuals became distinct. The raiders' wide, blood-lust stained eyes filled the world; their terrible cutting scimitars flashed in the moon and torch light.

And the moon dimmed. The wind blew cold. The shadows grew long and hard; knife-edged.

"Jaaaaaaaaaaaaaaaaaaaaaaaaaaaaaaaaaack!"

The voice was like the sound of the sky falling into a hole full of snakes. It promised the blood of ten-thousand years, spilled drop by drop.

Solly looked to Jack.

Jack closed his eyes. He looked up at Solly. Solly saw naked fear on Jack's face. Jack grinned his crooked grin, squared his shoulders, nodded and jumped over the wall.

From out of the darkness and cold, Lamia emerged. Solly could see every detail as if it were etched into glass. She was every disease, every lie, every broken promise. She was the Breaking-Whore, the hag-woman, the witch who eats the babies. She was everything dark and cold; all the damp, fungus-laden aspects of femininity given flesh. She was the eclipse, the vampiress who eats the moon. She was all of these and more. She was the world-killer; the serpent; the monster who lived under the darkness and poisoned everything light and good. She was the dark beneath, behind and below Yin.

She rode the winds, behind the attacking foeman, arrowing straight for Jack, who ran to meet her, bellowing defiance and knocking the foeman left and right.

She was thirty feet long. Every inch of her was covered in scales like rusted, iron plates. They were chewed and damaged, sharp-edged and mangled; blood-stained. Gore covered them. Solly could see pieces of meat dangling from them and straining behind her in the wind of her passage.

Her face was horror. Her teeth were like bent drill bits, and they tore through her lips, her cheeks and even through her chin. Hair, like tentacles, fell from the top of her skull. The strands moved with independent will, each ending in a cruel, spike-lined maw. Her eyes wept blood that fell and poisoned the sand, leaving it steaming and glassy.

Her body, from the waist up, was the body of a woman. Her belly was swollen with the scars of childbirth. Faces pressed against her abdomen from the inside. Solly saw the mark of tooth and claw on those faces, as if the children inside her warred among each other to be born. Her abdomen rippled. Lamia screamed. A star fell from the sky, staining the darkness around them with brilliant color for a few seconds. The noise was like the dying of a great beast. Her belly tore open and a mewling, puking, scuttling . . . something crawled out of the hole and skittered away on too many legs into the darkness.

From the waist down she had the body of a diseased snake. Her arms were bony sticks, ending in cruel, scythe-edged claws. Her skin was mottled and patchy, like a corpse's. Poison covered it, dripping from her claws, her teeth, her eyes and glistening like dew on her skin.

Her wasted dugs—a row of them, like a dog's—were gnawed on, marked with the scars of uncountable teeth. Wings, a hundred feet wide, spread from her back, and the moon shone through them. They were like a crypt-butterfly's, or a cockroach's; the multi-faceted, window-paned wings of an insect.

"Jaaaaaaaaaaaaaaack! I come!"

Her voice was the slide of the knife in the dark; the creak of bone in the grave.

Over the noise of the charging foe, Solly could just hear Jack's reply.

"Bring it, you fucking, ass-munching, three-dollar hooker!"

The tribesmen rushed toward the fort. Jack rushed toward Lamia. Lamia rushed toward Jack, now descending and killing tribesmen herself, snatching them up, tearing them in half, tossing them across the sand and eating them.

The noise was apocalyptic.

"Go!" he bellowed, hoping Jack could hear him. He had no time. Battle was joined in earnest.

With a small popping noise, Jack disappeared.

Lamia screamed in fury, threw a final tribesmen at the fort's walls with a noise like a lake being emptied and disappeared herself.

***

Jack rushed to the one place he knew he could hear Solly's True Name. He'd been there with Titiana, watching. He was a creature unfettered by time, and could go anywhere he wanted to, see anything he wanted to see. He could feel the unrestrained heat of Lamia's hate closing in on him. Working quickly, he searched his own timeline until he found the one place he'd needed to.

"Jaaaaaaaaaaack!"

He dove into the correct place and time just as Lamia's claw closed on an ankle.

****

The tribesmen reached the walls. Each eye was full of hate and vengeance. There were so many of them and they were all ready to kill, to destroy. Solly took a deep breath, readied himself to jump, and screamed a battle cry . . . in time to see them run, head-over-heels, directly into ten foot walls of stone that appeared in their path. There was a sound like five hundred pumpkins being dropped from a terrible height, magnified many, many times over, and the green men leapt to the attack. They operated without orders, without instruction. The faces, each one as green as frozen algae, were grimacing in a horrible contortion of concentration. Their feet had disappeared, knee-deep into the sand, and deep, booming, groaning sounds were coming from the ground all around.

Solly watched one of the green men throw a punch, and the ground responded in kind, knocking raiders flying.

****

Jack appeared in himself with Lamia's claw wrapped around his fist.

Solly Mont stood in front of Titiana. The scene was perfect. He'd arrived just as the man Jack knew was introducing himself to his queen.

"I am-"

Lamia, however, was paying no attention to the court. She burst through, ripping time and space like an over-infected wound, just as Solly Mont uttered his True Name. Jack heard it and shouted it as loud as he could while Lamia stuffed him into her mouth and closed her teeth on him. She ripped uncountable holes in his flesh, drank his blood and broke all of his bones, poisoning him, draining him, killing him, killing him, killing him.

Chapter Fifteen

In the still, watchful silence of the Beller Inn, Solly Mont lowered his hands. He sighed. The time had come.

Every eye was on him as he moved from his perch. Ana lifted a hand, unconsciously, Solly thought, and he touched it as he walked by. The folk watching were silent, patient and expectant as Solly moved to the woman who'd been sitting near the fire all this time.

Stars shone in her eyes and her skin was like radiant, salty dust.

Solly knelt at her feet, lowered his face to the ground, and kissed the floor three times. From his place, his voice could just be heard.

"What name did Jack shout, milady?"

The woman reached her hand out and gently caressed Solly's head. Her fingers moved through his hair and her eyes reflected unshed tears to the amazed watchers. Her face softened. For all her otherworldliness, she looked like a mother who has finally seen her son come into his own.

Her lips did not move, but everyone heard her just the same. They'd all heard her voice, for Wisdom never ceased calling out. Wisdom, and her sister, Understanding, raised their voices in their dreams every night, trying to teach, to lead. They'd each met her, on the heights or along their way, where paths met and where she took her stand.

Wisdom has raised her voice to all mankind.

She stroked Solly's hair. She touched his face, and she lifted him to his feet with a regal gesture.

"The name your servant Jack O'Green heard was Jedidiah, my dear, lovely son. 'Loved by the LORD.' But to the world at large, you are Solomon, king of kings, Wisdom's Servant and my own beloved son. I give you back to yourself, and I restore you to what you were."

She kissed both of his cheeks and embraced him exactly as a mother would her long lost son.

The cheering could be heard miles away.

****

And Solly wept. He wept as everything he'd been returned to him. He wept for the humanity he'd lost; he wept for the wasted years caused by his own ignorance and pride.

He looked at his hands. Light filled them. Light shone from his every pore: pure, radiant and beautiful.

And he knew them for his. These were the hands that taught the world about itself. These were the hands that had leashed the gnn: the spirits of earth, wind, air and fire. He took a step, and he felt the power of Errth beneath him. He greeted her in her own language and felt her return his greeting with the compliments fit a consecrated king.

Lifting a fingertip, he marveled at how easy it was, once again, to summon a spirit from the outer beyond to dance and cavort on the end of it.

"It's all so easy. It's just . . . It's just her voice!"

The words were whispered through numb lips and his eyes were full of the wonder of all Creation.

He remembered it all, now. All the sciences of man: mathematics, philosophy, astronomy. The magic world of the ants and the secret names the animals have for themselves; whispered to each other in dreams of predator and prey.

He could hear her voice again. Once again, he was whole.

He fell to his knees, and sobbed, just once, holding himself around the middle as it continued to pour into him like a dry crater filled with fresh, life-giving water.

After a time the light dimmed. Solly stood. Wisdom had gone. Solly looked around him at faces he knew and loved until he found his Ana.

"Hello. I'm back."

****

The name reverberated up and down the timeline. Solly Mont stood in the Beller Inn, embracing his beautiful wife. But he was no longer confined to time and space. Drifting free in his rediscovered power, Solly began to make the corrections, amendments and adjustments to the story that only Solomon could make.

In his palace, where he stood holding Titiana's hand, Solomon looked to where Jack was being devoured by Lamia.

"Stop."

The words shivered across her skin like lightning, but Lamia, elder goddess, hag-woman, witch-queen, Breaking-Whore and scorned woman ignored him. The taste of blood was in her mouth, and her prey was finally sliding down her throat. Nothing could stop her now.

The silvery blood of Jack O'Green drooled from her mangled lips and drill-bit teeth. She chomped, working them through a tougher bit of his flesh. He'd stopped moving and she couldn't feel his heart beating on her tongue anymore. The court was shocked into complete silence.

"I said stop!"

This time the words froze her. There was power here; power to match her own, and perhaps even more. Lamia looked at the little man in the crown; the one she'd ignored when she'd finally put her hands on Jack O'Green.

Light began to shine from him; light so like the light of the sun that her eyes boiled. Instantly. The light shining from Solomon began to steam the surface of her brain. She screeched and lifted a hand to cover her face, even as he strode toward her. Her skin smoked and blistered, as it would in the light of full day.

She cowered down on her stomach and tried to crawl away.

"I take my revenge!" she screamed, her voice whining and petulant in the mind of everyone there. ***"I take my revenge and I-"***

"I said, stop." Solomon grasped her by her hair. Lamia screamed at the contact. It was like a knife twisting deep inside her innermost being. Solomon threw her on the floor and laid his foot on her neck.

"Mercy, great lord! Mercy!" Lamia whined, as she smoked and writhed under Solomon's foot.

"I abjure you, demon. I cast you out. I command you to return to your place of torment. You will not return here, nor will you show your face." Solomon said, grinding his heel into Lamia's neck as she burst into flames. She scratched ineffectually at him, her claws having no effect, her strikes having no power.

Solomon drew his seal on her face. The floor cracked in a six-sided star pattern underneath them; the booming noise filled the palace and dust fell from the ceiling. Lamia screamed and fell into the floor. Solomon watched as she fell; the hole in the floor now an ever-diminishing hole in space, her voice fading as she disappeared.

****

He dusted his hands and returned to his place beside Titiana, queen of the Fae, whose mouth was wide and whose eyes were shocked. "I'm sorry about that, milady. It happens from time to time. Now. Where were we?"

Impressed into silence, Titiana smiled at Solly. Lamia could take care of herself, by silver!

****

In his place on the walls of Ft. Nowhere, Solly felt the transition. The battle in front of him was a horrifying rout. The green men did not fall, did not bleed, did not tire. The raiders couldn't cut them, and they moved like light beneath the trees; flitting and flying in horrible moving formations. They were as strong as five men and shook off blows that would've felled a tree. They moved in deadly, unnerving concert, ripping limbs from the raiders, and trampling everything in sight.

Filled as he was with his renewed self, Solomon saw that the battle was over. Earth herself was rising up to smash down upon ten, twenty men at a time. She moved like waves upon the sea, faster even. The enemy screamed in fear and tried to flee; tried to breach the moving walls of Earth, tried to get away however they could. Solomon stood atop the wall and killed anyone who came his way with a glance, a touch or a word.

The tribesmen attacked the green men in droves, hacking and cutting. They threw themselves with wrenching cries upon the waves of Earth, hoping to somehow stop the bloody slaughter.

There was no escape.

The living men of Ft. Nowhere watched, awe-struck. Not one of them fired his weapon. And then, it was over. The enemy fled, leaving scores of their dead upon the wasted ground behind them.

Solomon looked out upon a battlefield that resembled the floor of hell. There stood the green men, quietly dispatching the few remaining enemy survivors in a quick, efficient manner.

Knowing it was pointless and futile, but helpless to prevent himself, he looked back to where he'd last seen Jack.

He couldn't find him.

The foe-men lay in droves all around them. The green men moved off to the east, in the direction of the new-risen sun, but he couldn't find Jack.

The grounds were soaked in blood. Red blood covered every surface. His boots were soaked and he could feel it seeping into his trousers. The red covered everything. He came to a point of silver. A tree was growing there, in the dust of Ft. Nowhere. It had silver leaves. Solly could smell green things growing. The tree inclined toward him, though there was no wind, and he heard a gentle laugh.

A single, large, pitted seed, bright green, sat beneath the tree. It looked exactly like a stone.

Solly picked it up. "Still. There is always a price," he murmured.

The tree blew in the hot wind of the rising sun.

****

Cain felt the air move.

He was the only one who dwelt in this torn, blasted place of death. The sun, the moon, the stars, and even the wind had forsaken it. It was the final battlefield, at the end of all things, and nothing moved here.

And it was the one place Solomon knew he could be found.

Cain stood up, his eyes searching the dark horizon.

"You asked me, once, what the first magic is, Cain."

Cain threw a casting at Solly that blew the earth into fragments for a square mile around them. The cacophony was deafening. The earth flew into the sky and came back as meteorites, flashing across the horizon like streams of blood.

When the dust had settled, Cain felt a hand on his shoulder. He turned to see Solomon staring at him with sad eyes.

Cain sneered. “Talmidim.”

Solomon’s face was as hard as a gravestone and his eyes were dancing with might. “You will call me ‘student’ no longer, blood-spiller. I will teach you.”

Cain hissed through his teeth. “An insult? Very well, taaaaal-muuuuh-deeeeem. It seems you have found your balls again. Has your faggot lover returned them to you-”

Solomon didn’t bother with a physical attack. If he fought Cain’s way, he’d be fighting Cain’s battle for him. The man lived on conflict and battle.

He had other, more subtle tools available to him now. Instead, he poured all of the life, light, love and hope he’d felt in Wisdom’s arms over Cain’s soul.

Cain fell on his back, clawing at his throat. As if he were drowning.

“You said humanity wasn’t worth fighting for. You said that man had been formed from the muck; that it had degenerated from its first creation and become something much less.”

Cain rolled over onto his stomach. He threw up; blood poured from his nose and his eyes filled with tears. Coughing, hiccupping and cursing in fourteen different languages, he tried to crawl away from Solomon.

Solomon stayed where he was, watching Cain. He felt sad for this poor, tormented creature.

“And you were right. But only partly. Humanity has fallen, yes. It has degenerated and become something fit only for a sewer, yes. But there’s something you don’t know, Cain. Creation, the sole purview of the Creator, is about love. You have spent your entire existence in contempt for everything of man. But you don’t seem to realize that man is of the Creator, and the Creator is love.

“You were wrong. All of you. Love is the first magic, Cain-Bechor-Bar-Adam-shafn-durkh-Bashefer. Love! It is mightier than Story and Song, and everything else we know. Love is the first magic and the first power. Before anything else existed, love did. And it loved everything enough to share the gift of life with us. Everything that is, everything that was, everything that will ever be stems from one all-encompassing, eternal, magnificent and omnipotent love. It cannot be conquered. It cannot be stilled. It cannot be erased. Not by you, not by your maggot-wind, and not by all the forces of evil. Love will conquer the end of the universe, because love brought about its beginning."

Solomon walked over to where Cain was and lifted him to his feet. Cain could not meet his eyes, but Solomon held his shoulders and whispered the words that would haunt Cain for the rest of his life.

Solomon whispered them and walked, untouched, off the battlefield with an unhurried step as Cain sobbed on his knees.

"He loves even you, Cain. Even you."

****

Shadow smiled to himself. Taliesin hadn't been right about everything: you could find yourself, and you could leave a message with yourself. It took some doing, and you had to make a lot of mistakes, but if you looked hard enough, and tried enough times, it could be done. His teachers didn't know everything. How could they? They hadn't lived through the breadth of an entire universe and learned everything there was to learn, had they? They didn't have the time and the experience he did. There were some places you couldn't ever go, even if you knew how to find them. But you could create them. You could meet yourself, coming and going, because time and space were an illusion; spots on a map, and alternate streams of reality crossed all too often. It took Solly—or Shadow as he now thought of himself—several turns of existence to figure out how to leave a message for himself that he could hear and understand, and he had to die to do it.

So you did what you had to do. You died. And then you went to the only place you could be and built the only thing that could be there. You carved out a hole for yourself; a shallow grave in the surface of reality, and you waited on the far side of death in your little, black sphere with lightning dancing off it. Taliesin once told him it was "The Black Void."

Not quite accurate, nor very original, but the title fit.

It was the only place it could be, and it was the only thing that could be here. Shadow smiled. It was the very first place Taliesin had brought him when he was showing him how to travel.

You waited because you knew you would be coming by soon. Wisdom told you to go talk to yourself:

'Go to the desert of Takla Makan, my servant. Find the hermit of the desert, and do as he bids. Take no map or compass, no guide or seer.'

And you waited because maybe this time you'd get it right. Maybe this time you'd tell the newer, younger, fresher version of yourself how to do the job so it got done. Shadow took a deep breath.

"Maybe this time he'll get it right. Maybe this time I'll finally be free."

Solomon walked into the cave. His arrival was not heralded in any way. One moment he wasn't there, the next he was walking toward Shadow with thunder in his eyes.

"How long?"

Shadow smiled up at him.

"You look good. You look the way I remember being a long time ago."

Solomon sat on the floor, staring at the older, wiser reflection before him. Shadow sat back. His face, the worn leather skin of it so dark, so brown, so scarred and rutted with age, crinkled into a smile.

"You know what the hardest part was? Finding something that would make us sick. You couldn't just come here, sing me a happy little tune and not see a cancer. Mimicking life was easy. That's all about Story. But getting a disease that would thrive in the stainless-steel mechanism our body has become? That took some doing, buddy. Let me tell you."

The voice was Shadow's-Solly's-Solomon's, but the syntax was all wrong. Solomon knew he was looking at himself as he was, tens-of-billions of years older, but he missed the rhythm, the cadence of Shadow's voice.

"How long have you been doing this? Who are you? Who are you, really?" He knew the question was a stupid one.

Shadow kept talking as if Solomon hadn't spoken. "The thing was, I had to find something that I could kill myself with. Not suicide, no, but doing what was necessary to remove myself completely from the ebb and flow of existence so I could be in one place, waiting. To do that . . . well, I had to die. Of course, it was really just old age, but waiting here and educating myself every time I came through? I got pretty damn old doing that, and old age caught even me eventually.

"To answer your first question, I don't know how long. I've lost track of the rotations. I lead them into the north, I teach them how to live, and then I wait to see if they'll get it right. Humanity crawls down from the north, spreads across the world, and the whole thing starts all over. I've watched seas evaporate, mountains erode, and humanity foul its nest more times than I can count. And I always come find me, learn a little something more about myself, and come back again, millions of years later wearing a slightly different face. I change size, skin-color and even sex, but in the end it's always me come to find me. I come, I go. I get it right a little and then I screw it all up. I suspect it is entirely possible I'm older than the universe you come from."

"But . . . but why?"

Shadow stared at Solomon. "You know why, Solomon. You know why this has to be done. And if you don't get it right, you know why it has to be you that takes my place and waits for the universe to end and start up all over again; dragging humanity toward the light of perfection one bloody step at a time and waiting to educate yourself all over again.

"We rejected it once. We turned our back on everything that made us human. Remember? Remember when we couldn't hear her voice? And remember how it felt when it all came back?

"Humanity has lost the ability to hear her voice, Solomon. It's our job to teach them again."

"How . . . how much of this is real?"

Shadow smiled. The look that crossed his face was pained. "It's all Story, Solomon. Everything that I told you is true. It's true because we know it is. Jack, Titiana, Shadow, Weaver, all of it is true. The People lived and died. Jack served you. All of it is true."

"But how much of it is real?"

Shadow closed his eyes. "Does it matter? All of it, none of it, it's all-"

"A lie?"

"Ahh. You're angry. Alright. I tell you what: let's put the miseries of existence aside for a moment to soothe your tortured emotional state-"

"Don't patronize me."

"Who better, Solomon, then yourself? What was Wisdom's last instruction to you?"

Solomon stared at himself.

"Yeeeeees?" Shadow said.

"She told me to go to the desert of Takla Makan-"

"And you did."

"I was to find the hermit of the desert."

Shadow spread his hands in welcome.

"And do . . . as . . . he bids."

"Right. Would you like to hear my bidding or would you prefer to wallow some more?"

****

They talked long into the un-night. The not-wind blew outside. Shadow named it for what it truly was.

"It's death, Solomon. Entropy. It is the undoing of the Creator's love and the end of all flesh. We fight against its ravening hunger and lust for darkness, cold and not. It's simple: we fight for life and light."

They spoke of what was needed and they spoke of truth and reality.

And they spoke of Jack O'Green.

"You needed an ally. I've done this too many times without one. It took me forever to realize that the superhero needs a side kick. Even if only for comic relief."

"Is he real? Is he an actual living, breathing-"

"Solomon. Am I alive or dead?"

Solomon looked at Shadow; the ghost of his future and past staring at him with all-too-wise eyes. He didn't say anything.

"The answer, of course, is that I'm dead. But if I'm dead, and you're not, how are we having this conversation? The dead dwell in the land beyond. And you didn't go there to talk to me. You came here, to my little pinch-point in reality, that exists only because it must exist somewhere and somewhere everything that can exist does. Don't worry about it. Jack is . . . useful."

"Is he dead?"

"Am I?"

"But-"

"Let it go, Solomon. This universe is dying. The time for pointless, existential questions has ended. The time for action is now. Your world will end, and the not-wind will have a great victory. To spare the world of men, you have to be the hero again. But don't worry. You are returned to yourself and you have the strongest magic there is available to us: Story. Gather your allies, protect your friends, and do what must be done to save yourself, and me, finally and once for all."

****

The fire in the Beller Inn's great hearth died. The people surrounding him had gone still and quiet. Solly—for that was still how they thought of him—stood, stretched, and opened the door. The storm was gone. Morning birds were singing, crickets were chirping, and tree frogs were cheeping. Solly thought he had never heard prettier sounds.

They left, without being told, and without a sound, their minds still trying to absorb what they had been given.

Ana kissed him on his cheek, sensing his need to be alone. She touched his hand and her eyes shone with love remembered and love renewed. Solly embraced her.

"I'll be up soon."

She nodded and walked to the room above the inn, her steps tired but light.

Solly cleaned up, his movements drawing him inexorably toward the hearth. He never told anyone what Earth had demanded of him. It was a solemn secret; a charge he kept to himself and a burden he carried. But there upon the mantle sat a bright green stone that looked for all the world like a large, pitted seed. Solly touched it reverently, smiling hugely. He poured a glass of ale over the seed, and then, smiling hugely to himself and went to bed.

Chapter Sixteen

In his sewer of ages, at the end of time, Solly Mont lowered his hands. The bright weaves of Story coalesced around Ana-Titiana; Queen of the South; Sheba; Beloved; Queen of the May; Queen of the Air; Queen of the Fae and all the realms thereabouts, and the only woman Solly ever loved and trusted.

They were bright, those weaves. Solid, tangible, and all-entangling.

Ana's eyes were full of the color of them. Her face was slack, but wonder-filled. As Solly watched, she turned, took someone Solly could not see by the hand, and disappeared. When she left, the weaves went with her and the darkness was absolute.

He sighed. The noise was full of indescribable pain.

"That was a shitty, fucking thing to do. Oh, and I got to tell you, I could've taken that scaly, dick-breathed whore you set loose on my ass, too. And another thing! I damn sure don't appreciate you fucking infecting me with your bitch-ass sense of nobility! You make me sound like some kind of goody-goody pussy. What's up with that? I got a fucking reputation to be thinking of, dude. People start hearing I'm jumping out of the walls to solve mortals and I'll have all kinds of assholes crawlin' up on my jock. You got a lousy way of dealing with your friends, dude."

Solly looked up as Jack walked toward him, smoking one of his ever-present cigarettes.

"Oh, yes?"

"Yeah, dude. I mean, lying to her like that? What'd she ever do to you but love you?"

Solly looked into the water swirling around his feet. He didn't notice the smell anymore, nor the bits and pieces of filth riding the water. It was . . . home.

He swallowed. There may have been a sob.

"Tell me, Jack. Is she happy?"

Jack shrugged non-commitedly.

"Then I have given her the single greatest thing I can."

"Really? You don't mind that she's living a lie, then? In a dream-world of your creation—"

"The world is real, Jack. Story makes it real. It must be real, somewhere. Somewhere she lives in happiness with a man she loves. Somewhere, she is worshipped by the same man and given everything she needs in that love."

"Okay, whatever. But what about Lamia?"

"What about her?"

"I could've taken her, dude. That deal with the teeth fucking hurt."

"I know you could have, Jack. Does that soothe your wounded ego?"

"Fuck you."

Solly smiled into the darkness.

Jack smoked in silence for a moment, thinking his own thoughts. The darkness was warm and close between the two men.

"What about all that shit about being Solomon?"

"What about it?"

"Seems pretty shady to me. I mean, the man lived, died, did the whole mortal thing. It's all there in history."

Solly shrugged. "A convenient fiction. Story works with the truth-filled lies—"

"Yeah, yeah. Whatever floats your boat, dude. Tell me something, though. Why are you doing this?"

Solly looked up at Jack. "Because it has to be done. Someone has to do it, Jack. "

Jack made a derisive noise. "Says who?"

Solly ignored him and began to move down the tunnel. Jack's face went hard.

"How many fucking times have we been through this? How many turns of the wheel are you going to watch the whole damn thing burn down? We've seen them rise from the caves a hundred times cross space and descend back down again! We've seen the ice melt and cross the world more times than I can count! I've lost count of the number of times they've evolved. I've lost count of the number of times the fucking planet rolled over, changed shape, flipped poles! Lemuria; Hyperborea; Atlantis! You tried in Babylon three different times! You tried with the Olmecs five times! The Toltecs; the fucking Aztecs even built statues of you! You're the feathered serpent; the white god! In Camelot you were Merlin! The Egyptians, the Picts, the Celtics, the Inupiats! You've been President seven times, a king more times than I can count, and you've never gotten it right. You've done it with all of them, trying to be this "voice of reason!" All the stories, the legends, the prophecies; over and over again we've done this, and every time, one of them goes 'They have different hats! Stick a spear in them!' And it all starts over again! Don't you get it? Humanity doesn't want to be saved! You have a thousand years of renaissance, and sooner or later, they start fucking their sisters, eating their babies and sacrificing their children to the gods of dark, cold, blood and stone. It happens every damn time!"

Solly continued to move away.

"Don't you walk away from me! I'm talking to you!"

Solly ignored him. Jack ran to him, turning him around with a rough gesture.

"I'm tired!"

Solly stared at the creature in front of him, silent.

"How many times, Solly?"

Solly gripped Jack with his hands. Anger swelled inside him and he felt a surge of power building. His hands creaked and Jack grimaced.

He was old. He was older than the sun. And he had been even older once, elsewhere. He'd seen it all. He'd experienced it all. And though his long life had taught him to be deeply cynical about human nature, he still believed it was possible. There was no time for this kind of wallowing. If Jack couldn't see that this needed to be done, then Jack was a fool.

He took three deep breaths, one after the other. It would do no good to lash out at his only friend; his only ally.

Calmly, with his voice carefully neutral, he answered Jack. "As many times as it takes, Jack. If I have to watch them kill themselves over and over and over again, I will. I will watch them rise from caves to kiss the stars and I will try over and over again until they can do it right. I will watch them . . ."

He shook his head, lowered it and closed his eyes.

"Enough. This is the place? The time?"

Jack lowered his hands. "Who are you? Who are you really?"

"Answer me!"

Jack shook his head. "You're an albatross, Solly Mont. Or whoever-the-fuck-you are. You're an albatross of ill repute. The first time I saw you I should've run the other way as fast as my feet could fucking carry me."

Solly smiled despite himself. "Why didn't you?"

"You were a pussy. I could've taken you with one hand behind my back if you hadn't sucker-punched me."

Solly laughed. The noise was a quick snort of merriment in their grim, shared darkness.

Jack grinned his crooked grin. "Yes. This is the place. The fucking assholes don't even realize they're ruining the moon's orbit with their drilling. Then the asteroid smacks dead in their excavation. The pieces tear all kinds of shit up. Most of them die."

"Good. Do you still have your knife?"

Jack looked at Solly with what Solly believed were wary eyes. "Why?"

"You know the story as well as I do, Jack. We will need your knife to give them for the ceremony of blood-letting. Along with the guns and ammo we let them take; it will serve as a nexus point for their community."

Jack handed the knife to Solly. Solly unfolded it to its complete length and examined the beautiful blade. It was perfect in every way; unmarred and spotless.

"I thought it had been broken when you stabbed Molly. Is this the same knife?"

Jack shrugged. "I really liked that knife. It was a gift. You're not the only one who can tell a true story, Storyweaver. If it's not the same knife, it is now."

Solly nodded. "Good. Do you know where to find Weaver?"

"Yeah. I'll be waiting for him at Yggdrasil. It won't do any fucking good, and he'll probably be somebody else this time around, but I know where he is."

"Good. We will wait, then. And then we will lead them into the north."

Jack sighed. "Why? One man goes bonkers and starts killing all of them—"

"One, Jack! One man! One man fails! One man! We are almost there! We have almost led humanity to a perfection of existence! You heard the story! Only one man fails!"

Jack threw his hands in the air. His face was pained.

"Dude. The fucking throwback won't listen. How many damn times am I gonna have to explain that to you? His son died! He's fucking nuts! It's gonna keep happening the same damn way!"

"But we get closer, Jack. Ever closer, bit by bit."

Jack paced in a circle, muttering to himself. He lit another cigarette from the remains of the last. When he turned back to Solly, his eyes were hooded and his face was a careful blank.

"Seriously. Who are you? Why are you doing this?"

Solly licked his lips. He took his time in answering. "I am who I have been since I started, Jack O'Green: Solly Mont. Storyweaver. The Unknown One. The Wanderer. The Soldier. I am Wisdom's Servant, Wisdom's Slave. I am no-one. But I will see humanity shine. I will see them rise above the muck of their lives, and take their rightful place in the universe. I will see man sparkle like a handful of diamonds. I will see humanity make the Creator proud. I will lead them into the light, Jack O'Green, and I will do it until I get it right."

Solly wiped his face. He could feel a hundred billion years of experience etched into the skin. Something of that must've translated to Jack, for he stepped back several feet with wide eyes.

"And then, Jack, then perhaps I will be free . . ."

And in their place in the sewer at the end of time, the two of them, Jack O'Green, and Solly Mont, Storyweaver of The Ages, looked up into the sky, through the filth and stone surrounding them, at the rock that would fall from space to change the world of man forever, once again.
And once again, they looked up with hope, and they waited.

* * *

Epigraph

"All Storytellers Are Liars."

Neil Gaiman

Meet Our Author

Nescher Pyscher

Nescher Pyscher--his real name. Honest!--is a happily married, thirty-six year old author and poet living, writing and staying at home with his son in the Cambridge, Ohio area. His writing can be found at Weebly.com, Helium.com, Pablo Lennis, Surprising Stories, his aboutme page at http://about.me/nescher and elsewhere on the internet.

He writes a twice weekly column for the Cambridge, Ohio newspaper, The Daily Jeffersonian called Tattoos and Baby Food about his adventures in ineptitude with his son, 'The Pants'.

His first novel, *Tales of the Fallen*, is available from Argus Enterprises (www.a-argusbooks.com), Amazon.com and Barnes and Noble in paperback or eBook formats. His second collection of short stories, The Dreams of Trees, is available as an eBook at Amazon.com and his first book of short stories, Itchy Whispers, is now available from Trafford or Amazon.com.

11812333R0016

Made in the USA
Lexington, KY
02 November 2011